# THIRTY-TWO
## Going On...
# SPINSTER

## BECKY MONSON

*To my type B personality that starts so many things and never finishes them, I've beat you this time!*

*To my hubby and children who inspire me and make me crazy all at the same time.*

*To my friends and family that I love and adore. This girl didn't end up a spinster because of all of you.*

*Spinster Recipe*

*1 Pair of Cellulite Thighs*
*1 None-Social Life*
*1 Very Bad Sense of Style*
*1 Single-Wide Trailer (or Parents' Basement)*
*1 Cat (or more, according to taste)*
*1 Lack of Motivation*

*Directions: Mix together and then cry yourself to sleep.*

# CHAPTER 1

*Main Entry: spin•ster*
*Pronunciation: 'spin(t)-stər*
*Function: noun28*

*1: an unmarried woman of gentle family*
*2: an unmarried woman and especially one past the common age for marrying*
*3: a woman who seems unlikely to marry*

It certainly shouldn't come as a shock. I've always thought of myself as a recluse, a loner of sorts. Now I have a new title: spinster. I think I need some ice cream or an entire chocolate cake... or both.

I am a spinster... *I* am a spinster. It's true. I just looked it up in the dictionary, and there was a description of my life in plain view:

*1: an unmarried woman of gentle family.*

I'm an unmarried woman of gentle family. Okay, so I'm not quite sure what is meant by "gentle family." I wouldn't exactly call my family "gentle." More like obnoxious. Still, I'm an unmarried woman who is part of a family, so that counts.

*2: an unmarried woman and especially one past the common age for marrying.*

I believe that I am past the common age for marrying. I just turned thirty-two. What's the going age for marriage now? Twenty-five? Twenty-six? It doesn't matter because at the age of thirty-two, my clock is ticking. In fact, my doctor informed me of that last week. He actually told me that I seriously should consider finding someone and settling down because my eggs "weren't getting any younger." Pretty harsh when you consider that I haven't been on a proper date in over a decade, right? I seriously should find myself a new doctor, one who sugar-coats everything. I could use more sugar-coating in my life right now.

*3: a woman who seems unlikely to marry.*

This one has to be the worst of them all… a woman who seems unlikely to marry. That is *so* me. I bet when people look at me that's what they're thinking. I get that pity look all the time. The one where people tilt their head slightly to the side, purse their lips, and nod sadly at you.

Today was pretty rough as it was. With a rudely written e-mail from my boss, a ticket on my car when I poorly parallel parked to get some take-out, and a flip of the middle finger from some guy for no reason at all. Okay, I may or may not have cut him off, but was a hand gesture necessary? I think not.

Anyway, I came home and decided to watch the news. I never watch the news, but for some reason today I did. Big mistake. The lead-in story for the second half of the show — which I thought was ridiculous — was about this strange old lady who sat out on her porch all day, yelling at her neighbors. I thought it was bizarre that they were using this for a lead-in, but it worked because I hung around to see more.

So apparently, this lady caused quite a stir in her neighborhood. To me, she was the epitome of a spinster. From the trailer park, to the cats, to the scraggly hair and missing teeth. She was also wearing some sort of muumuu gown, and I'm quite sure there was no bra under there.

Then, I decided to see what Webster's definition was for spinster. Just for the heck of it. I looked it up on my smart phone, and there it was: my life in Webster's dictionary. You suck, Webster.

How did my life become so average? Truth be told, I'm just a plain old nobody. A nobody who swore she would be somebody. So much that when I was twelve, I bet my younger brother five dollars that I would be famous by the time I was fifteen. He's never let me live it down.

I was going to be a famous actress or singer or anything that would get me to meet Brad Pitt and marry him. I used to have dreams. I used to have hopes. But now I've settled into my little world, and I don't have much to dream about anymore.

This is crazy. I was clearly expecting a different definition of spinster when I looked it up. Something like, *"a woman who lives alone with multiple cats, in a trailer park."* Not so close to home as what I found. And yes, I do have a cat named Charlie, but only one. And no, I do not live in a trailer home. I live in my parents' basement, which I realize does not sound impressive to begin with, but has now taken on a whole new level of pathetic-ness.

Maybe I just need to accept it? I should acknowledge the fact that I am going to die alone and unloved with my cat (or cats at that point). I could start looking forward to the part where I get to start randomly screaming at people. I should stop deluding myself with any sort of dating (not that there has been any, anyway), cut to the chase, and start yelling now. "Get off my lawn, you damned hooligans!"

But my mom is always telling me to make the best of a situation. So instead of giving in, maybe I could try to find a silver lining? But how do you make the best of being a spinster? Just off the top of my head, maybe I could turn myself into some sort of superhero, like "Spinster-girl" or something. And I could go around doing nice things for other spinsters. Or finding all lost cats a home. Or even better (and more realistic), I could be a motivational speaker for women with no life or hope such as myself. We could bring our cats to some retreat high in the mountains and talk about our feelings. I would get up in front of them and tell them with as much enthusiasm and drive that I could muster: "It's okay to be alone. It's okay to have no one to come home to. It's okay to live in a trailer park or your parents' basement. Embrace your inner spinster, ladies! Embrace her!" This might be my calling in life. I could write a book. I would be famous. My brother would pay me back those five dollars from our bet.

Truly, if I am being honest, there is no positive spin on this. My only option is to fix it. Sadly, I'm not a "fix-it" person. If we were going down in a boat, and we all knew we were going down, I would not be one of those people who would be trying to bail us out until the last second. I would lie down and let it happen. It's much easier that way. But maybe I need to try this time? I need to get a bucket and bail myself out of my life, one bucket at a time if I have to.

Okay, let's see... What kinds of things do people who are the opposite of spinster do? Well, number one is most obviously to move out of my parents' basement. I mean, what kind of person lives in their parents' basement at the age of thirty-two? It's ridiculous. Of course, I do have a pretty sweet deal. I don't pay any rent, and technically it is the basement, but I have my own kitchen, bathroom, and living room. Except for my mom coming down to visit anytime she "darn well pleases," it's not that terrible of a set-up. But it's spinster-ish for me to live in my parents' basement. I seriously need to move out.

For the record, I have been telling myself to move out for the last ten years. Oh my gosh, it just hit me that I've lived here for ten years. And if you cut out the five years I went away for college (yes, I was on the five year plan), I have lived in this house for twenty-seven years of my life. I am *such* a loser.

Number two is to get some exercise. To be totally honest, I can't remember the last time I actually exercised. Maybe college? I sort of remember having a roommate in college that tried to get me to jog with her. Obviously it did not have a lasting impression on me.

Luckily for me, so far my genes have saved me from having to become a work-out-aholic. But I know I need to start doing something. I'm not what anyone would call fat, but I can certainly say I'm out of shape. So exercise needs to be on the list.

Number three on my list should be to eat better. I like food. I love to bake. In fact, it's one of the few ways I have to get away from my mundane life. I love to make sweets, and I even invent recipes of my own. I have to sample things to make sure they're not poisonous, of course. Again, I have some lucky genes. Because honestly, with the sweets that I eat, if it weren't for my genes, I might end up featured on one of those "They had to cut me out of my house" reality shows.

Number four on this list would be to get some new clothes and a new hairstyle. I do realize "the Rachel" went out of style a long time ago; however, I am a creature of habit. It took much arm-twisting and berating by my mom to get me to cut my hair into a style in the first place. I can't seem to change it. At least I have a style, right? Don't most spinsters just have oily and scraggily hair? So, then I'm a step ahead in that area.

Number five would have to be to get a social life. Baking and watching TV are what I do in my spare time. I don't hang out with friends at all. I get up, I go to work, I come home. I bake most nights, watch TV nearly every night, and then I go to bed. This has been my schedule for some time now, and I'm used to it. This really needs to change. I need a life. A real one.

Number six would be to do something else for work. I have to pat myself on the back for this one because I am already taking a step in the right direction. I'm not doing anything crazy like moving to another company or anything. That would be too much for me. Change and I don't mix well. To prove that point even further than I already have (ahem, parents' basement), I've actually been in the accounting department since I started there ten years ago. And I hate this department. I've hated it since the first day. Recently though, there was an opening in HR that is perfect for me and so I did it: I put in my request for a transfer and sent in my resume. I am dying to find out if I got it. I'm a shoe-in really, so I'm feeling pretty confident about it.

Okay, so considering how much I dislike change, getting myself out of the spinster category is going to be harder than I thought. I will persevere though. I must! I must rid myself of this new title. My life has to become something—something more than what it is now. I have a feeling it's going to be harder before it gets easier.

# CHAPTER 2

"So, have you seen the new guy?" Brown says as she enters my office and plops herself down in one of the cheap blue chairs that sit in front of my desk.

It's already been a rough morning for me. I woke up in a rotten mood, for obvious reasons. I'm starting to wonder if giving in to my spinsterdom wouldn't just be the better/easier option. I could toss the bucket aside now and stop trying to bail myself out. If I give in to it and accept it, I could learn to be happy with it. I could prepare for my future life with only cats to keep me company.

To top it off, today is another workday. Another dreaded day at Spectraltech. It's crazy that I have spent so much of my life in this place. I can't say it's flown by either. It's a software company, and to be perfectly honest, I'm still not entirely sure what we do. It has to do with back-up systems or software that makes back-up systems run or back-up systems that make software run. One of these days I'm going to have to ask. I'm not quite sure how to do that

9

without someone wondering how I have worked here this long without knowing what we do. It's not as if I'm the one developing the software or trying to sell it. So, why is it necessary that I know?

"Hello? Earth to Julia? Have you seen the new guy yet?" Brown brings my attention back to her with a look that says something like: why aren't you listening to me, don't you know I'm the center of the world?

"What new guy?" I finally respond.

"I haven't seen him yet. But I think he's a new hire in HR. That's what I'm hearing, at least." She looks at me as if she is waiting for a reaction.

"Wait, what? Are you serious?" My shoulders droop as I realize what she is saying.

"That's the word going around the office." She tilts her head to the side and gives me that pitying look I so loathe. "Don't worry, Jules, another opening will come along."

"You don't get it, Brown. That was my chance to get out of accounting. When is a chance like that going to come around again?" I put my head in my hands.

I guess I must resolve myself to the fact that I will be Henry Nguyen's assistant for the rest of my life. I will be old and brittle and gray (and wearing a muumuu) and still doing his stupid reports, staring at his disgusting extra-long pinky nail until the day I die. It is my stupid, crappy destiny.

"I know what will cheer you up. Wanna go on a smoke break?" Brown interrupts my thoughts of desperation. Of course, I say yes. Why would I want to do any work now? I know I will have to, but part of me wants to fake sick and go home so I can wallow in my spinsterly-no-new-job sorrow.

Unfortunately, there will be no going home. I have that report Mr. Nguyen asked me to do yesterday. The one I put off until today. Another stupid report that I swear on my life I have done before. I just know I have already run these numbers. I think he might be losing it. Is it sad that I actually welcome that thought? Mr. Nguyen losing his mind... happy thoughts... Maybe then I would get a new boss, and then something would be different in my life.

Brown and I head down the hall to the elevators. Spectraltech provides a smoking area out on the west side of the building; I can actually see it from my office window on the fourth floor. Brown and I meet down there quite often. I think at least four times a day, if not more. But no one actually cares, or at least no one has ever complained. We get our work done; that's all that matters.

I don't actually smoke, though. So, for me, these breaks are just... well, breaks. Brown is the smoker. I think it's unfair how just because you have an addiction you can't quit, you get more breaks than anyone else. It just doesn't seem right. But it would have been silly for me to go outside and take all these breaks by myself. Luckily, Brown and I hit it off when she started here, so I have someone to tag along with. The fact Brown and I love to gossip makes the breaks even more worth it.

You would think in a software company there wouldn't be much gossip... oh, but there is. It's pretty remarkable the information we hear. Between Brown in the sales and marketing department and me in accounting, we find out a lot of juicy stuff.

Brown is actually Betsy Brown. She hates her first name. Her friends in college started calling her by her last name and it stuck, I guess. I'm not sure why anyone would want to go by Brown, but somehow it fits her. She makes it quirky and cute. Just like, well, Brown.

Brown is the antithesis of me. She has blonde hair, I have brown. She has blue eyes, I have green. She is skinny and gorgeous, and everyone wants to be her, and well, I'm just... me. I don't think anyone has ever aspired to be me or be like me. But Brown is totally the kind of person people hope to be like. She has a life, and I am a spinster. That sums it up right there. She's been at Spectraltech for four years and is already working her way up the corporate ladder. I've already established how far I've gone in ten years. A big fat nowhere. Like I said, she is the complete opposite of me.

I genuinely like having Brown around; our breaks make my day more tolerable. I'm pretty sure she feels the same way about me. We are just work friends; we've never done anything outside of work. Not for lack of Brown trying, though. She is always trying to get me to hang out with her and her friends, go out clubbing, shop for some new clothes, and give me a makeover. She'd probably have me as her little pet project if I would let her.

Brown is dying to take me shopping. She is always saying that I have a "cute figure," and I need to emphasize it more. I suppose my wardrobe does leave little to be desired, if I actually cared about my wardrobe. What's the point in getting all dolled up for work? For Mr. Nguyen to see me? Or the nerdy software guys? There's no need.

I have my own uniform of sorts. Basically, I alternate between two pencil skirts, one black and one brown, and two pairs of slacks, also one black and one brown. For the tops, I have about ten different colored Polo-styled shirts, and I wear whatever is clean. Today is the brown pencil skirt with the navy blue Polo. It's plain, it's boring. It's, well, me.

"So, heard any gossip today?" Brown says as she leans up against the wall under the awning that keeps the smokers safe from the snow and what other crazy weather Denver likes to throw our way.

"Nah, I've got nothing," I say to her as I look out at the clear blue sky. There is nothing like spring in Colorado. It's beautiful. Except for the random snow storms. Those I could live without.

"Well, I do," she says with a twinkle in her eye. Brown does love to gossip. I think because she likes to know what's going on around her at all times. Not me, I like it because it's always fascinating to hear what is going on in people's lives. It's always much more exciting than mine.

"So, what is it?" I try to act as if it's no big deal, but Brown usually has the real juicy stuff. So, I'm dying to know.

"Okay," she says, lowering her voice as if someone else were around. "You know Martha in HR? She's totally having an affair."

"No way!" I crinkle my eyes in disbelief. "How? Who?" I am baffled. Big, overweight, Martha? Seriously? She has a crazy scandalous sex life, and I've got nothing? Really?

Brown takes a long dramatic drag from her cigarette and blows out the smoke. "I don't know who it is, but I suspect it's someone at Spectraltech."

"No! Who?" This is good stuff. Brown truly does get the most delicious gossip.

"I'm not sure, but think about it," she takes another drag from her cigarette and blows the smoke out. "She has been working late, and we both know that Martha is not the most stellar of employees."

I shake my head in agreement. On most days, you can find Martha in one of three places: the break room, eating; the bathroom on her cell phone; or at her desk playing computer games. I honestly don't know why she is still employed.

"I'm still wondering *who* would want to have an affair with Martha," I say, still confused by this scenario and trying desperately not to picture it. Ugh. Too late.

"Maybe Mike in IT? He likes 'em big," Brown says and we both laugh out loud. Mike is a total nerd as are most of the, dare I say, "men" at this place. Role playing games and online versions of *Dungeons and Dragons* run rampant around here.

We have to cut our smoke break short this time because Brown has a meeting. I'm still trying to wrap my mind around Martha and her crazy—and quite disturbing—life.

I am sure the answer to Martha's crazy love life is that, unlike me, she puts herself out there. I don't put myself out there because, as we have already established, I am a creature of habit.

The trek back to my office is a long one today. I didn't start the day in the greatest mood, and now I don't know if it's the lost dream of the position in HR or gross Martha and her crazy love life that has me feeling even bluer, but I'm feeling it. I'm sure having to work on the report for Mr. Nguyen is also not helping.

Like Martha, I guess I'm not the most stellar

of employees either. I actually do my job, but I hate it. My dad would tell me when I was a teenager to choose something I love to do, and I will always be successful at it. Well, I most certainly didn't choose something I love to do, and he was right—I am not successful. I am stuck in a job I don't love, and I have nowhere to go. And now my hopes of going to HR have been thoroughly crumbled by some guy who is probably a LARP (live action role-player—it's truly sad I know what that means).

If I were to do something I love, it would certainly be baking. I love it. I love everything about it. I love finding a good recipe. I love making recipes better, adding my own touch to them. I love the smells that come from the oven as my newest creation is baking. I love the first taste, how the flavors and smells come together to form that perfect bite.

I must say the best part of baking is sharing it with others. I know that sounds cheesy, like some message from an after school special, but it's true. Watching the expressions as they have their first delicious bite... Hearing all the admiration and praise of my hard work... I think that is when I am truly happy.

But baking is not something one can do for a living. It's just not practical. I mean, in order to make any kind of money at it, I would have to go to school to become a chef, and then work my way up in some kind of fancy restaurant or something. Or run my own bakery. That's all too risky, and I do not have the stamina, nor do I have the gumption, to do something like that. I know me, and it's just not in me.

Not everyone can be like Rachael Ray and take their hobby and make a fortune out of it. I can't even watch her on TV. Mostly because she uses too many hand gestures and talks too loud — well, okay, that's what I tell other people what my reason is. The truth, though, is I am totally jealous when I watch her. She has my dream job. How could I not be envious? And okay, she actually *does* use too many hand gestures, it can be irritating. But that's not the point. The *point* is that I'm stuck in my life and this job, and it's sad. I have become a pathetic person whose hopes and dreams have been ruined by Rachael Ray and, more recently, by some new guy that stole my HR position.

I seriously can't do this report right now. I'm not in the mood. I have time to procrastinate, so I might as well do just that. Perhaps a little catnap would lighten my mood. I *am* feeling pretty sleepy.

A little nap might be helpful for this mood I can't seem to get out of. And yes, I do realize I'm at work. How could it be possible for me to take a nap? Oh, but it *is* possible. And no, Spectraltech does not offer break rooms with cots in them, even though I anonymously left an article on the president of the company's desk about how napping during the day can increase productivity and morale in a company. He obviously didn't bother reading it.

No big deal because I am actually the queen of taking little snoozes at work. A self-titled queen, but a queen nonetheless. No one actually knows about it because it's not something one should brag about. But it is quite a talent if I do say so myself.

It took me some time to perfect it, but I figured it out. Basically, I just lean my head on my left hand while my right hand moves the mouse. It took practice to be able to sleep and move the mouse at the same time, but I mastered it. I've also made sure that my computer screen is placed strategically in front of me. That way, if anyone were to walk into my office, my face would be hidden from view. It's genius really.

Luckily for me, I don't have to use this technique that often (it tends to put a bit of a kink in your neck) because I have a little secret: Upstairs on the sixth floor is a rarely used conference room. It's mostly used for the Board of Directors' quarterly meeting. Sometimes they will use it for presentations to investors or buyers, but this is rare.

Since Mr. Nguyen is the VP of accounting, he is always a part of the board meetings. Being the next person ranked under Mr. Nguyen and his assistant, I know his schedule and, therefore, know if the conference room is in use. Today, like most days, it's vacant. This means I can grab some files (my disguise) and head up to the sixth floor to catch a little nap.

It's brilliant, right? Too bad I am the only one that gets to celebrate my napping-at-work discovery since it's not something one would want to share with one's coworkers.

Mr. Calhoun is the only person who has an office on the sixth floor. He's the head of the HR department and would have been my new boss had things worked out how I wanted them to. He's rarely in his office though. He likes to be downstairs where the action is. He sometimes sets up camp in the downstairs sales conference room, just so he can be near everyone.

So, napping in the conference room it is. I think it will revive me and help me get out of this funk I am in.

I will just sneakily maneuver myself up to the sixth floor. Really, it's not that sneaky; I just grab the files and walk like I have a purpose, like I have somewhere to be. No one cares what I do anyway (unless I'm dropping baked goods off in the break room), so it's not that hard.

Okay, so I can see how I am not making myself look like an employee who actually gets their work done with all the smoke breaks and the napping, but I swear I do. It's just that lately Mr. Nguyen hasn't been giving me all that much work.

He just keeps giving me reports to do, that I swear I've done before. I actually questioned him about it the other day, and he just gave me a look as if I were an idiot and motioned for me to leave his office. He didn't say a word, which is not unlike Mr. Nguyen (he is the quiet type for sure), and shooed me off as he usually does.

It doesn't matter because I honestly don't care much what Mr. Nguyen thinks of me. I do my job; he knows that I do my job. He has nothing to complain about. He never says anything to me regarding my work. In fact, my reviews are usually done via e-mail. I always get the standard raise, so that essentially says I do my job, right? Besides, I'm not the type of girl who needs constant reassurance. Unless it has to do with my baking, and then I do love the compliments.

As I enter the conference room, I notice it's a little messy today. Come to think of it, I actually haven't been up here in a while (proof that I don't nap that often). I'm sure people are using the conference room to store stuff again. Heads are going to roll—Mr. Calhoun hates it when people use this for storage. Well, I won't be the one to tell him. I am not a tattle, and he would wonder what I was doing up here in the first place.

The conference table is a long rectangle shape with chairs surrounding. Boxes are placed sloppily on the table, and the chairs are moved around a bit. No worries, the best chair — my favorite chair — is still in its proper place: right at the head of the table. It is the most comfortable chair. It's the biggest chair in the room. I suspect it was someone's desk chair and they got a new one or something. I don't know why anyone would give up this perfect chair. I've even thought of switching it out with my desk chair, but I wasn't sure I could get away with it.

It's got a high-back, nice reddish-brown leather. And it even leans back. Probably from years of usage, but it's quite perfect for snoozing.

I plop myself down in the perfect napping chair, kick off my shoes, and put my feet up on the conference table. I lean my head back. I'm so tired, I can actually feel myself drifting off already. Just as I start to fall asleep, it dawns on me that napping at work is truly quite spinster of me...

Voices.

There are voices right outside the conference room door, and someone is rattling the handle. The rattling is what woke me up, actually.

Who would be using the conference room now? I checked the schedule, and there was nothing. It's a good thing I locked the door, just in case. I'm fairly certain a key to this room does not exist. Hopefully, whoever it is will just try the handle and then give up.

The handle rattles some more. I can't make out the voices; it's too muffled behind the door.

I'm feeling groggy. I'm not sure how long I've been asleep. Whoever is out there needs to leave so I can get back to my napping. The rattling of the handle is keeping me awake.

Oh, no. Oh Heaven's, no. I just heard keys. I swear I just heard keys rattling. Who would have a key? I try to rack my brain, fully awake now, panic starting to set in. How will I get out of this? There is no other way out than through that door.

The keys keep rattling. Perhaps they are trying to find which one actually fits. It's buying me a little time, but I still have nothing. I don't know how to get out of this. This is bad, really bad.

They must have found the right key, the door handle is moving. What do I do? I have nowhere to go.

I make a snap decision and slip under the conference table, grabbing my shoes as I hide. I will just have to wait until whoever it is does their thing, and leaves. Hopefully it won't be long. Maybe it's the same people who are leaving boxes up here. Yes, that's probably it.

In hindsight, I should have considered the fact that if there are boxes up here, then that might mean more are on their way, but I was too tired to think straight.

Wow. What is wrong with me? Who takes naps at work? Who? Idiots like me and George Costanza, that's who. Oh my gosh, I'm *totally* the female George Costanza right now. And to top it off, I am wearing a skirt. I'm under a conference room table in a skirt. Lovely.

I hear the door open, and from under the conference table I can see two sets of men's shoes walk in. One pair is an older pair, very worn. Not from wear and tear as much as worn from having to support fat feet. I know right away who that is—Mr. Calhoun, the HR director. The other pair of shoes is fancy. I have no idea the brand; I don't get into shoes that much. I bet Brown would be able to tell. The fancy shoes are shiny and black. A pair of perfectly tailored and pressed pants hang over the tops of the laces. Whoever this is, I can already tell this person is a little too formal for the likes of Spectraltech.

Oh! I bet I know who it is. I bet it's *him*. The jerk who stole my HR job.

"I'm not sure how the door got locked," I hear Mr. Calhoun say, flustered. "Very strange. Anyway, it's open now. So, now how long do you think it will take?" Mr. Calhoun asks the job stealer.

"It usually takes a couple of months," Job Stealer says as I see his feet walk to the head of the table. He pauses in front of something.

My *files*! Oh no! I left my files just sitting there. I'm such an idiot. I don't even know what files they are. They could be something I shouldn't be leaving around. I just grabbed whatever was on the top of my inbox. I can hear papers ruffling. Job Stealer is looking at my files.

"What's this? I thought no one used this conference room," I hear him say, sounding a little irritated.

"I'm not sure? No one should be using this room," I hear Mr. Calhoun say, slightly out of breath. Mr. Calhoun is always out of breath.

"I was just up here not that long ago, and I left my things up here. Someone could have gone through them," Job Stealer says, now sounding even more irritated.

"Yes, well, I'll check into this right away. It doesn't look like anyone has gone through anything," Mr. Calhoun says, worried tones in his voice.

There is silence for a second, and I can see they're walking around the table, probably looking for more clues left by the perpetrator. Imagine their surprise if they knew that it was just a lazy junior assistant, taking a nap and now hiding under the table. I would be fired for sure.

I hear papers ruffling again. I'm trying to rack my brain to remember what they are. I'm getting nothing. I'm sending out silent prayers that my name is not on any of those files. This could be the end of my career at Spectraltech. Then what would I do? I've been here for ten years. I don't even know how to look for a job. I've been out of that mode for so long.

The good thing is, for now, I am safe under this table. Job Stealer and Mr. Calhoun will leave at some point. I will stay here all day if I have to. It will be fine, just as long as I don't have to cough or anything.

And there it is: I just jinxed myself.

And now there's the tickle. There's a tickle in the back of my throat. Oh, please, no. Please, no.

I have to cough. I just have to. This is not good. I'm horrible at lying. How will I get myself out of this?

The tickle is getting worse. I need some water. I need to cough. This is very bad.

I can hear talking between Mr. Calhoun and the new guy, but I am too consumed by this tickle to be able to concentrate.

I'm sweating. I'm now sweating from trying to suppress this tickle. I'm actually starting to feel a little claustrophobic under this table. I need an out. I need to get out of this office right now.

Here is comes... I cannot suppress it any longer: I cough.

Everything goes silent, and then I see fat feet move around to the side of the table, directly in front of me.

*Think, Julia. You have to think.* I look around hysterically and see nothing. I have no options. I must get out from under this table and come up with something that even remotely resembles an excuse. I am fired for sure. Who would be under a table in a practically abandoned conference room? A sad, lonely, and soon-to-be jobless spinster that is who.

Mr. Calhoun's body struggles to bend over to look under the table.

"Julia?" He says, his eyes opening wide in surprise.

I crawl out from under the table. I can't think of anything. I have nothing. No speech to give. I'm horrible at speeches as it is. It would be a near impossibility for me to come up with one on the fly anyway.

And then I see it out of the corner of my eye: a red stapler by the door. It's a long shot, but it's all I've got.

"Ah! There it is!" I say trying to sound convincing. I crawl over to the door and pick up the red stapler on the floor. "I knew it was in here, but I couldn't find it."

I clumsily stand up and tug on my skirt that was hiking up a little too high. Mr. Calhoun just stares at me.

"I... uh... left it up here when I was doing that project... um... the other day," said the Worst Liar Ever.

I'm holding out the stapler as proof that I found what I was looking for. This is the worst excuse I have ever come up with. I am going to lose my job. I will be fired for sure. What will I do? I don't even have a resume. I need this job. I have no other options right now, and the job market is complete crap. I'm so screwed.

I look up to see the man who stole my job and Mr. Calhoun staring at me. Job Stealer is looking at me like I'm a complete idiot, which I clearly am.

In hindsight, wouldn't it have been better if I had just stayed sitting at the desk, and looked as if I were studying the files I brought up? I could have told them I needed a quiet place to go over reports or something. I still would have looked like a fool, but not as much as I do right now.

I have to get better at thinking on my feet. I wonder if there is some sort of class I can take.

I look at Job Stealer, and as I suspected by his shoes and the cuffs of his pants, he is dressed flawlessly up on top, as well. He stands there holding my files in his hands, looking a bit confused, mixed with irritation, mixed with something else—probably total disgust. I must leave here, right now.

"Well, I guess I'll just be going, now that I... um... found it," I say as I shake the stapler at them and try to go casually to the door that was left open when they came into the room.

Oh, to rewind this day. Rewind and start over. How many things I would do differently.

"Julia?" Mr. Calhoun says. Here it comes. I'm about to get fired. I might puke.

"Yes?" I smooth my hair back nervously, trying as hard as I can to act calmly. I stand up a little straighter.

They can't actually fire me over this, can they? So I was hiding under a conference table. So I was in a room that is hardly ever used. So what? That's not grounds for firing, is it? No, it's not. But they might think I was spying. Maybe I should just tell them what I was actually doing so they won't think I was spying. No, sleeping on the job is certainly grounds for firing. I should leave it alone and just pray.

Mr. Calhoun turns to the job stealer and holds out his hand for the files. "Are these yours?" he asks as he grabs them and turns back to me.

"Yes!" I say a bit overly enthusiastic. "That is why I needed the stapler. To... um... staple these very important... um... files." I sound like a babbling idiot.

He walks over to me and hands me the files. I take them and stand in the doorway for a few seconds, still waiting to hear the words "you're fired."

Mr. Calhoun motions for me to leave the room. He just dismisses me. Like that. No other words. I don't say anything else. I just turn and walk out the door, shutting it behind me.

I stand close by the door to make sure I don't hear any words like "fire" or "terminate" or "crazy stapler lady." But I can only catch tidbits of their conversation. I can hear Mr. Calhoun say "in accounting" and something like "no need to worry" and I swear he says "has great cupcakes." I never knew him to be such a perv. Wait, he probably said "makes great cupcakes." That would make much more sense. Mr. Calhoun is a huge fan of my homemade cupcakes. Leave it to cupcakes to save my job.

I actually can't believe I just got away with that. I mean, how did they buy that? This is a miracle, really.

I hurry back to my office. I want to get there as fast as I can, shut my door, and probably cry a little.

I make it to my office and quickly shut the door behind me. I set the stupid red stapler on my desk and then sit down putting my face in my hands. My heart is pounding in my chest.

I am such a fool. I must promise God if I never sleep on the job again that He will make them forget about all of this. Just wipe it from their brains. That's probably not even possible. I'm quite sure God would not want me to get out of this so easily.

The phone rings and I say a silent prayer that it's not my boss who just got wind of what happened, and now he is going to fire me. Of course, someone who thinks rationally would realize that this is pretty much next to impossible. It has only been about two minutes since I got away from the conference room.

"Hey, nerd." It's Brown. She lovingly refers to

me as nerd sometimes—mostly because she knows how much the nerds that work at Spectraltech bother me. She enjoys categorizing me with them.

She asks me if I want to go on a break with her, and although I technically have done nothing as far as work goes today, I feel I need a break after nearly getting caught... taking a break. Whatever. I need some fresh air.

One thing is for sure, I will not be telling Brown what just happened. She would never let me live it down. And I'm not entirely sure I want to relive the episode just yet, or ever.

I head downstairs to meet up with Brown and I feel as if everyone is staring at me, which is clearly all in my head. It has only been minutes since the "episode." It's not possible that anyone could know. So why does it feel as if everyone is staring at me?

I take the elevator down to the first floor. The bright sun hits my eyes as I walk outside and Brown is already there waiting for me. The fresh air feels good. I'm starting to feel a little better, but there is still a hard ball of sickness in the pit of my stomach. At this point, I am feeling like it may never go away... ever. I have never been one of those people that can let things go easily.

"What's up? Got any gossip?" Brown says as she leans up against the building and lights her cigarette.

I have no gossip for her. No gossip I want to

share, at least. Just a rather embarrassing story I don't want to share with anyone, ever. I still want to throw up a little. The cigarette smoke is not helping.

I'm considering going into my normal tirade to Brown about how I hate my job (this happens on a daily basis), when out of the corner of my eye I see the door next to us open. And out walks, you guessed it, the new guy, a.k.a. Job Stealer, a.k.a. the-person-who-just-caught-me-under-a-conference-room-table. Well, isn't this outstanding.

"Hi!" Brown says as he comes out the door. She hides the lit cigarette behind her.

Brown likes to be on the up and up with everyone, so she is always eager to meet the new people. There haven't been any new hires in the past few months, so I'm sure she is quite thrilled to get her little paws on this one.

"I'm Betsy Brown. I'm in Sales. You must be the new guy in HR," she says enthusiastically, holding out her cigarette-less hand to shake his. I stand behind her hoping he will not see me or possibly ignore me.

"That's me," he says as he shakes her hand, "Jared Moody." He states his name in a business-like manner.

"This is Julia Dorning," she says as she gestures to me behind her. "She's in accounting. You got the job she wanted."

I will kill her.

31

"I believe we have already had the pleasure of meeting," Jared says with a slight smile, actually more like a smirk, on his face. "I didn't know I stole your job, sorry about that," he says as he sticks his hand out to shake mine.

I shake his hand quickly and then go back to being the deaf-mute standing behind Brown.

I have nothing to say. I pretty much want to die. He's looking at me as if he wants to let out a laugh, and he probably does. I am a joke to him.

It doesn't matter anyway. It's not as if I will be working with him. I'm in accounting, and he's in HR… *Stupid freaking job stealer*.

"So, this is the smoking area?" Jared asks Brown, who must have decided it was okay to smoke in front of him because she went right back to it.

"Yep. You smoke?" Brown asks as she inhales the cigarette.

"No. I don't," Jared says, still looking as if he might laugh. He keeps peering around Brown, looking at me. "Well, it was nice to meet you… Betsy, is it?" She nods at him and smiles her perfect little smile. "You too, Julia," he nods toward me. "And I'm really glad you were able to find your stapler," he says with that same smirk on his face, which at this moment I would like to slap off.

I shrink back behind Brown, once again humiliated as he leaves us and heads to the parking lot.

We wait until he is out of earshot and then Brown turns toward me, "What stapler?" she asks, looking confused, and then she punches me in the arm. "You are holding out on me, Julia! How come you didn't tell me you met the new guy already?" Her eyes are wide with disbelief as if I forgot to tell her it was the end of the world, or there's a huge sale at Bloomingdales. "And you also failed to mention how seriously good-looking he is."

"It was a brief meeting, names weren't even exchanged," I say, a little over-defensive. I rub my arm because, seriously, she hit me hard! I don't mean to sound like a wimp, but geez!

I look over in the direction of the parking lot and watch Jared Moody walking toward his car. "You think he's good-looking? I didn't notice," I say flippantly.

Of course, I did notice. He's tall, has sandy blonde hair, light blue eyes... So impeccably dressed... he looks like some sort of model or something. Although, my view of real-life good-looking men is a bit skewed. I am surrounded by nerds.

I suppose Jared "Job Stealing" Moody is good-looking. Possibly verging on hot really. And I just stood there hiding behind Brown, not saying a word.

I should have acted all calm and collected toward him, like it was no big deal. I could have said something witty about the stapler, laughing it off as if it were an inside joke between us. "Yes, the stapler and I are once again reunited; I was really lost without it." Our heads would fly back in laughter as we bonded immediately over that red stapler.

But that didn't happen. I just stood there like a little mute schoolgirl. So, now I've humiliated myself twice in front of him.

This day just keeps getting more and more horrid.

I make up an excuse to leave and go back to my office. Apparently in her annoyance of my neglecting to tell her about how I met the new guy, Brown forgot about the stapler. Thank goodness. I don't know how I would lie myself out of that one. I probably would end up telling her the truth, and she would remind me for the rest of my life. I'm already going to have to deal with this Jared person anyway—who is clearly not going to let it go.

The rest of my day is pretty mundane, which is good, mainly for my heart. I'm still having palpitations every now and then.

I do another dreary report for Mr. Nguyen, which seems very familiar. I'm having serious déjà vu. This has been happening a lot lately. I even do a quick scan of past files to see if I can find this particular budget report, but I can't find anything.

At the end of the day, Mr. Nguyen comes by my office to grab a report he requested. He looks at the report while in my office, and then he asks me a few short questions about it. Then, he acts as if I've done something wrong and as he leaves, I hear him muttering something about having to do it himself.

Well, he *can* do it himself if he wants to. He won't get different info than I did.

Not that I actually understand it. I mean, it's just a bunch of numbers to me. I get the data from Mr. Nguyen himself. So, if there is a problem with the report, it is most likely *his* fault.

I don't get my boss. He is odd. I'm not even sure if he likes me at all. He seems to act like I am just an annoyance he needs to have around.

He wasn't my original boss. I was hired by a woman by the name of Lucy who I actually liked quite a bit. She told me she saw my potential and had plans for me. But then she got pregnant and left to be a mom. I do admire that, but hate how she left me in the lurch... and then I had to work for Henry Nguyen.

I will never forget the day I met him. He came in to my office and introduced himself to me. He looked at me strangely and then just nodded his head, and that was that.

A short little man of Asian descent. He's a strange one, that's for sure. He has one long pinky nail on his left hand. I have no idea what it's for and I've never asked him. Brown jokes that it's his "coke" nail. I did not understand the reference at first, because of my lack of slang knowledge apparently. I doubt that Mr. Nguyen is a druggie, but you never know.

I noticed throughout the day the office was all a-buzz over the new guy. All the women are so excited to have something more appealing to gaze upon rather than the nerds we are surrounded by. He has brought a little bit of excitement to Spectraltech.

I can't lie, despite how we met and how I acted the last time I saw him, I, too, am feeling a little excitement myself. Mixed with embarrassment, mixed with annoyance from him taking the job I wanted. It's all mixed-up and confusing.

Brown is now preoccupied with getting info on this Jared guy. She makes it her job to know everything about everyone at Spectraltech. As usual, she has been doing her thing, diligently searching for information on him. I got an e-mail from her earlier:

Been searching for stuff on the new guy, have come up with nothing yet. Very mysterious. Do you have anything? Meet me downstairs in ten. -B

I wrote her back and made up some excuse for not meeting up with her. I just want to stay in my office and not see anyone today. Namely, new guy and Mr. Calhoun. Also, the more times I talk to Brown, the more chances I would have of her remembering about the stapler and then she would grill me about it until I gave in.

If I didn't know Brown better, I would assume she was trying to find out more info because she was attracted to Jared. But Brown isn't like that. She just likes to go digging in other people's business. It's her thing. Plus, she has a boyfriend that she claims to be totally in love with. I've only met Matt a few times when he has come to a company party or has met Brown for lunch. From what I can gather about him, he's quite perfect for her. Just as good-looking as she is, and also bubbling over with self-esteem. They are cute together—in a way that kind of makes you want to throw up. They have been together for five years, and she says this is "the one."

I have always been baffled by "the one" theory. Like there is just one person out there for us. I have, well, zero persons out there for me at this point. And according to Webster's dictionary, I may never find a "one" before I go to my grave. I shall die alone like all the other spinsters.

Well, whatever. I'm sure Brown will get info on this Jared guy like she always does. Then, she will share it with me, and I hope it's some good dirty stuff. Like he is actually a hermaphrodite or an ex-con. Or maybe even a stripper. Then I can be grossed out by him, and the embarrassment won't be mine any longer, but his. I will just feel sad for him and his stupid perfect hair and stupid perfect blue eyes...

At exactly 5:30 p.m., I pack up my stuff and start heading out to the parking lot. I rarely work late because... well, I hate my job. Why stay late at a place you hate? I don't have much to get home to though. No plans tonight, per usual. Tonight, I just want to get out of my work clothes, get into some sweats, and relax in front of the television. I need to do something mindless.

As I walk out the door of that dreadful building and head toward my car, I hear someone calling my name from behind. I turn around and see Mr. Calhoun struggling to catch up with me.

"Julia!" He waves at me as he gets closer.

Oh my gosh, did he follow me out to my car to tell me I'm fired? He probably did. I knew I couldn't get away with that.

But wait, he has a pleasant look on his face, so maybe he isn't going to fire me. Plus, we are in the parking lot. Firing me here would be highly unprofessional anyway, right? Not that I'm the best judge of what being a "professional" is.

"Yes?" I ask as he gets closer to me. I try to act all calm and collected, hoping he won't bring up the whole hiding-under-the-table incident.

"Julia," he says my name again and pauses to catch his breath. He's got to be at least three hundred pounds. Poor, sweet, Mr. Calhoun. He has a kind face, and I've always had a soft spot for him. He kind of reminds me of my grandpa... only bigger.

"I was wondering if you wouldn't mind making the 'proverbial' cupcakes for the new hire, Jared. I thought it would be a nice way to welcome him to the company." He uses air quotes when he says "proverbial." Mr. Calhoun always seems to add the word "proverbial" in most of his conversations and presentations. Most times incorrectly, I might add.

I smile slightly. I know what this is about. "Sure, Mr. Calhoun—no problem. Vanilla or chocolate?"

"Hmm, I don't know," he puts his hand to his chin as he ponders. "I would say, maybe a little of both?" He winks at me and smiles. I know very well that the cupcakes are not for Jared, but I will play along. Mr. Calhoun loves my homemade cupcakes and jumps at any chance to get me to make them. I don't know why he feels as if he has to have an excuse every time. He could just ask me. It's not as if I have a life or anything. Of course, he probably doesn't know that.

"No problem. I will bring them in tomorrow." I turn to walk toward my car.

"Thanks, Julia. Have a good night!" he says enthusiastically as he turns to walk back toward the building.

Mr. Calhoun never leaves the office early. He

is always here. I have even suspected that he has worked through the night before. I can't imagine him having that much work, but perhaps he is avoiding his home life or something. Brown heard that he was having some marital issues.

Oh! Maybe him and Martha?? Oh no... Don't picture it, don't picture it, don't picture it... too late. Gross.

So, at least I have some plans for tonight. Cupcakes! I love to make cupcakes, and I make the best if I do say so myself. Just the right touch of vanilla. But the secret is in the frosting. Two sticks of pure butter—the salted kind. Four cups of powdered sugar. One tablespoon of my homemade vanilla, and a touch of cream to thin it out. It's amazing.

I've been told that I should go into business, but I have no idea how I would venture into something like that. I don't think I'm daring enough to do my own thing. I also have an enormous problem with procrastination, which I'm pretty sure does not make for a good business owner.

I am thinking of ways I will decorate my cupcakes on the drive home, which is making it so much less mundane than the commute typically is. I'm a little particular about my cupcakes. One might say "anal-retentive" if one were being *rude*. My sister Anna has used those exact words when referring to my relationship with baking.

Speaking of the spoiled brat, I see her car in the driveway at my parents' house as I pull up. I'm sure she's here to ask for money, or new clothes, or a new car, or something like that. Either way, I'm sure she will get it. Anna is brilliant at getting things from my parents. They are so gullible when it comes to her. Neither of them will admit it, but I'm pretty sure she's the favorite.

Anna is what my mom calls an "accidental blessing." My parents thought they were done after my younger brother Lennon and I were born. They had a neat little matching set—a perfect family of four. And then when I was ten and Lennon was eight, they sat us down and told us that we were getting another sibling. We were not thrilled. I did not want another sibling, especially a sister. I liked having all the attention I needed from my parents. I didn't want to have to share my toys and my clothes and my room... I think I actually cried when my dad called from the hospital to tell us it was a girl. Lennon cried, too, but not for the same reasons. He would have loved a brother.

Anna lived up to all of my expectations. She was the most spoiled rotten little thing wrapped in a cute bratty package. Everyone would say how adorable she was, or how cute her little pigtails were, or how witty she was. It was annoying. At that point, I was no longer in the cute stage—I was in the awkward-bad-hair-with-braces stage. It was not pretty. Everything she did was so adorable to everyone. Everything I did was just... awkward.

We never quite got along, me and Anna. We have completely different tastes in everything. I like to bake, she likes to go shopping. I like to read, she likes to go shopping. I like to watch my shows, she likes to go shopping.

Since high school graduation, Anna has been in and out of school trying desperately to figure out what she wants to do with her life. I'm sure right now she is telling my mom about her newest idea and how this is "for sure" what she wants to do.

So far, Anna has wanted to be a doctor, a lawyer, a dentist, a hair-stylist, an esthetician, a court reporter, and I think the last time she dropped by, she was extremely excited about becoming an elementary school teacher. Her excuses vary for why she changes her mind, but they all have one thing in common—it takes actual work to get a license or degree in each of her ideas. And Anna does not like to work. She likes things handed to her, a trait my parents are fully to blame for. I have reminded them of this on many occasions, and they do not deny it.

Not wanting to go inside just yet, I sit on the porch and listen to the wind blowing through the trees. This has been the best spring in Denver in a long time.

Through the screen door, I can hear Anna

whining to my mother about something. I lean in a little further to hear their conversation.

"It's just not fair!" Anna says in her it's-all-about-me voice. The one she uses ninety percent of the time.

Wow, I wonder how long it took the whining to begin. Ten minutes after she got home? Fifteen minutes? My poor mother.

"I know dear, but Julia is just going through something right now."

Wait, they are talking about me? I move in closer so I can hear their conversation better. My ear is right up against the screen. They're in the kitchen, which is around the corner so they can't see me.

"She's been living there for ten years, Mom. Ten years! I think it's time that one of us got a chance to use the basement apartment. I would like to at least have the option."

"Anna, dear, I'm just not sure Julia would want to move out. She has a hard time with change. It's something she has always had a hard time dealing with. I can't ask her to move out." Move out? Change? What the heck are they talking about? And why does my mom make me sound like some sort of mentally handicapped child? Is that how she thinks of me? Really?

"Come on, Mom. You know she needs to leave. She's thirty-two years old! She needs a nudge. You just need to tell her to go. It would be good for her." Seriously? She's making a play for the basement?

"Maybe I could talk to her," I hear my mom say with doubt in her voice. She is not good with those kinds of conversations. If she were serious about it, she would have my dad talk to me.

Well, I've had enough of this conversation. I open the screen door, and it makes a creaking sound which immediately stops their talk. I should walk right in there and tell my mother that I am not some sort of invalid and then tell Anna where she can go. But I don't really feel like it, and I wouldn't have anything polite to say.

"Hi, Mom. Hi, Anna," I say with no smile on my face.

"Hi, sweetie!" my mom says a little over-enthusiastically, guilt all over her face. She hates talking about people behind their backs. She has never been any good at gossip. I apparently must have gotten that from my dad, although he's not actually a gossip either. I guess I can't blame that one on my parents.

Anna gives my mom a glance and nudges her to talk to me, even though my mom clearly does not want to have this conversation right now. She shoots a look to Anna telling her to shut up, and Anna rolls her eyes. She has lost this battle.

The silence is awkward and we all just keep looking at each other.

"Well, I guess I will go downstairs, I have

cupcakes to make." I head toward the stairs. No reason to sit around there and feel uncomfortable.

"Save me one!" Anna calls out after me. At least there is one thing Anna appreciates about me — my baking.

I am kind of sick to my stomach right now, and actually the thought of making cupcakes is not cheering me up like it usually does. Anna wants to use the basement apartment, which she should have every right to. And my mom kind of agrees with her. I am feeling a little embarrassed that I have not tried to venture out in ten years. Ten years! That's a long time. Heaven knows I have enough money saved up from living here to put something down on my own place. Why can't I just do that? Why is it so hard for me?

Feeling frustrated, I start grabbing the ingredients I need to bake the cupcakes. I know it will make me feel better to just get started. Baking is freeing for me, I actually think it's therapeutic. It probably has kept me sane all these years. Although from what my mom was saying to Anna, perhaps I'm not quite as sane as I thought.

I look around at this great setup I have. It really is the coolest basement apartment. My parents originally made it so that any of their parents could move in and they would be able to help take care of them. My dad's father died when I was pretty young, and his mom remarried fast and has been traveling the world. She's in terrific shape for being eighty-two. My mom's parents refused to move in — instead, they moved into a retirement village in Miami with a bunch of their friends.

So this fully furnished apartment, which my parents worked so hard on, was left for no one to use. It was just too perfect for me not to move in right out of college. I didn't have a job quite yet, and I needed some place to go. It was a way to live at home, but *not* live at home. My parents never asked for rent money, and I never offered. In hindsight, that would have been nice of me to do. But instead, I saved all the money. Now, I have a nice little nest-egg to use on, well, I'm not sure yet. But something. Perhaps a refuge for cats, or a down payment on a trailer.

Right now, I don't want to think about Anna and her wanting to live in the basement. It's just too much for me to consider. Finding a new place to live, finding furniture, moving in, signing paperwork, living by myself... it's just too much. I know I need to leave at some point, I know I need to get out on my own, but right now I just want to bake.

I get started on the cupcakes, and I take care to mix the batter just so, not over-mixing it, but not under-mixing it either. My pink KitchenAid mixer is one of the greatest purchases I have ever made. I've had it for a while now, and I still get a little giddy when I look at it.

I make the vanilla batch first, and then I do the chocolate. I use different colored paper cupcake holders, which I bought at the restaurant supply store last week, to bake the cupcakes in. One set is white with a black damask print and the other is a pink-gingham. So adorable.

Once the cupcakes are baked and cooled, I meticulously pipe the frosting on with a star tip. Then, for decoration, I use different colored sprinkles. I like a uniform sprinkle, none of that tossing it on for me. I use pink sugar crystals for the damask print holder and chocolate jimmies for the pink gingham ones. When I'm done, I stand back and look at my work. All works of art really.

After I'm done baking, the conversation I heard earlier between my mother and Anna doesn't seem as daunting as it did before. Maybe Anna will just forget about wanting to live here, and I can stay and keep my life the way it is. I'm used to my life. I know I probably need to make a change, but I want to do it on my terms and not because I'm forced to.

As I get into bed after I have put all the cupcakes in boxes to transport them to work tomorrow, I think over my day. Besides the silver lining of baking cupcakes, this truly has been such a crappy day. And I thought yesterday was awful. I mean, realizing you are a spinster is one thing, but getting caught hiding under a conference room table by a guy who stole your job — strike that — a hot guy that stole your job... well, that is just a whole other bad day in itself. I honestly can't compare the two. Both days sucked. I wonder if this is how the rest of my week is going to go.

# CHAPTER 3

Cupcakes are in the main break room. Enjoy! – Julia

I'm not going to lie. It took me over an hour to come up with this e-mail. Other drafts consisted of "Cupcakes up in the break room, y'all! Go and get ya some!" and "Yo, cupcakes in the break room. Peace."

I'm feeling pretty solid with the one I went with.

It's ridiculous that I'm all in a tizzy (yes, that's right, I said tizzy) about these cupcakes. I'm feeling... I don't know how to describe it... vulnerable? I think I might know why.

So here is the deal with me: I live inside my head a lot. This has always been a part of who I am. Perhaps it's not that abnormal. Of course, I have to because as I have already established, apart from work and baking, I have no life. So, I tend to exaggerate things in my head a bit. I say this because it is highly possible that, in the late hours I was up making cupcakes, I may or may not have had a few, ahem, fantasies about the new guy, Jared. And no, they were not *those*

49

kinds of fantasies.

They mostly consisted of... no, really, they are just too stupid to admit. Okay, fine. They mostly consisted of him taking one bite of cupcake and falling madly in love with me, and then we ran away into the sunset. It varied a little, but that is the gist of it. In my fantasies, he was no longer the job-stealing-smirking-jerk that he actually is, but this incredible guy who says and does everything right. You know, the type of guy who doesn't actually exist.

It's ridiculous, right? I mean I don't know the guy at all, and what I do know of him is that he's a big ol' jerk. He stole my job for one. And then he was practically laughing at me about my red stapler incident, and while I'm sure it will be one of those funny things I look back on, I'm not finding it so funny right now. Just very, very, very embarrassing.

If I honestly think about it though, it's not that ridiculous. Not the part about me fantasizing about a guy I don't even know—no, that is totally ridiculous. But I work at an office full of complete and total nerds (and, by the way, I looked up "nerd" in the dictionary, and it said: "an unstylish, unattractive, or socially inept person," which is so incredibly fitting, it's scary) and along comes someone who is *so* not a nerd. Well, I couldn't help myself. Jerk or not.

I usually like to hang out in the break room after I drop off the cupcakes to see everyone enjoying them. But today I just couldn't. I dropped them off, grabbed a soda, and went back to my office as fast as I could. I then proceeded to spend the next half hour (or more) writing up an e-mail to send out to the office that Jared would inevitably read. So, it's pretty understandable why it took me so long.

My phone rings and it's Brown wanting to go on a break. Perfect timing because I'm pretty much drained from having to write the cupcake e-mail, so I figure I deserve a little break. Then once I come back and play a game of Spider Solitaire to clear my head from our break conversation, I will finally get some actual work done, but by then it could be lunch time. Oh well, I'll just take the day as it goes.

"Great cupcakes, Julia!" a software engineer named Brian says to me as I walk out of my office.

"Thanks!" I say to him and smile. I make sure it's a you-and-I-work-together-and-that-is-all smile because — well, once at an office Christmas party, I was in exceptionally poor judgment, and Brian and I made out in the upstairs conference room. Yes, the place where I used to take my naps. It was not one of my better moments.

In my defense, Brian is a sweet guy, and when you are stuck in an office full of not-so-good-looking people, one of them is bound to become good-looking. You just keep lowering your standards until someone meets them. It's true. Plus, it had been a really long time for me, and I mean a *really* long time.

I made the mistake of telling Brown, and she has never let me live it down. Apparently, although I don't see it, Brian may or may not resemble a troll. At least, that is what Brown says. I don't see it because I am not as shallow as Brown. Or perhaps I don't want to admit it because that would make me even more pathetic, but I'm pretty sure it's because I'm not shallow.

The spring breeze feels pleasant on my face as I open the door and step outside to meet up with Brown. Brown is, of course, looking adorable. She's wearing a black pencil skirt with a soft white blouse with some kind of ruffle-y thing on it and black patent leather shoes probably made by someone name Christian Blah-blah-tin (I can never remember). Whatever his name is, he's her favorite. Brown's hair is perfectly done, soft blonde curls about half-way down her back. Her hair is definitely something people covet. It's long and is always perfect. I feel like sometimes she's going to swoop her head toward me, and in a deep sultry voice say, "And I'm worth it," like those Clairol commercials.

Her eyes scrunch up, and she smiles slightly as she sees me, "What's up, Jules?"

"Not much," I tell her as I lean up against the wall next to her.

"I saw the cupcakes in the break room, you

outdid yourself." She winks at me, cigarette lit and in hand.

"Did you actually eat one?" I look at her, knowing the answer already.

"Nope." Brown never eats my baked goods because she claims she doesn't like sugary stuff. I think that's something she's told people for so long, she actually believes it's true herself. Because honestly, who actually dislikes sugar? I will hold her down and force her to eat a cupcake someday. I swear I will.

"Got any gossip?" she says, and then inhales her cigarette.

"Nope. I've just been doing dumb reports for Nguyen," and taking a half hour to write a one-sentence e-mail, but I'm not telling her that. "Did you ever find out any info about the new guy?" I'm seriously hoping she found out something about him, something that could stop me feeling embarrassed — shamefully fantasizing — about this man I hardly know.

"No, nothing yet. Very frustrating. Give me time and I will find something," she says confidently. And she will. Brown is amazing at digging up info about people.

The door from the building opens quickly and out walks, guess who… Yep, the star of my absurd fantasies, Jared. He walks right by us, talking on his cell phone. He walks about ten feet away from us and stops. Brown and I look at each other, and then both lean toward him to see if we can hear what he is saying.

"I told you, I don't have time to do that." He does not sound happy. "What do you mean? I did what I was hired for!" His voice got a little louder with the last statement.

Brown mouths to me, *What is going on?* and I shrug. How would I know?

It's quiet as he listens to the person on the other line. He looks over his shoulder and glances in the direction of Brown and me. We quickly look away, Brown at the floor and me at the ceiling. I have this overwhelming feeling to start whistling as I look up, but I stop myself.

I expect him to walk further away, but instead he turns completely around and walks toward us.

"I'll have to call you back later," he says, and ends his call, slipping his phone back in his pocket.

"Betsy and Julia, right?" he asks as he walks up to us. He wants to talk to us? Oh geez. Here comes deaf-mute girl again.

"Hey!" Brown says and waves at him. Why is everything she does so perfectly cute? Even the way she says "hey." It's so annoying. I'm sure if it were me that said it, it would come out sounding like the bearded-lady or something.

"Do you guys come out here often?" he asks. He's got that same smirk on his face, and I'm feeling the need to slap it off.

"Just when the weather is decent," Brown

says, and then takes a drag from her cigarette. This is a total lie, of course. We come out here at all times of the year. Minus during a blizzard, which doesn't happen that often.

There's an awkward silence for a moment, and then Jared turns to me. Here it comes — more comments about me and my red stapler. Just fabulous.

"I had one of the cupcakes, Julia. Really good stuff," he says, the smirk turning into more of a genuine smile, and of course my heart flutters a little, which is so annoying and unfounded. He has a seriously great smile. A great smile that I hate, of course. I must keep reminding myself that he stole my job, great smile or not.

"Thanks," I squeak out and nod my head, nervously pursing my lips together, and that's pretty much all I've got at this point. Brown looks at me strangely and then nudges me lightly in the ribs with her elbow.

"So let me guess," he looks from Brown to me, "you two must be the gossip girls around here."

Brown and I look at each other, and my eyes widen. How the heck would he know that? Did someone say something? Are we that transparent?

"What makes you think that?" Brown says, sounding a little insulted.

"Just a hunch." He shrugs. The fluttering suddenly goes away. *Who is this guy?*

"Well, you're wrong," Brown says, and looks at him like he's got some nerve.

"Whoa, hey, I don't mean to offend," he smiles genuinely at us, and just like that, the flutters are back. "I just wondered if you two are the people that have all the information. You know, the good juicy company stuff. I like to know what's going on around me."

Brown looks at me and shrugs. "Well, we might know a little bit." She smiles slightly at him.

"Great. Well, then, let's start with you two. How long have you worked at Spectraltech?" he asks, looking from Brown to me with those intense blue eyes. Oh, and now the flutters have turned to butterflies in my stomach. What is this? Fifth grade? I soooo hate me right now.

"I've been here for five years," Brown says, her voice full of confidence.

He gestures over toward me. "Ten" is all I can say, and then I blush. Why would I even blush at that? What is wrong with me?

Brown looks over at me like I am some sort of idiot and I'm sure she's a little shocked at seeing me at a loss for words because that doesn't happen very often. Her eyes open a little wide and then a smile comes across her face. And just like that, Brown knows. She knows I'm being a ridiculous schoolgirl, and, of course, she is not used to this, never having anyone at Spectraltech to look at in, well, ever. Then, an evil smile spreads across her face and I shoot her a glance like "you wouldn't." Oh, but she would.

"Now it's our turn. So, where did you go to school?" Brown asks Jared and flashes a conniving smile.

"CU," he says, and smiles at me.

"That's so funny because Julia went to UNC. Isn't that so funny, Julia?" No, it's not funny, it's not funny at all.

"Why is that funny?" Jared asks, looking confused.

"You know, they're both universities... in the same state... anyway, I've got a meeting to get to, so you two can chat about that." Then in some sort of lightning-fast speed, she leaves me there by my deaf-mute self, alone with ridiculously hot job-stealing-Jared.

"So UNC, huh?" Jared says, clearly not planning on leaving as I had just prayed for him to do.

I nod my head yes. *Say something!*

"So, CU, huh?" Really? Is that the best I could come up with?

Jared gives me a kind of you-must-be-slow smile. "I guess I better get back to work." He starts to open the door, and then turns back to me. "That cupcake was one of the best I've ever had, you should think about selling them." Then he flashes me a genuine smile that makes my stomach turn, in a ridiculous way. I goofily smile back, surely confirming that I am, in fact, slow.

Back at my desk, I have a report to work on for Mr. Nguyen but before I get to that, I need to send the most hate-filled e-mail to Brown. If our e-mails weren't monitored for cussing, I would be using some very choice words as well.

I start to write the e-mail, but then I realized two things. First of all, my anger would be lost on Brown. She truly wouldn't care. And second of all, I don't want to give her the satisfaction of knowing how irritated I am.

I decide I deserve a soda from the vending machine, but as I am about to leave my office I am stopped short by Mr. Nguyen who does not look at all pleased. Although, that is how Mr. Nguyen always looks.

"Julia, do you have that report I asked you for?" he asks sternly.

Report? Report? Report? Please say I did it yesterday. "Which report was that, Mr. Nguyen?"

"I e-mailed it to you this morning."

Craaaaaaaaaaaaaaaaaaaaap! "Yes, I am... um... nearly done so I will just... uh... get that right to you," I stammer, very unconvincingly, and head back to my desk. I have done absolutely no work today. Oh please, don't let this be a long report! With all these new people in the office — okay, new *person* in the office — I'm forgetting to do my job. I cannot be *that* girl. I am not that girl.

It was not a long report, but it was not an easy

one. I kept re-running the numbers because they didn't make sense. How could profits be down so low last quarter? I feel confident that I did the report correctly, so I shoot it off to Mr. Nguyen.

I spend the next few hours in my office, doing various reports and designing a spreadsheet Mr. Nguyen asked me to do for a big meeting we both have to attend tomorrow. I work my way through lunch, just eating at my desk. I guess I'm feeling a little guilty for not doing my job, and I also feel a little stupid for letting some weird schoolgirl crush get in the way of work. That is the kind of girl I make fun of, not the kind of girl I am.

"I feel that, as a friend, I need to tell you something," Brown says to me as we go outside to the smoking area. It's near the end of the day and Mr. Nguyen had a meeting, so I figured I could take a little break.

"What is it?" I ask, not truly caring. I am still annoyed with her. I want to say something, but there is no point. She wouldn't care anyway.

"Friends do not let friends go around with *that*," she says, pointing to my upper lip.

"What do you mean? Is there something on my lip?" I ask, walking over to the door to see if I can see my reflection in the glass. I can't see anything.

"Yes, there is something on your upper lip... *hair.*"

Whaaaaaaaaat? "Are you serious? I have a moustache?" My hand immediately goes up to my mouth, covering it and my upper lip. "But... I... How bad?" Somehow this is very fitting. A spinster with a moustache.

"Look, it's not bad. And we do not call it a 'moustache,' it's referred to as 'upper lip hair,'" says the perfectly-put-together prom queen. "You have sort of... always had one. But it was always blonde hair, so I never said anything. But now, all of the sudden, there are brown hairs as well as the blonde."

I guess right now would be a good time to die. I mean, I recently had a conversation with a good-looking man and this hasn't happened in, well, over a decade. And I realize it wasn't a real conversation since I couldn't say more than three word sentences. But he was talking to me up-close and — oh my gosh, he could have seen it. Of course he did because that is how my life goes. I am an under-a-conference-table-hiding-deaf-mute-possibly-slow-spinster... with a moustache. Next comes sagging boobs and trailer parks.

"Relax, it's not *that* bad. I just thought you might want to take care of it, just in case, you know, you see your little lover boy, Jared." She says "lover boy" in a sing-song voice.

I roll my eyes at her, still covering my mouth

and upper lip with my hand. I will have to walk around the rest of the day like this, just in case I run into... someone... anyone! I don't want *anyone* seeing my moustache. Unless it's Martha, and then maybe I could get some tips from her—she's got one as well. Maybe Martha and I could start a moustache club.

I can't believe the one thing I have in common with Martha is our twin moustaches, but our love lives—oh no, those are polar opposites.

"Oh, get over yourself, Jules," Brown says, seeing the horror on my face. "I'll e-mail you an address for a little place I go to. You can have it taken care of and be upper-lip-hair free by tomorrow." She pats me on the head like I'm her little dog.

I relax a little. Thank goodness I can have this taken care of tonight, I was seriously considering calling in tomorrow because of it. But I can't because of the meeting I have to attend with Mr. Nguyen.

A freakin' moustache... seriously.

"Listen up, I have some fantastic gossip," Brown says, turning my attention quickly away from my upper-lip.

Apparently Jean in sales, who is going to be out of the office for the next three weeks because of some family illness, is actually going to get a boob job. A boob reduction, actually. I have to say, in Jean's case, this is a necessity. But isn't everyone going to notice? I don't know, maybe breast reductions are not as obvious as implants. We soon shall see.

After our break, I hurry back to my desk because I don't want anyone to see my moustache, or upper lip hair — whatever. I stop by the bathroom on the way back just to take a closer look at myself, and sure enough, I am a spinster with a 'stache. Kill. Me. Now.

As promised, Brown sends me an e-mail with the info I need to prevent me from being an upper-hair-lip-girl for life. It's a little mani-pedi place just down the road from here. Apparently, they remove hideous lady-moustaches as well.

I make an appointment for just after work. I want to get this over with. I've never had my upper lip waxed, and it honestly doesn't sound like fun. It sounds quite painful, actually. I e-mailed Brown back, freaking out a little about the possible pain, but she wrote back and said it was no big deal.

I successfully make it out of the building and to my car without running into anyone, namely Jared. Not that it would matter, he has no-doubt already seen my man-lip. Maybe that's why he is always smirking at me. Maybe it's not about the stapler at all, but my mannish appearance.

The place is called "Mimi's Nail." Yes, that's right, "Nail," as in just *one* nail. I don't know what I was picturing it to be, but I am pleasantly surprised by the spa-like feeling inside. I check in, grab a seat, and pick up a copy of *Cosmo* from five years ago, which is probably right up my alley since I'm about five years behind in anything stylish—or maybe ten years. I'm sure my sister would say a lifetime behind.

The magazine is full of the usual—clothes that no one should ever wear in public. One of the models is wearing a plaid scarf-type-thing across her chest and a skirt about as short as underwear. No shirt underneath, just the scarf. The adjacent article says, "What to Wear to the Office: It Doesn't Have to be Boring Anymore." Are they insinuating that one could wear this barely-there scarf and skirt to work? Really? That is pretty ridiculous if you ask me, but what do I know.

Oh! The next article is interesting: "Dating 101: How to Date a Coworker." This is definitely more appealing than the other article.

It says forty percent of workers have dated someone on the job during their career. Ha! Well, none of them has ever worked at Spectraltech. The dating pool has left much to be desired, until recently that is. And even then, it's only up by one.

This part is intriguing: *"Before making a move, it's a good idea to suss out whether your work crush has the hots for you, too. Some tip-offs are if he starts hanging around your work space frequently, or asks you to grab lunch or after-work drinks."*

Well, I think I might have to read this entire article. I look around carefully to see that no one is looking at me and quickly rip it out and put it in my purse.

What? Everybody does it. I need it just in case the offer ever presents itself. You never know, Brian the Troll and I could be destined to be together, and I would, therefore, need to know how to properly date a coworker.

A small Asian woman approaches me, asking me to follow her. We go to the back of the spa to a small dimly-lit room. She tells me to lie down on the massage table that is taking up most of the tiny space. I'm feeling the not-so-good kind of butterflies in my stomach. Have I mentioned before that I seriously hate pain? Well, I do. I avoid it all costs.

I lie down on the table and close my eyes. Maybe closing my eyes will make it all better. Or maybe it really isn't that bad, and I might even fall asleep during the process... I am feeling quite comfortable right now.

"You ready?" She says to me, and I give her the go ahead. *I can do this, I can do this...*

Oh! Okay, the wax is kind of hot. Is that normal? I'm sure it is. But it feels pretty hot. Really hot. I think I smell something burning. Should I say something? No, that would be stupid. Okay, it's kind of cooling off now. That's probably what it's supposed to do.

Now she is putting some sort of paper on the wax. She pulls the corner of my mouth down and taut and here it comes, here it comes, here it comes!

Rrriiiiiiiiiipppp! Oooooowwww! Okay, that freaking hurt. What the heck was Brown talking about? I feel like my upper lip was just pulled entirely off. People do this? Seriously, I'm not exaggerating. It's burning! My entire upper lip is on fire.

I can't believe people do this on a regular basis. This is my first time, and I already know that there is no way that I am doing this again. I am just going to have to find an alternative for next time.

Okay, okay, now she's putting some soothing cream on my lip and it's feeling a little better. Wow, that was crazy-painful.

She helps me up from the table, and we walk to the front of the store. She asks me if I want to get a pedicure, and although I totally need one (surprise, surprise), I decline. Maybe I'm being a bit of a wimp here, but my upper-lip is hurting pretty bad. The cream she put on is no longer helping, and now it's throbbing.

Geez, what we women do to ourselves to be more appealing is ridiculous. If my upper lip hurts this bad, I can't imagine how a bikini wax would feel. I shudder at the thought.

I pay her and quickly exit. The cool evening air stings my lip as I head out. I make a call to Brown on my cell phone as I get into my car.

"What's up, Jules?" She answers after the third ring.

"Oh my gosh, Brown, why didn't you tell me getting my upper lip waxed hurt this bad?"

"What? What are you talking about? It doesn't hurt *that* bad," she says sounding confused. I thought she would be laughing like "the joke is on you!", so I'm confused as well.

"No, seriously! It killed!" I say, pointing to my lip, although she can't see me.

"Geez, Julia, you are ridiculous. You have, like, the lowest tolerance for pain of anyone in history." She starts laughing a little.

"It's not funny! I'm telling you, the whole waxing thing hurt really bad. And now my lip is still hurting! Can I put something on it?" The burning intensifies even more when the cool air starts moving through the car vents, so I turn them off.

"I guess you can put some aloe on it or something. You really are ridiculous." I can imagine her eyes rolling at me, just by the tone in her voice. "But think, now you will no longer have upper lip hair."

"Yah, at least I got it over with." It's still burning! Seriously, this cannot be normal. Who does this?

"Anyway, I'm glad you called because I have some good gossip," she says in a little sing-song voice that she gets sometimes when she is excited about gossip.

"But... My lip!" I say because I am not done whining about it.

"Oh geez, Jules. Get over yourself. Now listen up," she says, and I do because I like gossip and, at the very least, it can help me forget about my lip, even if for a second.

She tells me that she left work a little later than usual, and as she was walking out to her car, she saw Mr. Calhoun walking Martha to her car and it looked rather intimate. No hand-holding or kissing or anything, but it certainly didn't look all business either. I tell her how I had recently had the same suspicions.

"So, Mr. Calhoun and Martha, huh..." she trails off.

"Yah, don't picture it," I say, and smile to myself.

"Oooh, Julia! Nasty! I hate it when you do that," she says, clearly having pictured it.

"So now, back to my lip — which is still throbbing, by the way."

"Oh, brother. I have to go, Jules. You will be fine, I promise," she says. She then quickly says goodbye and ends the call.

I don't have much to do tonight. When I get home, I just throw on some sweats, take my hair out of my normal ponytail, and sit in front of the TV. I did find some aloe, which is definitely helping the upper lip situation. After an hour, it is still hurting, though not as bad.

I surveyed it in the mirror, and despite a lot of redness, there is not a hair there. So that's good. I look a little bit like a clown, but I'm hopeful that will go away. At least before tomorrow. I really do not need to go to work looking like a clown. I have acted like one all week—no need to look like one.

# CHAPTER 4

Remember when you were in high school, and it was more exciting to go to school when there was the off chance you might run into a cute boy? Remember that feeling? Now imagine having that feeling in your thirties, only it's not school, its work... and you will see why I need to be committed.

Yes, so I'm finding myself a little excited about going into work today. It's totally ridiculous and baseless. But after so many years of dragging myself into the office, never wanting to be there, it's not a totally horrible thing, right?

Here's what I know about Jared: first of all, he stole my job. But I am starting to get over that. I mean, I don't even know if I'd have gotten the job, even had he not popped up and stole it. Secondly, he's incredibly good-looking. And third, and most important of all, the cupcake I made him is the best cupcake he's ever had. Ever.

Here's what I don't know about Jared: Everything else. Seriously, this guy could be a psycho stalker for all I know. I'm being totally ridiculous.

This is what I keep telling myself, and yet, here I am actually feeling a bit of excitement to go to work today. I am probably the most pathetic person in the world. At least I can admit it. Most people who are pathetic don't know it.

After my shower, I put on my one pair of black slacks and a dusty-rose colored Polo because I have been told it looks good with my skin. This morning, I am finding myself wishing I had more to wear than what I have in my closet, and let-me-tell-you, this is a first for me. Maybe I will have to go shopping. However, I wouldn't know where to begin. We have already established that I have no sense of style. As a spinster, it is my duty to know nothing about the fashion industry.

Just for fun, I picture myself wearing the sash and extremely short skirt from that Cosmo article. How hilarious would that be? I mean, I seriously couldn't pull that off. Brown couldn't even pull that off.

I give myself a once over in the mirror, my first of the day. Unlike most women, I don't stare at myself in the mirror forever, primping and such. I know — surprise, surprise. But I don't wear makeup, I normally pull my hair back so I don't have to round-brush it, and I wear nearly the same thing every day. So, what is there to see? I already know what I look like.

But today I find myself looking a little longer

than just the once over. Wow, that dusty-rose color really does look good with my pale skin and dark brown hair. Even my green eyes seem to shine a little brighter…

What the… What is *that*?????

Oh my gosh, please no. Please nooooooooooo!!! There's a scab. There's scab on my upper lip. I totally forgot about the moustache waxing debacle from last night! This is not happening. Please say this is not happening.

It's not a small scab, either. It's a long, thin, brownish scab above my upper lip.

I look… like… Hitler.

What am I going to do? I don't own any makeup. There is no way in hell I am going to work today. I can't show up with this! What would people say? It's offensive in so many ways.

That's the answer then: I will just call in. It's Friday, which means I have an entire weekend for this thing to heal.

Okay. It's going to be okay.

Wait, I just remembered that I can't call in! I have a budget meeting that I'm required to go to. Of course, I do. Of course, on the day that my upper lip has a scabby-growth, I would have a mandatory budgeting meeting.

I am going to murder Brown. How did I let her convince me to do this? Something must have gone wrong … horribly wrong. I've never known anyone to get a scab from waxing. Yes, of course, this would happen to me.

What am I going to do? I have to go to work. Okay, I can handle this. I'm a smart person. There is only one person who can help me right now.

"MOMMY!!!!" I scream as I run upstairs.

"Mom!" I say frantically as I find her at the kitchen table reading the newspaper and drinking coffee with my dad. "Mom! You've *got* to help me!"

"What is it, Julia?" my mom says, getting up from the table, looking concerned.

"Look at my lip!" I say as I point to my scabby-Hitler-upper lip. I really want to cry right now.

"Oh my!" she says as she gets close to me and then takes a step back, obviously a little shocked by what she's just seen. "How did you... what is... what happened?" she stammers out.

"I got my moustache waxed, and apparently it went horribly wrong!" I hear my dad stifle a laugh and my mom shoots him a look telling him to shut it.

"What can I do? I have to go to work! I can't go like this!" I start to tear up a little.

"Well, sweetie, I'm not sure. I guess I could try to cover it with some makeup or something? I'm not really sure I will be able to cover it, though," she says, reaching out to touch the scab. "Wow, that's bad. They must have taken some skin when they pulled the wax off."

"Ya think?" I snap, a little too sarcastically. I reach up and run my finger over my upper lip, feeling the bump of the scab. "Do you think makeup might actually work?"

"Well, I don't know dear, but we can try," she says, looking at me in a pitying way.

"Mom, please, just try. I'm desperate. I have to be at a meeting this morning, and I can't miss it. But I can't go into work looking like Hitler for crap's sake!" I say as I point my upper lip. My dad is desperately trying not to laugh and actually covers his mouth and pounds his fist once on the table trying to keep himself from letting it out.

"Dad! Just... whatever," I say and roll my eyes at him as I follow my mom into her room and into the master bathroom, silently praying she will be able to cover the scab.

It took about fifteen minutes of working on it. At one point I had to wash all the makeup off so she could start again (which really stung!), but she was able to cover it pretty well. At least from a distance you couldn't see it.

Why does completely horrible stuff like this always happen to me? Seriously. What did I ever do?

My mother also convinced me to put on some other makeup as well. You know, to help take the focus off my scabby upper lip and put more focus on my eyes. Somehow she got me to wear blush, eye shadow (a light cream color, which I fought for — she wanted to do something brighter), eyeliner, and mascara. I think I can count on both hands how many times I have worn makeup. I'm feeling a bit whore-ish. I hope she is right though, I will take anything that might take the focus away from this horrible wax job. I should have just left the hair. That would have been one hundred times better than *this*.

At work, the first thing I do is make Brown come up to my office and bring some makeup with her just in case I need some touch-ups. In all my stress to get to work on time, and hopes of no one noticing my scab when I got there, I actually started sweating on my upper lip.

"Oh my gosh!" Brown says as she sees me, a humongous smile spreads across her face.

"I know! It's horrible, right?" I say as I cover my mouth and upper lip with my hand.

"No, Julia… you look beautiful! You're wearing make-up!" She is practically jumping up and down at this.

"Yah, because I have a huge scab on my upper lip, thanks to you," I say, pointing to my lip.

"Seriously, Julia. You look so pretty!" she says, sounding absurdly giddy. I mean, the makeup is not the important part here.

"Brown, you are missing the point. I *had* to wear makeup to take the focus off of this growth on my upper lip. It's not about the makeup. Focus, please!"

"Okay, let me see this lip," Brown says as she gets up close to my face. "Oh geez, Jules, it's not that bad," she says as she inspects it.

"Because my mom covered it up. It's horrible! I looked like freakin' Hitler, for hell's sake!" I squeak out. All she cares about is that I'm wearing makeup, not that I'm a super-freak show.

With that, Brown starts to giggle. And then the giggles turn into laughter until she is hysterically laughing and can't catch her breath. She is so rude. I guess it is kind of funny, in a horrible why-does-this-crap-always-happen-to-me kind of way. I can't help myself though, and despite it all, I start giggling and all of the sudden I am joining her, out of breath with laughter.

"Oh no! My meeting!" I say as I look at the clock bringing us back to reality, tears streaming down our faces. "Fix me!" I point to my face and Brown grabs her makeup bag and gets to work.

I have only a little time to make all the changes to the budget spreadsheet that Mr. Nguyen asked me to make, and then it's off to the copy room to make enough copies of the report for everyone in the meeting.

On the way to the meeting, I stop by the bathroom for a quick moment to check myself out and my upper lip disaster. I've got to say, I do look pretty good. I mean, scabby-upper lip aside (which has been covered up nicely thanks to my mom and Brown—you can hardly see it), the other makeup my mom put on me actually does look pretty good. Huh. Maybe I could use a little makeup? Just a little, I'm not going to get crazy or anything. But just a little bit wouldn't hurt. I'll have to think about that.

Feeling a slight bit of confidence I guess due to the makeup, I walk into the meeting with a new skip to my step. Well, I didn't actually skip, that would be stupid. That was until I actually looked to see who was in the room. Yep, you guessed right—Jared Moody. Front and center. Nervous schoolgirl flutterings immediately start in my stomach mixed with a bit of confusion because I honestly have no idea why he is here. HR has never been a part of this meeting.

He looks up at me from whatever papers he was reviewing and smiles at me, and just like that I don't care that he's not supposed to be at this meeting. His smile is stunning. And then without thinking, I smile back at him. Just like a normal human would do. Geez, put makeup on a spinster and watch out! She'll start acting like a lady. Who knew?

I hear a throat clear behind me and turn around to see all of Mr. Calhoun standing in front of me.

"Hi, Mr. Calhoun!" I say much too cheerfully. What has gotten into me? This makeup stuff must have leaked into my brain or something.

"Well, hello, Julia," he pauses and weaves his fingers together placing his hands on his large belly. "Will you be bringing in any of your famous cookies anytime soon?"

"Um, sure. I can do that," I say and smile at him.

"Let's get started," Mr. Nguyen says from behind me, and I awkwardly find a seat. I make sure it is not next to Jared. Hey, I successfully smiled back at him without tripping or burping or doing something that would be ridiculously embarrassing. No need to rock the boat.

"Before we begin, Ed Calhoun has a few words," he says with no inflection in his voice. Almost as if he is annoyed, but Mr. Nguyen always seems annoyed.

"Thank you, Henry," Mr. Calhoun says extra jovially, and his belly moves a little Santa Claúse-like as he smiles at everyone. "Sorry to be hijacking your 'proverbial' meeting everyone." *Oh geez.* "I just want to take a moment and introduce our newest hire, Jared Moody," he says and motions to Jared, who is leaning back in his chair.

"I know that HR isn't usually in your weekly budget meeting, but I have asked Jared to sit in on this meeting just so there is an HR presence. In an attempt to be more efficient, we want to make sure we have a presence with all company departments. Jared has been kind enough to help me out with this," he says and nods to Jared. "Do you have anything to add, Jared?"

Jared stands up and looks around at everyone. "Nothing to add, I'm just glad to be here. I don't want anyone to think that HR is hiding under the table or anything," he says and then sits down, looks at me, and gives me a sly smile and a wink.

Well. I. Never.

Okay… technically, I did, but I can't believe he just said that. I quickly spin my chair around so I am facing slightly away from Jared, but still looking somewhat forward. To say I am blushing would be an understatement.

"If that is all, then I will now turn the time back over to Henry," Mr. Calhoun says and shoots us all a wave as he waddles out of the room.

Mr. Nguyen goes to the front of the room. "We have a lot to cover, so let's begin."

He goes into an interesting description of the quarterly budget and where the company is and where we need to be and blah, blah, blah. Okay, it isn't interesting. But I make it seem as if I am particularly interested in what he has to say. I nod my head yes when I notice everyone else doing it, and every once in a while I rest my chin on my fist in a pondering way to make it look as if I am contemplating all that he's saying. I need to act cool here, like I don't care that Jared just secretly insulted me in front of everyone. But was it actually an insult if no one else knows what he's talking about?

I really need to hate him right now, but he looks so incredibly good today. He's wearing a perfectly pressed light blue shirt that makes his eyes pop. He makes eye contact with me, and I quickly turn my attention back to Mr. Nguyen.

"There has been a downward turn of sales as of this last quarter, and adjustments have been made in the budget to compensate for this as you will see on the fifth page of the report..." Mr. Nguyen continues his presentation, which is about as exciting as having teeth pulled.

My mind starts wandering to food because that's what I do when I'm bored. Right now I'm craving a cream puff I had recently. Last week, I was at the restaurant supply store looking at some new baking tools (they know me by name there, embarrassingly enough), and afterwards I stopped by this little pastry shop and had the most amazing cream puff I have ever had. And I mean a.maz.ing. It had just the right amount of cream and puff. I will have to try and recreate it.

"Julia?" Jared's voice pulls me out of my cream puff thoughts.

"Yes?" I say as I look up from the report that I am not actually reading, and then I see all eyes in the room are on me. I look at Jared, and he points to Mr. Nguyen at the front of the room.

"Julia, could you please hand out the reports?" he says, shooting daggers from his eyes at me.

"Um, yes, sorry! I was just… Um… reading the report. Very interesting stuff! Sorry everyone!" I say as I get up and start handing out the report to everyone in attendance. I hear someone snicker in the back of the room. I wonder how long Mr. Nguyen was trying to get my attention. I must have looked like a total fool.

I was supposed to hand out the report to everyone *before* the meeting started. I guess Jared and Mr. Calhoun caught me off guard, which is not actually an excuse that is even remotely acceptable. Mr. Nguyen is not going to be happy.

I try desperately to focus for the rest of the meeting, to attempt to make up for my indiscretion. Mr. Nguyen is seriously anal (it's the only word that best describes him) and hates it when things don't go smoothly in his meetings. I can't believe I was the cause. There will be a strongly worded e-mail coming my way very soon.

"Julia," Mr. Nguyen says my name rather tersely after the meeting ends, and motions for me to come to the front of the room as everyone else starts to leave. "I need to speak with you."

Oh my gosh, he's going to yell at me in person. In front of everyone? In front of Jared? Really? But he rarely says anything to my face. He usually just sends e-mails. I can't believe this.

How will I respond? I don't even know... I have no speech prepared.

"Yes, Mr. Nguyen?" I say as I get up from my seat and walk to the front of the room. "Great presentation, by the way!" I say and smile cheerfully. I hate how I get overly-patronizing when I know I'm in the wrong.

"Yes. Well, I need you to do something for me," he says as he looks down at his long pinky nail, which is so long it's starting to curl. So gross. I'll be telling Brown about that later.

"Sure! No problem! What can I do?" Really, I am being so pathetically butt-kissy right now. I can't help myself though. It's a very annoying trait of mine.

"This is Jared Moody," he says, motioning to Jared.

"Um, yes, we've met," I say, turning around to see Jared leaning back in his seat, the little smirk spreading across his face.

"Mr. Moody is new here, and he needs to have the quarterly report explained to him," he says as he grabs all of the paperwork he used for the meeting and stuffs them into a manila file folder. "I don't have time to do it, so I need you to."

What? Is he crazy? I can barely get out a sentence in front of Jared. How am I supposed to explain this report?

"But... I honestly can't. I have so much to..."

"Yes, well, you will have to do all that later. I

am unable to do this, so I need your help." He looks at me sternly, and my heart sinks.

"Sure, no problem," I say to Mr. Nguyen as he leaves the room, clearly done talking. Well, this is… awkward.

I'm honestly confused by all of this. I heard Mr. Calhoun's explanation, but the job Jared got—the one I wanted—is supposed to be more of a support role under Mr. Calhoun. It should have nothing to do with accounting, or any other department for that matter. I don't know why I even have to explain this report to him when it should have nothing to do with his job. I guess I didn't truly understand the job description when I read it on the interoffice posting board. In a way, I'm now glad I didn't get the HR job. I was trying to get away from accounting, so it wasn't the perfect position for me after all. Hopefully there will be another opening soon, far away from accounting. Far, far away.

"Julia, the cupcake girl," Jared says as I turn around nervously and see him smiling at me.

It's just him and me in the conference room now, everyone else has left. I am about to have an actual conversation with him, and I have yet to be able to do that. And in order to give him the full rundown of this report, I will have to use more than one-word sentences. This is not good.

I sit at the opposite end of the table from him and look down at the report. I don't even know where to start. Stay tuned for yet another embarrassing moment in the life of Julia Warner Dorning. I've had so many lately, I think I've lost count.

"So what's the story?" he says and smiles at me, and my stomach does a couple of flips.

I smile at him nervously and wonder what in the heck I am going to teach him about this report. I don't even know where to begin.

"Well, this is the... um... budget report," I say to him, holding the report up by the corner like this is show-and-tell or something. So. Stupid.

"Yes, I know," he says, and smiles. He stands up from his seat and walks to my end of the table and sits right next to me. "Do you mind? I figure it would be easier if I sat closer to you. I don't bite, promise," he says, and holds up his hands in an "I'm innocent" way.

"Sure," I say and smile slightly at him. He smells really good. Dang, he smells really, really good. The fluttering in my stomach gets stronger.

"So, what can you tell me about this report?" he says as he sits back in his chair looking at me.

There is no time like the present to start acting like a human with a brain and show him I do have a personality and can say words, and that I am not actually slow like I'm sure he has been wondering.

I breathe deeply.

"Okay, as Mr. Nguyen talked about in the

meeting, this report is done quarterly. So, this report is from the last quarter's earnings." Holy crap, I just got out a sentence. A miracle has just happened. Well, it's a miracle for me at least.

Jared nods his head like he understands, and—feeling a little more confident that I can actually speak around him—I continue. "This first part of the report is the overall sales from last quarter. As you can see, they are down substantially."

"Is that the number, right here?" His hand brushes mine as he points to the report and instantly my entire arm has a warming sensation that goes directly to my cheeks. Please don't blush, please don't blush... too late.

"Um..." Breathe Julia, *breathe*. "That's right." I keep my face focused on the report hoping he isn't looking at me.

I glance just slightly in his direction and see him sit back in his seat. It looks as if he is pondering the numbers I just showed him.

"I'm starving," he says all of the sudden.

"Oh, okay... um... we could do this later?" I say, feeling slightly relieved yet disappointed at the same time.

"Actually, I was thinking I might order some lunch, and we can eat it here while we go over this. You hungry?" he asks, and smiles slightly at me.

"Um... I..." Eat lunch together? There really is no room for food in my stomach because it has been taken over by nervousness and butterflies. Plus, I'm about ninety-seven percent sure I will do something stupid like spit food on him while we are talking or snort soda out of my nose if he says something even remotely funny. Let's look at my track-record here: It's not stellar.

"Sure," I say totally against my better judgment. Stupid-giddy-high-school-girl, one point. Rational-adult-who-should-know-better, zero.

We briefly discuss what to get. Well, he throws ideas out, and I just nod my head like an idiot. I can't even make a decision about food around him. Food—the one thing I know a lot about, the one thing I am most always certain of.

We decide on pizza (actually, he decides on pizza, I just nod in agreement), and he pulls out his smart phone and makes an order for delivery, paying for it with the company card.

So, if I had gotten his job, then I would have had a corporate card? Dang. How impressive would that have been to pull out in front of people?

While we wait for the pizza, we discuss the report and he asks questions. Every once in a while he will have me repeat something, or stop and contemplate something. When he contemplates something he almost always looks out the window, and I use that time to study his face a bit. Not stalker-like, of course. Just a little peek here and there. It's the only way to get a good look at him since it's hard for me to make eye contact with him when we are talking because it makes the butterflies in my stomach flutter and then I start to blush. So, it's better that I keep my eyes mostly on the report.

I get a short moment to myself when he goes to the break room to get us something to drink, and I take this time to compose myself a little and try to breathe deeply. *In with the normal thoughts, out with the spinster thoughts.* If only I could breathe myself into a normal-acting person right now. I can't believe I am going to eat lunch with this super fabulous looking guy. It's so… unlike my life.

The pizza arrives, and we each grab a piece and start to eat. We eat in silence, and as I eat I look out the window mostly, or down at my food. It's feeling a bit awkward, really. I don't have anything to say, and I guess neither does he. I should just be grateful for the silence. I'd most-likely embarrass myself anyway.

"So, tell me a little about yourself," Jared says, breaking the silence I was just feeling grateful for.

Of course, he asks this just as I take a huge, and I mean *huge*, bite of pizza. So much so that I am barely able to shut my mouth around my food. So, I have to sit there and cover my mouth with my hand so he can't see me chomping, and it's taking me a while to get it down. There is this terribly awkward silence while he watches me chew my food.

Aren't I the picture of loveliness?

"Um…" I choke out, and then take a quick sip of my soda. "What do you want to know?" What could this super-hot guy possibly want to know about me?

"Where did you get your name from? Is it a family name?" he asks, and then takes a bite of his pizza.

Well, that's easy enough, thank goodness. Kind of odd, but easy.

"Um, well, my parents are huge Beatles fans. So, my name comes from one of their songs. My sister Anna's name also comes from a song, and my brother, Lennon, well, that doesn't need much explanation," I say, eyeing my pizza. I am tempted to take another bite, but I really don't want him to ask me another question while my mouth is full, which I'm sure he will do. So I wait.

"That's interesting—naming you all after the Beatles. That's some true fans right there." He ponders that for a moment. "My father was a fan," he says, and I see a glimpse of something in his eyes that seems like sadness, but I can't tell, and it passes too quickly to be sure.

"Yah, my parents were a bit on the hippy-ish side in the sixties. You know, peace, love, and all that other crap." I smile to myself. They certainly didn't grow up to be hippies. More like ultra-right-wingers.

He laughs at that. "What does your dad do for work?"

"Lawyer. He has a firm not far from here off Twelfth Street. He keeps threatening to retire, but I don't know if it will ever happen. "

"And your mom?"

"She's a teacher. Stayed home most of my life, but once we were all in school, she went back to teaching... at the same school I was going to, actually. It was very annoying. You can't get away with anything when your mom works at your school." Not that I ever tried, but it would have been nice to know I could. I don't tell him that part, though—just to make myself seem a little less dull, like maybe I was a bit of a rebel instead of the opposite.

"How long have you been in Colorado?" he asks, his blue eyes shining in the sunlight coming through the window.

"My whole life. Born here, will probably die here," I say, and smile as I see him smile at that. "How about you?"

"Same. Except I travel a lot for work." He looks down at his hands and then quickly up at me. "Or, at least I used to."

"Is that why you took the job at Spectraltech?"

"Yah... I guess," he says as he grabs another slice of pizza. "So, do you like working at Spectraltech?"

This is an interesting question. Do I tell him

how I hate this stupid job? Or do I tell him it's suddenly become a lot more appealing since he started here? Neither of those answers is going to do, so I settle for: "Well, it's a job."

"So, it's not your dream job, I take it?" he asks as he takes another bite of his pizza.

"Um, no. Not my dream job."

"So, what is your dream job then?" he asks me with what seems to be sincerity. I'm not sure why he cares.

"I don't know, I guess something to do with baking," I say, nonchalantly. Of course, baking is what I would love to do. That is my real passion. Who would have a passion for doing accounting at Spectraltech? No one.

"You've been at Spectraltech for ten years. Don't you want to spend the next ten doing something you actually enjoy?" he asks, head cocked slightly to the side as if he is trying to figure me out.

I want to tell him this is just what spinsters do. They stay at the same job until someone finds their body half-eaten by cats. But he wouldn't get that, so I just say, "Change and I are not the greatest of friends."

For a moment he looks like he is contemplating that. "So, where do you live?" he asks, changing the subject to something equally as uncomfortable. There is no way in heck I am telling this amazing-smiling-good-smelling-hottest-man-ever that I live in my parents' basement.

"In Denver," is all the information I am willing to give, "and you?"

"Same," he says, and grabs another piece of pizza. I think he's on his fourth. I, on the other hand, have barely been able to eat my original piece. Had this been Brown or anyone else, I would be on my third by now. I can't seem to eat, which is a new feeling for me.

"So, what do you like to do when you are away from Spectraltech?" he asks, and takes a bite of his pizza. Clearly we are not going to get back to the report anytime soon. I should be glad about this, but he keeps asking me questions I seriously don't want to answer.

"Not much," I say and shrug my shoulders.

"Really?" he says as he leans back in his chair and looks at me like he doesn't believe me. He is quite horrible at reading people, that's for sure. I don't look like a person who gets out much.

"You sound surprised," I say, curious.

"I just figured you were the type of girl that went out every night, living it up," he says, and smiles a half-smile.

He must be teasing me. I am in no way, shape, or form the epitome of a party girl. Anyone with eyes can see that. "Um, no. I do not go out and live it up every night," I say, throwing in the "every night" at the end so maybe he might think I live it up every once in a while, rather than never, which is the truth.

"So, no boyfriend then?"

I half cough my drink out my mouth, nearly snorting it out of my nose and quickly grab a napkin to clean up my face. Is this guy for real? A boyfriend?

"Um, no," I say through my coughing, trying to compose myself.

"Ah, getting too personal, am I? Sorry. Forget that." He picks up his napkin and wipes his mouth.

"It's fine, really. Just caught me off guard," I say, which is a total understatement. "Why do you ask?" my mouth says before my head can stop me.

"No reason, just curious." He smiles a dashing smile at me.

"So… do you?" I say, not being able to help myself.

"No. I don't have a boyfriend," he deadpans, and I laugh a little too hard at that. The laughter eases the butterflies I had been giving myself.

My laughter at his little joke makes me relax. I'm feeling a bit more at ease, and so I sit back in my chair and look up, our eyes meet. The butterflies are back, but this time I don't feel like I'm going to blush, I feel more comfortable.

I quickly grab another piece of pizza, since all of a sudden there is a little more room in my stomach now. I also don't want this to end. Now I feel like I want to prolong this lunch as long as I can. By eating more, maybe I can do just that.

I think that it's now my turn to ask him a bunch of personal questions, but before I can muster up enough courage to ask him something, his phone rings.

He picks up his phone and looks at me as if to ask my permission to answer, I nod my head. "This will only take a second," he says as he puts his phone to his ear.

"This is Jared," I hear him say and then silence as he listens. He turns his chair slightly away from me. "I thought we took care of this. This is not how I do business."

Whoa, he suddenly doesn't sound very happy. I try not to eavesdrop too much, but how can I? He's sitting a foot away from me.

"No, no, I will not tolerate it. You are unprofessional. How could you let this happen? There was a contract." His voice escalates at the last part.

Um, I think he forgot I was here because I'm not quite sure I should be hearing this. Seeing him mad like this is quite interesting though. I will be telling Brown all about this at our next break. One thing is for sure, he is *not* ugly when he's angry.

He stands up from his chair, cursing under his breath. "Hold on," he says, and holds the phone away from his head. "Julia, I'll be right back."

He goes out to the hall to finish this odd and out-of-nowhere conversation. I'm very curious about what they are saying on the other line. Jared must not know the walls at Spectraltech are paper thin. I can still hear everything he is saying.

"Look, I don't care how you fix it, just fix it. My name cannot be associated with this, it's too important I remain anonymous." What, is he involved in something illegal? Or is he in some kind of trouble? This is getting interesting. I can't wait to tell Brown.

His voice quiets a little, and I can't exactly hear what he is saying, but I think he mentions something about a lawyer. I hear him say goodbye and so I move my chair quickly back up to the conference table and grab my pizza that I was eating so I can look like I haven't been paying attention at all to anything he's been saying.

"You okay?" I ask as he takes his seat. "That sounded intense, I mean the part I heard when you were in the conference room." Oh geez, could I sound like more of a buffoon? I just basically told him I heard it all.

"Just my last job. Some information got out that wasn't meant to," he says, his composure easing back.

"Where did you work before here?" I ask, super curious now.

"In Boulder," is all he offers. So evasive. Interesting... Brown and I have much to discuss.

The conversation turns to more of a small-talk-between-strangers genre, and eventually we get back to the report and I finish telling him everything I know about it, feeling a little sad because once he knows the report, this lunch is done. And this is about the best lunch I've had in a long time. This is sad to admit, but true nonetheless.

"Well, thanks for telling me about this most interesting report," he says as we finish up, adding sarcasm to his voice when he calls the report interesting. We stand up at the same time and end up just inches away from each other. Our eyes meet, and my breath catches in my throat a little. He smiles and then looks at me for a moment. Then, he gives me some sort of weird look as if he's concentrating on my face. I quickly turn away hoping there isn't a piece of food or something… worse… like, coming out of my nose. Oh please, not *that*.

We clear off the table and walk silently together to the break room down the hall to dispose of everything. I want to say something, but nothing is coming out.

"Can I ask you something personal?" he asks after we throw everything away and are about to leave the break room.

"Um… I guess," I say, wondering what kind of personal question would be coming this time.

"What's going on with your lip?" he asks, pointing to his upper lip.

Oh. My. Hell. My freaking Hitler lip! I totally

forgot about it, and I must have wiped off the makeup with my napkin after I nearly snorted soda out of my nose!

I think I might die.

I quickly cover my mouth and lip with my hand, and try to think of something to tell him.

"Is it like a cold sore thing or something?" he asks looking concerned.

Oh my gosh, he thinks I have *herpes*?? What do I tell him? Herpes or moustache? Herpes or moustache?? HERPES OR FREAKING MOUSTACHE???

I want to die. Just let me die right now.

"Um, I just... burned myself... somehow." I say and cringe.

"How did you burn yourself there?" he asks confused and rightfully so.

I pause for a moment and then I breathe deeply. "I really don't want to tell you," I say and turn away from him quickly, my hand still covering my mouth. Why does this stuff happen to me? Is there a large rock I can hide under or something... for like, ever?

"Why not?" he asks, sounding somewhat offended that I won't tell him.

"Because it's really embarrassing, and we really aren't close enough for me to share that kind of information," I sputter out.

"Well... I hope that changes," he says, and smiles at me. My heart races a little and the butterflies multiply in my stomach, and even though he can't see it because my hand is covering my mouth, I smile right back at him.

"I'm sorry…" Brown trails off, giggling to herself. She's not apologizing because she's actually sorry, she's apologizing because she can't stop laughing at me.

We're in my office and Brown is trying to fix my upper lip once again. I'm filling her in on all the details as she tries to reapply some cover-up. In normal circumstances, I would've left that whole moustache/herpes part of the story out, but since I need her help, I've had to give her all the details. Which is why she can't stop laughing. I can't say I blame her. In any other scenario, I, too, would be finding it hard not to laugh. But I'm still reeling in the embarrassment. It's too soon for me. The wound is still fresh.

"You are really focusing on the wrong parts here," I say, rolling my eyes.

"I know, sorry," she says, sniffling and wiping a tear starting to form in the corner of her eye from laughing so hard at my expense. She grabs some sort of little sponge and blots lightly on my lip.

"Anyway, don't you think it's weird about the phone call, and then how evasive he was about his last job?" I try to speak with my upper lip pulled taut over my teeth so she can do her magic.

"Not really," she says as she stands back to look at her work. It must not be good enough because she puts more cover-up on me and starts blotting again.

"Why not?" I ask, creasing my eyebrows together, confused at her lack of interest.

"For many reasons." She shrugs her shoulders. "Maybe he got fired from his last job and doesn't want anyone to know about it. Maybe that's why he was talking about a contract when he was on the phone. Maybe there was an employment contract that was broken." She nods her head like she has just solved a mystery. "Anyway, people don't always want to share where they worked before. It's really not that big of a deal." She stands back to look at me and seems satisfied with her work.

"Well, I guess you had to be there, had to see the look on his face when he was on the phone. It seemed like a bigger deal," I say grabbing her compact to look at my lip in the mirror. Much better. I was just going to hibernate in my office for the rest of the day, but I couldn't risk running into Jared, or anyone for that matter, with this thing on my lip so exposed.

"Yah, maybe…" she trails off, grabbing her makeup and putting it all back in her case. "Anyway, at least we know his last job was in Boulder. I suppose I can see if I can find anything out with that bit of info," she says with a twinkle in her eye. Brown does love to snoop. I think she should've been a private investigator or something. She may have missed her calling in life.

I brighten up with her last comment, hopeful she will find out something more about him, hopeful that we can discuss him more. My schoolgirl crush has escalated to a new level now, not as pathetic as it was before. Okay, it's just as pathetic, but I can't help myself. It's been a while since I've had a crush on anyone and I have to admit, it's kind of fun.

Brown leaves her press powder compact with me before she goes, just in case I need to do touch-ups. I don't actually plan on leaving my office, but if I have to for any reason it will be good to have it as back-up.

After she leaves, I get to work on the reports Mr. Nguyen told me to do earlier, before the meeting and my lunch with Jared. I keep coming back to lunch and replaying parts of it in my head. Not the bad parts (ahem, mustache), just the good stuff — the stuff that made my stomach turn in a good way, full of butterflies.

My computer beeps and I look and see I have an e-mail from one Jared Moody. My heart starts to thump in my chest as I double-click on it.

Thanks for your help today. Any chance there are cupcakes leftover from yesterday?

I try not to get too caught up in how I honestly want to react here, which is spending forty-five minutes writing a one sentence reply. I need to reply now. So without thinking it over too much, I write this:

You're welcome, anytime. Cupcakes are gone, I'm afraid. They never last past the first day.

I push the send button and wait, hoping for a reply. It doesn't take too long for my computer to beep again.

I figured. Too bad. I was craving one. What can I say to convince you to bring some more?

I should say something witty here, right? Like "only just the promise of your firstborn." But that's stupid and contrived... Can't I come up with something better? I have nothing though, no good reply. I'm rusty when it comes to bantering with the opposite sex. I reply quickly not allowing myself to over-think it.

No convincing necessary. I'll bring some on Monday. :)

Crap. I just added the dreaded smiley face to the end of my e-mail and hit send too fast before I could erase it. Stupid, stupid spinster. Not only that, I just essentially told him I have nothing better to do this weekend than make cupcakes. I seriously need to go back to over-analyzing everything. It's better that way.

My computer beeps:

Excellent. That will make for a better Monday. ;)

Oh! Okay, he just sent back a smiley face, too—and a winking one at that. That means something, right? It's like a flirty-smiley face. Or it could also be that the colon and the semi-colon buttons are on the same key and can easily be mixed up. Whatever. Clearly, I have some considerable reading into and over-analyzing of this little e-mail chat.

Who needs to do work when there are so much more important things to do?

# CHAPTER 5

It's been two weeks since Jared and I had our lunch together, and we are now officially boyfriend and girlfriend. Oh yeah, and they found some unicorns in my parents' backyard playing with Bigfoot and I also found a leprechaun with a pot of gold at the end of a rainbow. Okay, so, not so much.

Seriously though, Jared and I have actually started to become good friends, and it has made work so much more exciting. I'm actually starting to find my place of employment enjoyable. Well, I still hate my job, that has not changed. In fact, if it were possible, Mr. Nguyen has even gotten weirder. Such a loon. But that's a whole other story and who'd honestly want to hear about that anyway?

Let's get back to Jared, which is so much more compelling. So, this is what I now know about Jared: He grew up in Colorado (like me — I think we might be soul mates, even though that's actually the only thing we have in common, so far), he graduated in marketing with an HR emphasis, he loves his mom (so cute), his dad died when he was in college (so sad), he likes sports — especially football, his drink of choice is a Coke… and well, there are other details that I have figured out about him, but I'm feeling a bit on the stalker side right now so I will just leave it at that.

Oh, but there is one extremely important thing about Jared: He loves to gossip. I know, totally gay, right? Brown and I (mostly Brown) were a bit suspicious of this incredibly good-looking guy with the most incredible smile, and his love for gossip. He's been joining us sometimes during our breaks, and he is *very* interested in the goods on the employees at Spectraltech. We were skeptical (mostly Brown) because we didn't know him that well, and he does work in HR, but eventually we decided he seemed pretty trustworthy. Plus, it's been quite fun having him around, if nothing else but to just look at. He doesn't have much to offer in the way of gossip yet since he is new and all, but that doesn't matter because Brown and I have so much info that it's taken us some time to catch him up. We've sort of taken him under our wings.

Anyway, so Brown and I did have some gay suspicions. It was just too good to be true — him being hot *and* loving gossip. So we came up with a list — a list of reasons why Jared couldn't possibly be gay. First of all, he is too good-looking. This was quickly debunked because let's face it, back in the day, George Michael was a total hottie and even though my dad swore up and down he was a "fruit," I knew in my heart he couldn't possibly be. He was going to wake me up before he go-goes, and we would live happily ever after. I guess my gaydar is not hugely reliable.

The second reason Jared couldn't possibly be gay is because he loves sports. Although that is really just a stereo-type, I'm counting it.

He is a big fan of the Denver Broncos and, lucky for me, my brother Lennon is a huge fan as well, so I happen to know a lot of stats and names and crap like that because Lennon used to bore me with them. Who knew all that information would eventually be useful? I must thank him for that.

The third, and most important, reason Jared could not possibly be gay is because... Brown flat-out asked him. Leave it to Brown to say what is on her mind. When she asked, he looked at her like she was a complete idiot and seemed a little offended. He emphatically said no, and although he just might be an exceptionally good actor, it did seem as if he were being sincere. Plus—and Brown will attest to this—there has been a lot of flirty-flirty going on between him and I. So. Much. Fun. And honestly, quite unexpected for a spinster.

I'm not sure, but it might have to do with the fact that I am now wearing makeup. Oh, yah, totally forgot about that part. So, after the Hitler-lip incident, I did find myself wanting to wear some makeup. I mean, at the age of thirty-two, you would think I would have started this years ago, but I just didn't get into the whole makeup thing. I rarely wore it, and so I got used to how I looked without it and when I'd put some on, it didn't look like me anymore. I guess every other time I had makeup on, it was too much because that day my mom put a bit on me, it opened up a whole new world.

So, I bought some. I did the unthinkable though. I was going to ask Brown to help me pick some out, but I never got around to it. Then, it was the weekend, and so I asked… Anna (she happened to be home for a few days). Crazy, I know. I mean, Anna and I have never gotten along, ever. But the girl does know her makeup, and I was sort of desperate. I would not have been able to do it on my own.

I have to admit, it was actually kind of fun. I never realized Anna and I could have a conversation on a normal, non-bratty level. But apparently, we can. She loved helping me pick out makeup, and she was quite good at finding colors and tones that matched my skin and didn't make me look like a hussy (which was my biggest stipulation). I suppose that one semester at beauty school rubbed off on her or something. I think we have finally found some common ground. I don't know anything about fashion;

she thinks she is the queen of it. Therefore, we are a good match. I even asked her to help me pick out some new clothes. We are going tonight.

I guess I'm starting to come out of my spinster shell? Don't get me wrong, I still live in my parents' basement, and I still have my cat... I'm still hating my job, and I have no boyfriend or social life or anything of the sort, except for the little bit of attention I've been getting from Jared, but that probably doesn't truly count. I guess the only change is that I am wearing makeup, and I'm buying new clothes. That does make me a little less spinster-ish, right? One step at a time, I suppose.

So back to the flirty-flirty between Jared and I. I wasn't actually sure it was flirting because, as was stated before, I am a bit rusty. There have been a few things here and there, and Brown has seen some things right before her eyes, and she is quick to point it out—after Jared leaves, of course—and then we discuss it at length like two little schoolgirls.

The other day something pretty huge happened. Well okay, it was huge for a spinster. Anyway, so the other day he caught me in the break room practically having a PMS breakdown over the soda vending machine. It ate my dollar, and I seriously needed a drink. A Dr. Pepper to be exact. He actually joined in on the kicking and fist-beating of the machine and even used his manly muscles (so sexy) to shake the machine, but there was no such luck. We finally gave up, and so totally irritated, I met Brown downstairs for a break (sans Jared). I was still ticked about it when I traipsed back to my office, and when I got there, lo and behold, right there on my desk, was a Dr. Pepper. It was ice-cold even. Love. Him.

It took me about a half hour to compose an e-mail to him about how much I appreciated that blessed Dr. Pepper. After many drafts, I ended up sending him one word, "Thanks." After refreshing my e-mail about one hundred times, I got a reply back that simply said: "You're welcome," which I took as: "Please have my babies."

That's flirting, right? I think it is. Brown even thinks it is. I don't want to get my hopes up because it probably isn't, not the kind of flirting I want it to be at least. And one day, I'm sure, he will show up at work engaged to some supermodel, and I will be devastated. I don't want to be devastated so I must pretend in my head that he is just a super-hot guy that simply wants to be my friend. I can deal with "friend." Even though at night, when I am home baking something, I am thinking about him the whole time. And the other night, after watching *Grey's Anatomy*, I gave him one of those "Mc" names... McManly. Because that is truly what he is, manly and just too freaking cute.

I have mixed feelings about work today. Part of me doesn't want the day to end because this is the only time I get to see Jared. The other part of me is excited for the work day to be over because I am looking forward to going shopping. I'm not sure why I'm feeling excited, but I am. This past week Anna has lent me a few of her tops, just to mix it up a bit, and Brown, of course, had a complete (and unnecessary) cow about how excited she is that I am wearing something other than my standard outfit.

Are my work clothes honestly *that* terrible? I suppose that's the spinster in me because I really didn't think it was horrible. What's wrong with being practical? I guess Brown thought it was totally wrong because this morning on our break I told her I was going shopping tonight with Anna, and she said something like "there is a God" and looked to the skies as if she were actually thanking Him. Whatever.

Work has gone by slowly today. I have taken a few necessary walks around the building hoping to "accidentally" run into Jared. Okay, they weren't necessary walks, but I pretended like they were. You know, just grabbed a couple of files and walked around the office as if I had somewhere to go. It didn't work today like it usually does. Maybe he's not even here. That thought just made my heart sink a little. How pathetic of me.

Suddenly there is a beep from my computer

telling me I have e-mail and my heart skips a beat as I see in bold type: Jared Moody. It's addressed to both me and Brown.

Feel like a break? Downstairs in ten. –J

Now butterflies have started in my gut, and I'm getting a bit of a dry mouth. I hit reply and type "Sure!", and then decide to erase the exclamation point to avoid sounding desperate. "Sure" with a period is much more laid back and cool as I am trying so hard to be. I send my reply and then tap my fingers nervously on my desk. Ten minutes is not soon enough. I decide I will use that time wisely by working on a spreadsheet for Mr. Nguyen that's due by the end of today. Yah, right. I think my time would be more useful if I went to the bathroom and checked my makeup.

As I enter the bathroom with my lip gloss in hand, I step back and look in the full-length mirror on the wall. The soft pink button-up blouse I borrowed from Anna really does compliment my hair and eyes as she had said it would do. The slight bit of makeup I'm still not totally confident about applying correctly, is still intact, thank goodness. I apply a little bit of lip gloss in just the way Anna taught me and then I adjust my black pencil skirt. Not bad for a spinster.

I make a quick trip to my office and drop off

the lip-gloss. A slight bit of self-consciousness seeps in as I think about the lip-gloss and I feel like maybe I am trying too hard. Brown knows me well enough to read my thoughts; I seriously hope Jared does not. I pray I am not that transparent. Yes, I have a crush on Jared, and of course he doesn't have one back because that just would not be possible. Cute guys do not like spinsters. It's in the spinster rule book, which has not actually been written yet, but I'm pretty sure it would be one of the rules. Just under the rule about spinsters only having lasting relationships with cats.

I head downstairs. As I go outside, Brown is already waiting for us, cigarette in hand. Jared is not there yet.

The temperature is pretty warm, even after the snow we got over the weekend. The perfect run of spring weather we'd been having was totally ruined by snow. Denver weather is seriously schizophrenic. It's warm, no wait it's cold, no wait it's warm again. Make up your mind already.

"I can't get over how good you look," Brown says as she sees me. "I should have gotten them to hire someone good-looking a while ago. Who knew it would have such an effect on you."

"Shut up," I say flatly and roll my eyes at her. "Besides, who says I'm doing this for some good-looking guy? Maybe I just need a change."

"Riiiiiiiiight," she says, sarcastically.

"Whatever you say, Jules."

The door swings open and out comes Jared, eating one of my chocolate chip cookies. I put a plate of them in the break room earlier. My heart speeds up a bit at the sight of him and butterflies flutter in my stomach.

"Good stuff, Julia." He points the partially eaten cookie at me, "What's the secret?" He winks at me and the butterflies multiply.

"Like I'd tell you." I fold my arms and lean up against the wall, trying to act like his presence isn't making my heart pound in my chest.

"Come on..." he chides, knowing full well I will give in because I always do. He is always interested in my little baking secrets.

"Okay, fine." I give in way too quickly this time. "It's my homemade vanilla, extra flour, and milk chocolate chips," I say, and smile at him. "But I'm not telling you the measurements. I think you might be trying to steal my recipes."

"Who me?" He feigns innocence and then he scrunches up his eyes at me, "Homemade vanilla? How do you make that?"

"It's pretty easy," I shrug my shoulders. "I just put about thirty vanilla bean pods into an expensive bottle of vodka, and then let it brew for about four months."

He looks at me, clearly impressed, and I wonder how he could be impressed by that. But I'm glad he is.

"So what's new, Jer?" Brown says bringing attention to her. I had kind of forgotten she was there, actually. "Got any gossip for us?"

"Actually, I do today." He smiles mysteriously.

"Really?" Brown and I say at the same time, shocked. He's never offered any gossip before. What could he possibly have?

"Okay, but this is just between us," he lowers his voice.

Brown and I look at each other and roll our eyes. Who else would we tell?

"Okay," he pauses to look around to make sure no one else is there. "I think Mr. Calhoun and that Martha person in HR might have a little somethin'-somethin' going on." He nods his head and smiles conspiratorially at us like he has just given us the juiciest gossip ever.

"Oh geez," Brown says, and then leans back against the wall taking a drag from her cigarette.

"You're going to have to do better than that if you want to stay part of this group," I say pointing between Brown and me.

"What? You guys already know?" He seems genuinely shocked this wasn't news to us.

"Of course, we do," Brown says, rolling her eyes at him. "We know everything around here, remember? We know all about your dirty boss and Martha. Now run along and try to dig up something better." She shoos him away with her hand.

"I really thought I had something there," he hangs his head in mock-shame. "I can't compete with you guys."

"I don't even know why you bother trying," I say, and smile.

It's so fun having Jared around for our breaks. He is adorable, and I really just want to grab him and make-out with him right here. Of course, that would be a little awkward with Brown being here and all. Of course, there is also the issue that he wouldn't reciprocate.

Jared looks up at me and smiles, and my heart skips a silly beat. "So, I had to get my computer fixed by Mike in IT this morning. What's the word on him?" he asks as he eats the last bite of the cookie.

Brown gives him some info on Mike, which isn't much. Mike kind of keeps to himself for the most part. Except for his love of the ladies with a little junk in their trunk—at least that's the kind of girl he brought with him to the last Christmas party—we haven't found anything scandalous. He's pretty good at what he does and is quite busy with all the computer stuff that happens in an office the size of Spectraltech. I honestly don't know how anyone would want to work in IT. I mean, it has to be the most mundane job in the world. Even accounting seems more compelling to me than IT.

Satisfied with the rundown about Mike, Jared asks us about Kelly who works at the front desk.

My stomach sinks a little. Kelly is a young and cute little brunette that has only been working at Spectraltech for two years. All the nerds try to flirt with her. Maybe Jared is looking for info on her because he finds her attractive? This is not good. I must think of something juicy about her, and if I can't find anything I will have to come up with something. What? It's just a little innocent sabotage. Besides, she's too young for Jared, so I am actually just helping him.

"Oh, Kelly," Brown jumps in before I can respond. "Well, there's not too much to say about her. She does a pretty lousy job of answering the phones and can never seem to transfer calls right. I think she might spend a little too much time texting her boyfriend." She rolls her eyes, and then as soon as Jared looks away, she looks at me out of the corner of her eyes and smiles slightly. Brown is *such* a great friend. I could kiss her for that. I wonder if any of that is true. I'll have to ask her later. Either way, Jared looks indifferent in regard to the information.

I could stay out here all day long gossiping with Jared, and just looking at him and wondering what he's thinking about, what he's doing tonight, if he ever thinks about me for any reason besides work and baking... stalker-ish stuff like that. But, of course, the break has to end because Jared gives some lame excuse about how he has to get back to work. I mean, who really cares about work.

It's then that I remember I have to get that spreadsheet done for Mr. Nguyen before the end of the day and it's past three o'clock. I guess the flirting break must end, and I should do some actual work. Because if I don't do my job, I'll get fired and then I would never see Jared again, and just the thought makes my heart drop. That would be horrible.

Back at my desk I do my spreadsheet while intermittently thinking about Jared, which is making it way too hard to concentrate. But I have to get through it because it must be done by end of day.

The spreadsheet I'm trying to work on is infuriating. One of the formulas must be wrong or something because I cannot get the final numbers to match. Have I mentioned lately how much I hate accounting? I do. I truly hate it.

After about an hour and a half of trying to figure it out on my own, I resolve to the fact that I will have to ask Mr. Nguyen for help, and I truly hate doing that because he's not the kindest person to talk to. Plus, he will inevitably be annoyed that I can't figure out the formula, and he will roll his eyes as if he should have done it himself.

"Mr. Nguyen?" I say as I enter his office. He's just sitting at his desk staring at some paperwork, abnormally long pinky nail intact.

"Yes?" He looks up at me. He does not look

thrilled to see me, which is a normal reaction.

"Um," I say as I walk into his office and take an uninvited seat at one of the gray guest chairs facing his desk. "I'm having a problem with this spreadsheet." I show him the printed copy I made before I came to ask him for help. "I can't seem to get the two bottom numbers to match."

"It's fine," he says not even looking at the report as I set it in front of him.

"But... I think one of the formulas is messed up or something." I point to the bottom of the spreadsheet where the problem is.

"The formula is correct," he says briefly, looking at the numbers.

"Are you sure? I thought they were supposed to match." I'm almost positive I'm right. Like ninety-nine percent sure.

He looks at me like he doesn't have time for this, and how could I even insult him and his intelligence. "It's fine," he says again, flatly. I can tell by the look he gives me, this conversation is over so I get up and leave.

Back at my office, I'm surprised and incredibly happy to see that it's already five thirty. I gather my stuff and head out to my car. On the way, I stop by the break room to get my empty plate of cookies and wonder how many of them were eaten by Jared.

I'm meeting Anna at Nordstrom's in the mall. Anna is always late so I will inevitably have to wait for her, but it will give me time to pick out a few things on my own and see if I can actually find something stylish. I don't know if I have it in me.

To my surprise as I arrive at the department store, Anna is already waiting for me with a bunch of clothes in hand.

"Well, look at you," I say in a silly high-pitched voice. "You beat me here. Wonders never cease."

"I guess shopping with someone else's money made me want to be on-time." She shrugs, her curly, dark hair bouncing on her shoulders. Anna and I look remarkably similar, except for the curly hair. I was always jealous of her curls.

"Just remember, we are shopping for *me*," I say, just in case she has some crazy notion that I'm going to be buying clothes for her.

"Duh. I know." She purses her lips together, annoyed. Then she smiles, "Let's get started."

She ushers me into a large dressing room, probably meant for someone in a wheelchair, but clearly it's the only one large enough for all of the clothes she has already picked out for me. Anna is in her element.

"Start with this," she says and hands me a pair of wide-legged brown pin-striped pants. The growing fear of looking like a clown when I put them on vanishes instantly as I cautiously glance at my reflection — they actually look cute. She hands me a white blouse with short, slightly puffy sleeves, and I put it on.

116

She looks me over. "I don't like the shirt." She holds out her hand as I take it off and hand it back to her.

"What's wrong with the shirt?" I thought it looked cute.

"Your shoulders are too broad for puffy sleeves," she says as she looks for another shirt to pair with the pants.

"My shoulders are broad? Like a man?" I look in the mirror at my shoulders. They actually *are* broad. Yes, that would make sense. A mannish looking spinster. It is all coming together now…

"No, you don't look like a man." She rolls her eyes. "You just have broad shoulders. You are definitely a girl." She points to my boobs. "How did you end up with those? And I got these little mosquito bites? So not fair."

I look down at my chest and think about that for a second. "I have nice boobs? I never really noticed." I smirk at myself in the mirror, and then turn to the side to inspect.

"Yes, well the problem is that bra." She points to my old cotton bra I bought at a discount store. "That is not doing you any good. I'm going to go find you something better. I'll be right back. Try on that dress while I'm gone." She points to a little black dress hanging in the corner.

I take off the brown pants and then slip on the dress. It's a simple dress that hugs to my figure nicely. The lining inside is a satin-like material, and it makes me feel so classy and feminine.

Who knew clothes could make you feel like that? I honestly had no idea.

I'm looking in the mirror as Anna enters the dressing room with a bunch of lacy, trampy, and uncomfortable looking bras. What is the point of having pretty bras? I don't get it. I'm supposed to wear something lacy on the off-chance someone will ever see it? We all know, for me, it's a *very* off-chance. Besides, as a spinster in the making, I should just stop wearing a bra altogether and let nature take its sagging course.

"How did you know what size to get?" I ask as she hands me a lacy white bra to try on.

"I'm just good, I guess," she says, and smiles slightly at me. I glimpse a bit of something in her eyes, but I'm not sure what it is. Something like worry, maybe. It's hard to tell with Anna.

I make her turn around as I try on the bra and it's a perfect fit. It's amazingly comfortable even with all the trampy lace.

"See how this bra lifts and separates? Yah, that's what it's supposed to do." She looks at me condescendingly, but I don't take offense. She certainly knows what she's doing.

"How did you get so good at this shopping stuff?" I ask as she hands me another outfit to try on.

"I don't know, I guess I just really got into styles and fashion when I was in middle school, and then it just kept going." She adjusts the shirt I have on so it hangs nicely over the flowing black skirt I am also wearing.

I think back to Anna in middle school, and I can barely remember what she looked like. I had just moved back into my parents' house when she was thirteen. We were in such different worlds. We never paid much attention to each other. I find myself feeling a little sad that I don't really know her all the well.

I'm feeling all these cheesy after school special feelings, and I want to say something sentimental to her, but I can't bring myself to do it. Sappy, cheesy moments have never been a strong suit of mine. It's just too much for me to handle I guess.

"You're really good with this stuff," is all I can say.

She just smiles slightly at me, and then throws me another outfit to try on.

We spend the next couple of hours trying on clothes and putting them in piles of "keep" and "don't keep." The amount of clothes in the "keep" pile is getting quite large, and I'm starting to get scared at how much this is going to cost me. Then again, I have been living at home for free for the past ten years. Thank goodness I saved money. What else did I have to do with it? Besides the many baking gadgets I own, I've actually lived quite frugally. So, there is one silver lining in my spinsterly existence: I have saved up a nice little nest egg. Look at me finding a silver lining. My mom would be so proud. It's actually quite a large nest egg if I'm going to be honest. Ten years plus no social life, no traveling, not anything fun at all, equals a lot to save.

After finally deciding that we've done enough damage for the night, we grab all the clothes and take them to the sales agent. The total was under two thousand dollars, but not by much.

I realize I am starving as we leave Nordstrom's so I ask Anna if she wants to get something to eat, expecting her to decline. To my surprise she says yes, so we go to a restaurant in the mall.

We are seated by the host and place our orders with the server. There is an awkward silence as we sit at the table together. What kind of conversation do you have with someone you should have a relationship with, but don't? It's very strange.

"I'm moving back home," Anna says, breaking the silence.

"Really?" I say, nodding my head, and then my eyebrows shoot up at the implications of that statement.

"Don't worry, I'm not going to make a play for the downstairs apartment." She looks at me flatly. "I'll just move into my old bedroom upstairs."

"Oh," is all that comes out of my mouth. Then I quickly add, "Well, that will be fun." I smile at her as genuinely as possible.

"Yah, not really," she says flatly. "I mean, who wants to move back into their parents' house in their twenties?" She looks over to the table across from us and then quickly moves her head back to me. "I mean, no offense to you. I just never imagined my life like this." I see a little sadness in her eyes as she says this.

"Tell me about it," I say and laugh an awkward laugh. "Never thought my life would be like this, but here I am." I open my arms in a presenting myself kind of way. "So, why are you going to move back home?"

"I sort of have no other choice," she says unhappily, and stirs her soda with her straw.

"Why?"

"I don't know, I guess I've gotten myself into a little bit of trouble." She smiles weakly at me.

"What kind of trouble?" I ask her, feeling concerned—which is a new feeling when it comes to me and Anna.

"You really want to know?" She sounds surprised that I would care.

"Sure, why wouldn't I?" How sad is it that my own sister doesn't think I care about her?

"Well…" she hesitates and then sighs, "I've sort of gotten myself into some credit card debt."

"That doesn't seem like that big of a deal," I shrug my shoulders at her. "How much could it possibly be?"

"Um, I don't know. I guess somewhere around fifty thousand dollars." She looks down at the table, shamefully.

I can't keep my eyes from bugging out of my head. *"Fifty thousand dollars*? How is that even possible? You've hardly had a job. Who would give you a credit limit that high?"

"Oh, it wasn't hard." Anna looks at me with guilt in her eyes. "Anybody will give you credit cards these days."

"Yes, but not for that much," I say, thinking there is more to this story than she is letting on.

She looks down at her drink again and stirs it. There is a pause while she collects her thoughts. "Um… well… I applied for some of them using Mom's information," she says and then looks at me, biting on her bottom lip, guilt written all over her face.

"Anna!" My eyes bulge. "How could you do that to Mom?"

"I was desperate!" She holds her palms as if to plead her case. "I just didn't know what to do. I started small, figuring Mom and Dad never check their credit reports because why would they? They will live in that house until they die, and they never buy cars on credit, only cash. It was just like borrowing, only I didn't have to bother them with all the details. I am going to pay it all back."

"How? You don't even have a job!" I'm trying hard not to yell.

"Look, I don't need you to lecture me. I know what I did was wrong, and I know I can fix it.

Don't start acting like you're my all-knowing big sister that actually cares about me because we both know you don't. The only reason you are even paying attention to me right now is because you need shopping help. Otherwise, you would be totally ignoring me like you usually do." She blinks back tears.

I don't know what to say. Her words sting, as they were meant to. Sadly, Anna is right. I probably wouldn't be paying attention to her in any other circumstance. If I took the time to look back, would I see our rift was from both sides? Or was the truth that she had always tried, and it was me that kept pushing her away? I'm not sure I want to know the answer.

"I'm sorry, Anna." I say, "I don't mean to sound like I'm lecturing. And for what it's worth, I have had a fun time shopping with you, regardless of how we got here." I look down at my hands, feeling ashamed.

We sit there in silence for a while, and soon after, the server arrives with our food. We both just sit, looking at it. I'm no longer feeling hungry, and she probably isn't either.

"Are you going to tell Mom and Dad?" I say breaking the silence.

"No, and please don't tell them." She puts her face in her hands. "I've really messed things up."

"I won't tell them... but Anna, you probably should. If it comes out in some other way... I just don't think that would go very well."

"Yah, I will have to figure it all out," she says finally picking up her fork and stabbing her food with it, but not putting any in her mouth.

Still feeling the remnants of the sting from her comment about not caring about her, I feel the sudden need to start. "I could help you," I say, and she looks up at me.

"Julia, I'm not going to ask you to bail me out. I wouldn't do that," she says, a bit of insult in her voice.

"I'm not saying I'll bail you out, but I could help you. I could help you find a job and… and, I could move out of the basement," I say and regret the words immediately. Did I really just say that?

"What? You? Move out of the basement?" Anna says, equally shocked.

"Um… yes," I say, trying to fake resolve in my voice, when I actually want to throw up a little. "I… I think I have been there long enough."

"You don't have to do that, Julia. It's not your fault I'm in this mess."

"I know it's not my fault, but maybe I can start acting like a big sister and help you. Plus, it will probably be good for me." The regretful words keep spilling out of my mouth, and the more I say, the more I can't take it all back. This is not good.

I guess the thought of having the basement apartment is making Anna's move back home seem much more appealing to her because her appetite seems to be picking up and she is starting to eat her dinner. I, on the other hand, have lost my appetite altogether. Actually, I may never get it back again.

How am I supposed to move out of the basement? I mean, I know I should for heaven's sake. Who lives in their parents' basement for ten years? Spinsters do, that's who. But I don't even know where I would go. I've never lived on my own, never rented an apartment, never even thought about buying a place. I'm not ready to move into my spinster trailer home yet. I feel like it's just too much to think about. It's too overwhelming. I've always thought I should move out, but I never actually thought about moving out.

One thing is for sure, I will have to figure a way out of this. I can't move out. Not yet. I will just have to find an excuse, and convince Anna that living upstairs in her old bedroom is the way to go. Yes, that is what I will do. I will think of a plan. I just can't do it; I'm not ready to move out.

I'll make Anna understand, I have to.

# CHAPTER 6

So, apparently, I love to shop because I have gone the past four weekends. I've bought new clothes, new shoes, new makeup, and even accessories. It's amazing! Why didn't anyone get me to do this before? Oh, they did. I just resisted. Well, whatever. The point is I have now found a new hobby.

Fashion is compelling. I had no idea how much talent and ability goes into designing and making just one shirt. It's truly astounding. My new favorite show on TV is *Project Runway*, and I realize I'm most likely the last person in the world to catch onto it, but I love it. The talent is overwhelming. It puts baking to shame, really. Who can't read a recipe and bake something? It's not that hard... but to design and sew an entire evening gown in one day? That's incredible.

I sometimes dream that I'm a contestant. I realize this is an impossibility because first of all, I can't sew, which is pretty key to being on the show. And secondly, I just found out about all this fashion stuff a month ago. So, I'm kind of new to all of it. I actually owe any fashion sense I have to Anna anyway. Left to my own devices, I have been known to pick out shirts with shoulder pads, which, according to Anna, are "totally revolting."

Speaking of Anna, she has officially moved back home, and it's actually been really fun. She's been hanging out with me in the basement apartment a lot. I bake goodies, and we talk. We also watch a lot of TV together. We love all the same shows. She is the one who got me into *Project Runway*, of course.

As for moving out, well, I am pleased to say (and a little pukey also) that I am actually going to do it. I came up with many ways to get Anna to see why I couldn't leave, but every idea had holes in it. There just was no convincing argument.

I have a job so I couldn't say I needed to save the money (I did contemplate quitting, so it was no longer an issue… obviously that would have been stupid in this economy… or any economy, really). Besides saving money, there was no valid excuse. I knew Anna was not going to accept "I hate change" or "I can't live on my own" or "I just don't wanna"… so I had to give in and bite the bullet.

I asked my dad to help me look for apartments, and he convinced me that, with all the money I saved "mooching" off of him (I know he was joking but I must admit that one cut right to the core), I should just purchase a place. So, we spent one weekend looking, and that was all it took for me to find the perfect place for me. It's on Fourteenth Street in a newly-renovated high-rise building. I actually signed paperwork at the bank yesterday and have my keys sitting in my purse. It all happened so fast, which has got to be a gift from the gods. If it had dragged out in any way, I would have ended up running back to the basement, I'm sure.

So, I have a new place in downtown Denver! Just me and the bums. And yes, Jared also lives downtown. But that is not, and I repeat, *not* the reason I was even considering downtown. Okay, that might have been part of the reason. But once I saw my new place, I fell in love with it, and it just seemed right. Jared or no Jared.

Anyway, so about Jared. We are soooooo in love. Okay, we aren't. But there is love there — he loves my baking (which he has told me on many occasions), and I love his... well... everything. Seriously. And, yes, I do know it's not "love," it's actually "lust," and blah, blah, blah. I've already heard it all from Anna, which is extremely annoying to take from someone who is ten years younger than me. Sadly though, she has more experience.

She actually said, "Trust me Julia, I have so so so so so so so so so much more experience in this area." I may have added a few so's for emphasis, but that is essentially what she said.

Actually, it has been fun to have Anna around to talk to about Jared. I love to tell her all the details of my day. I have Brown at work to talk to, and I thoroughly enjoy reading into things with her, but I can sense something else from Brown. Like maybe a small bit of jealousy? It's probably not true, but it sometimes feels like it is. Brown can only take so much of my endless chatter. With Anna, it's so entertaining to talk about him, and she seems genuinely interested and wants to hear all the details, even the ones that are probably boring.

Anna has had some interesting experiences with the opposite sex. I had no idea. She has given me the gory details of her past relationships, and she's actually suffered a lot of heartbreak. It's sad to hear and makes me thankful I've avoided all that, thus far.

Honestly, I don't know what to think about Jared and me. There actually is no "Jared and me," so that notion is ridiculous. I realize I have little (to no) experience in this area, but I swear he actually seems to like me. I don't know if it's a "like-like" situation, but it sometimes does seem that way. Brown sees it, but then tells me not to get too excited. He may just be one of those guys who are overly flirty. But he doesn't flirt with her. And that's truly shocking because Brown is the picture perfect girl—every guy's fantasy. He genuinely seems to like Brown, but he's just different in the way he talks to her and the way he talks to me.

For example, a couple weeks ago, we were out on a smoke break and Brown casually mentions going to lunch.

"Um, I'm not sure…" he said, and then he turned to me. "Are you going?" Which, of course I said yes because—well, do I seriously need to explain? And then he turned back to Brown and said, "Sounds good, I'm in."

We decided on where to go and just before we were leaving, Jared called my office phone to tell me that he was running late and would meet us there. I thought it was interesting that he called me instead of Brown since she was the one that did the inviting. However, as was already established, I tend to over-think things a little… Or a lot.

On the drive over, Brown said, "Let's try a little experiment." She gave me a devious smile, and I was a little nervous at what she was about to say. "Let's ask for a booth when we get to the restaurant and see where Jared sits when he gets there."

I do love Brown and her little high school antics because it really is so much fun… but then, as we took our seats in the booth, I started to get a little sick thinking about what would happen. And of course, I had to think too much about it. How could I not? You see, no matter where he sat, there were many different reasons for his choice. If he sits next to me, then he most obviously picked me. But then if he sits next to Brown, then he obviously likes her more than me. But then, maybe he sits next to Brown so he can look at me. Of course, if we are going to go there, then if he sits next to me, it might just be to look at Brown. So, you can see my conundrum.

Anyway, in walks Jared to the restaurant. I'm feeling even sicker at this point because I have over-thought my brain into a tizzy. But he didn't even flinch or look like he was even thinking about it. He walked right in and sat next to... me.

Brown looked over and winked at me, and we gave each other conspiracy-type smiles over the tops of our menus. Of course, then I went back to thinking maybe he was sitting next to me because he wanted to look at Brown, but that notion pretty much died down when he mainly paid most of his attention to me. He even touched me a couple of times on my arm, and actually put his arm around me after we were done eating and waiting for our checks. Okay, it wasn't so much around me, but resting on the booth behind me. But it was near me, and I'm going to count it.

Lucky for me that I have Brown, right? And what's also great about her is she has way fewer inhibitions than I do (like, way way less), so I can get her to ask him questions about things I want to know about him. Stuff I'm not willing to ask him myself.

She's just better at digging into people's business. Plus, it won't make him think that I have this super-duper crush on him, which of course I do. I do realize that I'm acting like I'm in high school. I'm just not good at this, and since this is my first crush in like a bajillion years, plus the fact that this guy is completely out of my league, I am doomed to rejection. So, I will drag this out until I finally give up and move on or die of old age. Whichever comes first. Probably the latter.

So, here's what we now know about Jared: His birthday is September 22, which makes him a Libra, but on the cusp of a Virgo. He didn't tell me the sign part (he doesn't seem like the type that gets into that stuff), I looked that up on my own. But it just so happens our signs are quite compatible. Of course, this must be fate. His favorite color is navy blue. I found this out when I wore a navy blue shirt to work. Then Anna had to talk me out of picking everything that was navy blue the next time we went shopping. I swear it was subconscious, I didn't even realize I was doing it.

He loves cars and everything to do with them. I told him I drove a Honda Accord, and he then told me all the specs about my car. I pointed it out to him in the parking lot one time during a break, and he could tell me the year just by looking at it. I was totally impressed. Probably a little overly impressed, at least that's what Brown thought. It is, after all, just a Honda Accord. Not like he was guessing the year of some car people rarely drive. But I did find it manly and impressive. I even checked out a *Car and Driver* magazine when I was at the grocery store just so we could have something else to talk about—just him and me—and I made it to page two before I totally lost interest. Cars are *not* my thing.

Oh, and on a side note, one time when I was exceptionally bored at work I found this website that tells you your personality based on the car you drive, and under Honda Accord it said, "You have no creative ability and are basically a lemming." I found this to be somewhat true and a bit depressing.

Anyway, so more about Jared. Oh, this was interesting: He doesn't drink. At all. That was kind of weird and awkward, actually. What happened was when we were out on a smoke break, Brown asked him if he wanted to go out for drinks after work and he said, "I don't drink." And Brown laughed and said, "Okay, but that doesn't mean you can't come hang out with us." And he was all, "I don't like being near alcohol, at all." He seemed kind of short with us after that, then excused himself and went back to work. Brown and I, of course, discussed this in detail and tried to break down everything to figure out this mysterious behavior (high schoolers back in business). I think we deduced that he must be a recovering alcoholic, or perhaps someone close to him died from alcohol. All I know is it made me want to hold him and let him know everything would be alright. And if he was a recovering alcoholic I would be his sponsor or something. Of course, I think you have to have been an alcoholic to be a sponsor, but whatever. I would be his support.

I did get Brown to ask him about past girlfriends. Just to see if he is still hung up on one of them or something. He was not particularly forthcoming, but we did get a little information from him. Apparently, the last girlfriend he had was for three years, and it was one of those off and on tumultuous-type relationships. He got pretty burned by it and hasn't really been looking for anything for a while. He did look over at me and wink after he said that which was quite strange, and was promptly discussed in detail with Brown after he went back to his office.

Jared has actually been out of town the past week, and I've got to say, it has been dreary at work. Like, agonizingly dreary. First of all, Mr. Nguyen has been on a rampage having me do all these stupid reports that are still not making any sense to me. I'm starting to wonder if he is losing it. I mean for real this time. He's always seemed a little loony, but I think it's getting worse.

For example, today he gave me some handwritten numbers to plug into a report I was working on, and I couldn't tell what one of the numbers was. It looked like a squiggly mark or something. What the hell am I supposed to do with that? So I asked him about it, and he told me I must be mistaken and shooed me out the door. So now I'm not quite sure what I should do with this report. I tried using my detective skills and looking at what number he might have meant, but I'm still at square one.

So currently, since I can't figure out this stupid report, I'm rereading the article I ripped out of the *Cosmo* magazine when that awful incident happened with my upper-lip/mustache. Which, by the way, I noticed the hairs were starting to reappear, and for fear of having to lock myself away forever, I decided to try one of those pads that are supposed to rub the hair off. I ended up rubbing myself practically raw and looked like Yosemite Sam for the better part of a weekend. My dad could no longer control his actions, and laughed until he cried when he saw me. Thank goodness I was smart enough to try it on a weekend, instead of a weeknight. I seriously can't win in that area. Next stop is electrolysis, although I have heard it's incredibly painful. So, I will be putting that off indefinitely.

Okay, so, back to the article. The one about

how to date a coworker, aptly titled "How to Date a Coworker." This, of course, is not because I have some visions of grandeur and think Jared and I are dating, but it does have some clues into how to tell whether it's a thought that may have gone through his head.

For example, it says: *"It's promising if he's in an unrelated department yet asks your opinion on a project of his — it indicates that he is looking for an excuse to talk to you and values your opinion."* He has never asked me to work on a project with him; however, he is still very interested in my and Brown's knowledge of the company and the people in it. I'm grasping at straws here. I think I'll move on.

Another article I just happened to bookmark, you know, for posterity's sake or something like that, was "Three Ways To Tell if You Are More Than Friends." I found it to be very intriguing... for posterity's sake. The first way, according to the article, is to simply ask. I laughed out loud at that one, and then got a little queasy when I envisioned myself actually asking. It said if you do that, it's kind of like ripping the bandage off, you will know one way or the other. I'm not sure I'm ready. I'm a take-the-bandage-off-slowly kind of gal anyway, so it's a no-go for me.

The second way to tell, according to the article, is to ignore the person. This one I found intriguing. The theory is if you back off from the person and not pay attention to them or go out of your way to see them, then one of two things will happen: he will either miss you and then make an effort on his part to see you, or he will back off altogether and then you have your answer. That way there is no confrontation, and it's in your control. Here is the biggest problem with that: how do you avoid the one person you actually want to see? How long would I have to suffer? And if he just backed off and went away (the likely of the two), then there goes the flirting, the fun, the excitement, my will to live…

The third way to tell if you are more than friends is to hang out alone as much as you possibly can. According to the article, this is the most honest approach instead of the game playing that ignoring someone truly is. This one is obviously the most appealing way to me, but how do I do it? We have never hung out outside of work (except for a few lunches), and when Brown casually mentioned going out for drinks, we were quickly shot down. So, the only way to hang out alone with him is to get assigned to a project that he is working on, or to go to lunch alone with him. The project sounds the most appealing because it's the least unnerving to me.

We have had some lunches together, but Brown has been there, which is how I like it. The only lunch Jared and I had alone was stressful, to say the least (he also thought I might have herpes, but why relive that part). I don't know if

I can handle it alone again. Granted, I didn't know him very well back then. But now I have come to rely on Brown too much as a buffer; it's much less stressful for me if she is there.

Okay, so a project it is. How the heck do I get put on a project with Jared, though? I guess the best way to do it is go to the source: Jared's boss, Mr. Calhoun, and ask him.

By now I realize, I've established myself as a complete idiot, but truthfully I am not that stupid. Of course, I am not going to march up to Mr. Calhoun's office and ask to be put on a project with Jared. First of all, he would just scoff at me and then probably ask me to make him some cupcakes. And honestly, it just wouldn't make sense—me in accounting, Jared in HR. The whole notion is silly. No, the only hope I have is to throw it out to the universe and hope that the chick who wrote that *Secret* book is right.

So there, I'm sending it out. Show me what you've got, universe.

"Julia?" A voice pulls me out of my self-serving universal wish.

I look up to see none other than Mr. Calhoun standing in my door way. Whoa, that is crazy.

"Yes?" I say and quickly click off the article I was reading, and then say a prayer of thanks that my computer is strategically placed so no one can see what I'm doing.

"I need you to help me with something," he

says as he comes into my office and shuts the door behind him. He takes a seat in one of the guest chairs facing my desk.

"What can I help you with?" I ask, slightly concerned that his shutting of the door means this is serious business.

"I need this to be top secret; please do not discuss this with anyone including your boss or any of your friends at work." And by "friends," he must mean Brown and possibly Jared, although I'm not sure how much he knows about my friendship with Jared.

"Sure, no problem."

"I need you to…" he trails off as his Blackberry vibrates and he pulls it out of his belt loop holder, looking at it quickly to see who is calling. Probably Martha requesting a quick rendezvous in the supply closet.

"Make cupcakes?" I chime in without really thinking.

He gives me a weird look. "Um, no," he says, squinting his beady little eyes at me, shaking his head no. Then he does this little fake uncomfortable laugh.

Oh dear Lord, I have just insulted him. I've just insulted my boss's boss. By insinuating his super-secret request is cupcakes, I am actually saying he's a Fatty McFat-Fat. And not just a run-of-the-mill fatty, but one who eats in private and doesn't want anybody to know about it, secretly hiding the evidence down deep in the trash can. I try to cover my faux pas up by laughing like I was just joking, but it's not really working. It's just awkward.

He shakes his head quickly and closes his eyes like he's trying to remember why he was here in the first place. Or perhaps he's changing his mind and will fire me on the spot. I can't say I'd blame him.

"Um, Julia, what I need you to do is help me out with some reports, and I need it to be the 'proverbial' hush-hush," he says and smiles thinly at me, making air quotes around his usage of proverbial.

"No problem, I can do that," I say, relieved he has quickly recovered and moved on from the cupcake comment. I'm wondering what the heck kind of report I would do that Mr. Nguyen can't know about.

"This means you will have to do this after work since I don't want anyone to know about what you're doing," he says, looking at me like I don't really have a choice, and honestly after insinuating that his fat butt wanted some cupcakes, I am not at liberty to argue about it.

"Sure, that won't be a problem," says the spinster who has no life after work anyway.

"Great. Just meet me in my office after work, and again, I cannot stress enough about keeping this secret, a… um… secret."

With that, he squeezes himself out of the guest chair and heads to the door. He turns back to me before leaving, "Cupcakes would also be great, by the way," he says as he winks at me, and then he opens the door and leaves my office.

Okay, so one thing is for sure, when you throw something out to the universe, it answers quickly. And the other thing that is for sure, either that book is complete malarkey or the universe is hard of hearing. What part of "put me on a project with Jared" meant "put me on a super-secret project with his boss"? Stupid universe. Stupid book.

I manage to get out for a smoke break with Brown later in the afternoon, and I have to bite my tongue about five times to keep myself from almost telling her about my super-secret reporting with Mr. Calhoun. And I mean, I literally had to bite my tongue, it was that hard not to say anything. I tell Brown practically everything, so of course, it would just come naturally to me to have verbal diarrhea around her. Especially when I have something juicy to tell her. Also, I needed her to help me break down the cupcake comment I made to him and see if she thought it was as horrible as it seemed. But I was able to make it through the break without saying anything.

I sulk through the rest of the afternoon, dreading having to stay and work after hours. I really don't want to prolong my stay at this mundane place, especially when Jared isn't here.

I know Jared has only been away this week,

but it feels like a lifetime. I dread coming to work without him here. It's just no fun. What kind of HR conference takes a week anyway? It must be agonizingly boring. I can't wait to show my fake curiosity while he tells me all about it when he gets back. Sadly, I won't actually be pretending I'm interested. Anything out of Jared's mouth is exciting to me, as pathetic as that is.

I wait until five thirty to leave, and grab my purse to go. I walk casually by Mr. Nguyen's office. I glance at him through the open door and see him working on something, long pinky nail tapping away on the keyboard as he types. I say a quick goodnight, which he, as usual, never acknowledges, and I walk down the hall to the elevator. This time instead of going down to the parking lot and away from this dreadful Jared-less place, I have to take the elevator upstairs to hang out with Mr. Calhoun.

I wonder what kind of super-secret reports he's having me do? Whatever it is, I'm sure it will be super boring. Although the thought of doing something away from Mr. Nguyen has piqued my interest a bit. But then it's ruined by the fact that I have to stay after work to do it. I wonder if I will get overtime for this. I better.

I make it to the sixth floor and feel a bit of the butterflies when I see the door to the conference room that has now become Jared's make-shift office. I know he's not in there, but just knowing he has *been* there gives me butterflies for some reason. It's ridiculous. I'm ridiculous. I internally roll my eyes at myself.

Mr. Calhoun is on his phone with his back turned toward the opened door as I approach his office. I stand there for a few moments as he talks in hushed tones. I honestly can't understand anything he is saying. Then, I realize if I don't make some kind of noise notifying him of my arrival, he will wonder if I was eavesdropping. So I knock on the opened door and clear my throat, just to make sure I've covered all bases. He spins his chair around, sees me, and gestures for me to come in and have a seat. Beads of sweat appear on his forehead. Mr. Calhoun is a rather sweaty person, so this is no surprise.

"Thanks for helping me with this Julia," he says after he wraps up his phone call with various "uh-huhs" and "no problems" and "will-dos." Along with a few "proverbials" thrown in there for good measure, of course.

"No problem," I say, wishing I was anywhere in the world but here. Then again, I have nothing to do. Even nothing sounds better than this. "So, what is this report you need me to do?" I say, wanting to get started. The sooner we start, the sooner I am home and in my PJs watching McDreamy on my DVR.

After reminding me about fifty times that this was, in fact, the most proverbial of all proverbial

143

secrets (he actually said that), we got started. The report didn't seem to be anything out of the ordinary, nothing I hadn't done for Mr. Nguyen. I was tempted to ask what this was all about, but I felt like I might be questioning something I have no right to know. Although, I *am* staying after work to do this, so why shouldn't I have the right to know? Brown would have asked by now… I just don't have that kind of gumption.

Luckily, I don't have to spend much time with Mr. Calhoun. He got me set up on his computer and has been running around the office doing… whatever he is doing. I have no idea. Probably seeing Martha. Probably eating something. Who knows? He makes it seem like it's of the utmost importance, whatever he is doing. And although he is a sweaty man, he seems extra sweaty, and a bit stressed out tonight. It really can't be good for his heart.

The report is mainly just plugging numbers from one spreadsheet into another larger spreadsheet. I've had to make up a few formulas so it all totals out in the end, but it's nothing I haven't done before, and certainly doesn't feel super-secret. I am feeling less and less important as the time ticks on. Anyone could have done this. Why did I have to stay after work for this? Good thing I'll soon be done with this, and can get back to my regularly scheduled life of baking, watching TV, and settling into my spinsterly ways.

The next time Mr. Calhoun comes back in the office, frantically looking for something, I tell him I'm nearly done. He tells me to save the file to his desktop, and that I can leave when I'm finished.

"So, tomorrow after work then?" he asks as he bends over to pick up a large manila envelope that had fallen onto the floor.

"Um…" I say, trailing off. I thought this was a one-time thing? And tomorrow is Friday! I mean, come on, how can he expect me to work late on a Friday? But what do I say? I mutter out a "Sure," and try to fill it with as much disgust and loathing as I can. The idea of working late on a Friday night at Spectraltech makes me want to cry.

The spring air feels good on this May evening as I leave dreaded Jared-less Spectraltech because I am finally done with my super-secret reporting. Ugh. Spectraltech without Jared is like chocolate chip cookies without the chocolate chips. Actually, I sometimes like that last cookie you scrape from the bowl—the one that has one or two chips in it. So, that is a bad analogy. Spectraltech without Jared is like sugar cookies with no sugar. Just a ton of extra salt. Nasty.

Tomorrow, I have to endure another stupid day at Spectraltech without Jared, and then to make it even worse, I have to stay late… On a Friday night, even. If I didn't have a new mortgage to pay soon, I would quit right now.

When I get to the basement apartment, Anna is waiting for me on the couch, looking a little frazzled. My date with McDreamy will apparently have to wait a little longer.

"What's up?" I ask, looking concerned at her, but not *too* concerned. Anna hates receiving any sympathy toward her. Something I have learned only recently.

I set my stuff on the floor, and plop myself next to her on the couch. I lean back against the soft brown leather. I love this couch; I may try to steal it when I move out.

Anna puts her hands in her face. "They're after me," she says through her hands in a slightly muffled, but clearly paranoid tone. I stifle a laugh, because seriously? "They're after me"? That's a little on the dramatic side.

"What do you mean?"

"The creditors!" she says in a how-in-the-hell-do-you-not-know tone.

"The creditors? What creditors?" I say, knowing full well what creditors. But for some reason, I ask her like I don't know.

"The credit card companies are calling me!" she says, head still in her hands.

"About what?"

"About my bills!" She uses her condescending tone. She removes her hands from her face and sits back on the couch, slouching low and closing her eyes in a super dramatic way.

"What about your bills? Aren't you paying them?" I look at her like she's a fool, because she is. I mean, of course she is paying her bills, everyone knows when you have a credit card, you pay the bill.

She looks at me, throwing daggers with her eyes. "No, Julia. Of course, I haven't been paying my bills. Why do you think I moved home? Because I felt like it? Because I had nothing better to do? I have no money!" Her head goes dramatically back against the couch, eyes closing again.

"But some of those credit cards aren't yours, they're Mom's!" I say, realizing what she is implying. If the creditors are after Anna for her credit cards, they are also going after Mom for her credit cards—the cards Mom doesn't know she has.

She looks at me like I'm a complete idiot. Almost as if this is all my fault. I realize she's just taking it out on me, which is kind of annoying. I suppose as the big sister I should allow it, especially since I've only recently started acting like a big sister.

"When they call, aren't they calling Mom?" I ask, wondering how she's going to be able to get away with it all.

Her hands go back up to her face. "No, I only put my cell phone on the applications. But all my mail is being forwarded here, so I'm getting stuff in the mail, too. I've been staying home all day waiting for the stupid mailman so I can grab the mail and get my stuff out before Mom and Dad see it."

"Anna, you have to tell Mom and Dad." I try to pull her hands away from her face so she can see the serious expression on mine.

"No way!" she says, bursting into tears. "They will kill me!"

"They are not going to kill you—they'll be pissed, sure—but they are not going to kill you." Although, I wonder if the thought won't briefly cross Dad's mind, when he finds out.

"Anna, it's just going to get worse. You need to tell them. Why didn't you ask me for help? I didn't know you weren't paying your bills. You're not only killing your credit, you're also killing Mom's!" I say that last part like it just dawned on me—because it did just dawn on me. I totally spaced the credit history part of this.

With that, she cries even harder. That was not the right thing to say, apparently. But what do you say? I mean, it's true—she is majorly screwed. She's not paying her bills, and now she has creditors after her. She's likely killing hers and my mom's credit. Plus, I'm not sure, but applying for credit cards with someone else's information is probably illegal. Actually, I'm *quite* sure it's illegal.

"What am I going to do, Julia?" she says as she pulls her hands back from her tear-stained face and looks at me rather pathetically.

"I don't know…" I trail off. What is she going to do? I guess the first thing she needs to do is find a job and start paying her bills, and she definitely needs to tell Mom and Dad. I tell her this and the crying starts up again. I want to feel sorry for her, and I do—but she dug herself into a hole. Now I'm wondering if *I* should say something to our parents. But I seriously don't want to jeopardize this newfound relationship that we have just started. She would hate me for sure if I went behind her back. I don't know if Anna is a thank-you-for-it-later kind of person. She seems more likely to hold a grudge.

"Well, have you even started looking for a job yet?" I ask after the crying lets up a bit.

"I haven't had time. I've been sitting around all day waiting for the mail," she says as she wipes her nose on the sleeve of her sweatshirt. I get up and go down the hall to the bathroom to get some tissue because that is disgusting, and what is even more disgusting is it is *my* sweatshirt. I will have to burn it.

"Well, you are just going to have to take a chance that Mom and Dad won't bother looking at your mail," I say as I walk back into the room. "You're going to have to get out there and get a job." I hand her the tissue.

We sit in silence for a bit while she contemplates that. "I guess you're right," she says finally, and then blows her nose into the tissue.

"I'll help you," I smile at her.

"Thanks," she says, sniffling and looking at the balled-up tissue in her hands. "I hate working, though. Couldn't I just win the lottery or something?"

"Yah, 'cause that kind of thing just happens when you need it the most," I say sarcastically. "Come on, join the rest of the world and get a job. It's not that bad." I nudge her arm in a way that is sure to annoy her.

"Oh yah, because you're such the poster child for loving your job." She rolls her eyes at me.

"I'm totally offended by that comment. I love working at Spectraltech. It's all I have ever aspired to do," I deadpan.

"Okay. Whatever. So, are we gonna watch some McSteamy or what?" she asks, still sniffling.

"Well, we probably should get online and start looking for a job for you, shouldn't we?" I feign a condescending tone.

"Let's just start tomorrow. I don't want to think about it tonight." How typical of her to put it off for one more day. I don't feel like arguing with her because, honestly, I don't really want to help her look for a job right now. I think we both need a little escape. A little pajama/DVR time should be just the trick, I think.

# CHAPTER 7

Did you know that, on a regular standard keyboard, the "T" and the "G" keys are really close together? I just realized this today when I sent out a three-department-wide e-mail that was signed "Retards, Julia."

Thank goodness Jared wasn't here to see it since he is still away at his conference. It really has been the never-ending week for me. Of course, before Jared came into my Spectraltech world, every week was never-ending. But I can't seem to remember that part of my life. It's as if my life started the minute he caught me under the conference room table. Wow, that was cheesy.

I can't believe I have to endure another evening with Mr. Calhoun and more reporting. It's been so hard to keep it all from Brown. We're the gossip queens, for crap's sake. We know everything that's going on in this company. I hate having to keep gossip from her. Especially when it really wouldn't hurt because I don't even know what this report is all about anyway. But I promised Mr. Calhoun, and I will keep his secret. I may be a gossip, but I am an honorable one. Well, as honorable as a gossip can be, that is.

Anna and I stayed up way too late last night watching TV. It was fun, though. She seemed to feel better as the night went on. I came up with this grand idea that maybe I could find her a job at Spectralcrap (I came up with that last night, hard to believe it never dawned on me before). After all, our front desk girl, Kelly, is probably on her way out since she rarely does her job anyway. How fun would it be for Anna to work here? It might make the endless weeks when Jared is not here, seem less... endless. Hopefully there will be no more of these trips to stupid conferences. But if there were, and Anna was here... well, at least she would let me talk nonstop about Jared. Not like Brown, she can only take so much of my obsession.

Currently, I am working on Anna's resume because Mr. Nguyen is out of the office for the rest of the afternoon. So, why bother doing work when he is not here to impress? Not that I have ever impressed Mr. Nguyen. He mostly just stares down his nose at me, probably disgusted with my questions and my lack of understanding his handwritten numbers.

I've got to say, I'm pretty good at the resume writing thing. This is good because Anna needs some serious help. Considering the fact she hasn't worked much, except for a couple summer jobs at The Gap and Anne Taylor, she has mostly just been going to school and letting my parents pay for stuff. Oh, and using credit cards like some crazy lunatic. So proud of her.

My computer makes a beeping noise and an e-mail pops up in my inbox from Brown requesting a smoke break. Sounds like a great idea.

Before I go, I shoot the finished resume off to Mr. Calhoun with a quick note telling him if they're looking to hire, I have a candidate that would be perfect for a start-up position. It will be quite obvious it's a relative since we have the same last name, but I doubt that will bother him. Maybe he will think because I bake, Anna bakes, too, and then he would have two Dorning sisters to bring in baked goods to the office. She will be a shoe-in for sure.

I'll just make sure I mention a little something to him about it when I'm doing the report for him tonight. Just so the e-mail doesn't get lost in his inbox as so many of them do.

Currently, it's raining in the lovely city of Denver. May is full of rain and sometimes even some snow for us Coloradans. It makes for a beautiful June, which I am definitely looking forward to. June is my favorite month in Denver. Everything is green and lush. Then, July and August show up and bake the crap out of everything, and it all turns to an ugly brown, which stays until the following June.

"What's up, nerd?" Brown says as I meet her outside. She's tucked up against the wall under the awning, protected from the rain.

"Not much. Just working." A little fib. Obviously working on Anna's resume is not technically working, but it *feels* like it, and, therefore, I'm going to count it as actual work.

"What's crazy Nguyen having you work on now?" she asks, and then takes a long drag from her cigarette. I honestly do not understand how Brown can have as good of skin as she has and smoke. It's just not right. It will probably catch up with her at some point, as will emphysema.

"He's gone for the rest of the day. So, I'm just biding my time until I have to go help Calhoun." The words fall out of my mouth before I can even stop myself.

Dang it! I'm the worst super-secret keeper, ever. How could I do that? I only made it one freaking day.

"What do you mean?" She crinkles her eyes at me, looking full of interest.

How the heck am I going to get out of this? I pause too long trying to think of what I'm going to say. "I can't tell you," is all I can choke out.

"Julia Dorning, you are holding out on me," she says, pointing a burning cigarette at me.

"I know, I know." I put my head in my hands. "I was sworn to secrecy, and it's been killing me not to tell you."

"Well, you're going to tell me, right now," she

says, still looking like she can't believe I would keep something from her.

"No, seriously, I promised. Mr. Calhoun told me not to tell anyone, including Mr. Nguyen. I honestly don't even know why it's a secret anyway. It's really not that big of a deal," I say, looking down at the floor, ashamed of myself for making Brown feel bad that I kept something from her, and ashamed for not being able to keep one stinking secret. I really could never work for the CIA or FBI. I would end up in jail for unintentional treason.

"I'm annoyed with you right now, Julia," she says, and takes another drag of her cigarette.

"I know! I'm annoyed with myself! I'm sorry. I will tell you everything when I have something to tell you."

"How did it happen?" She crinkles her eyes at me.

"Mr. Calhoun just asked me to help him with some stuff after work and I was not supposed to tell anyone. Brown, you can't tell anyone, okay? I will fill you in when I actually know what the heck I am keeping a secret for. I really don't know what I'm doing. Just some different types of reports." She looks so annoyed at me right now. I just wish I could keep my big trap shut. The thought does cross my mind that perhaps keeping a secret from her isn't what's truly bothering Brown. Maybe she is feeling a bit of jealousy because *she* wasn't asked to work on this project. That would be very Brown-like.

"That's interesting…" she trails off, looking like she is putting the pieces together to something in her head.

"It's really not," I say emphatically.

"I'm not talking about your work for Calhoun. I'm talking about something I heard earlier today. I didn't think it was gossip worthy because I wasn't really sure… but now I'm thinking it might be…" she trails off again.

"Don't leave me hanging, Brown. Tell me!"

"I'm sorry, I was sworn to secrecy." She smiles slightly and looks at me out of the corner of her eye.

"I'm sorry. What more do you want me to say? I will tell you when I have it all figured out, I promise. Now tell me what you've heard." Oh how I love the possibility of juicy gossip, it makes my blood race. It's my only vice.

"Okay," she says in hushed tones, moving closer to me. "I walked by my boss's office earlier today, and I think I heard him say something like Nguyen was on his way out. I wasn't sure because it wasn't clear. I didn't even remember it until you said that Calhoun asked you not to tell Nguyen. Now I'm wondering if that is actually what I heard."

"Oh, that *is* interesting…" I say, smiling conspiratorially at her.

"Think about it. It kind of makes sense. Why would Calhoun want you not to tell Nguyen, and have you work after hours to do it?" Brown says, nodding her head like she has just uncovered something huge. Such the detective.

We ponder on this for a bit, tossing around ideas for why Mr. Nguyen would be on his way out. The guy has worked for Spectraltech for years. It's hard to believe they would let him go. So, maybe he's going to quit? However, then what's with all the secretive stuff? Maybe he's going to be fired for something big, and they need me to help catch him.

If that's true, in an odd way, it makes me feel a little sad. I mean, I know I think Mr. Nguyen is a crazy person who should have been committed along with his abnormally long pinky nail, but it doesn't mean I want him to be unemployed. Maybe Brown is wrong, although it sort of makes sense.

It's odd how I don't even have an inkling of his life outside of work. I don't even know if he's married or has children. In the ten years that I've known Mr. Nguyen, he has never revealed anything about his personal life. When he comes to company parties, if he comes, he's always alone and leaves quickly. The longest conversation we've ever had has been maybe five minutes, and it's always been about work. Nothing else.

I don't even know how long he has worked here. He was here before I got here, and when I asked around everyone said he was part of the buy-out deal that is now Spectraltech. No one knows where Henry Nguyen came from. Maybe he's a spy for another country or something and he's been working undercover for all these years. His long pinky nail marking his allegiance to his terrorist group.

Yes, well, most likely that is not what is going on. The thought of three hungry children crying because there is no money to buy food, and Mr. Nguyen going postal when he is fired and coming in with a gun (it's the quiet ones you're supposed to worry about, right?), keeps running through my head. Although, I've already established I have no idea if he has a family and who are we kidding—Mr. Nguyen would have saved money for something like this. He's definitely not the frivolous type. The postal type, though, is a possibility.

I decide not to ponder this anymore because I am clearly jumping to conclusions. I spend the rest of the afternoon catching up on work since I spent so much time in the morning working on Anna's resume.

At five thirty, I get my stuff and head to the elevator, feeling a twinge of guilt/sadness as I walk past Mr. Nguyen's office. I realize I'm being a bit dramatic. I can't help myself though.

I can't believe I am spending a Friday evening with Mr. Calhoun. This really ranks high in the book of pathetic spinster activities. Pathetic, even for a spinster. Although, I have to say this whole Mr. Nguyen twist has got me intrigued. Now, I really want to find out what the heck I am actually taking part in. Even though there are a million other things I'd rather be doing right now, at least that has piqued my interest a bit. I'm also feeling a bit on the important side considering how annoyed Brown seemed at not being asked to be on this super-secret task. It's like I'm some sort of spy. A spinster spy. Well, that doesn't really roll off the tongue remarkably well. I'll have to think of a better name.

As I get on the elevator, for no particular reason, I start to feel a little giddy and move around the small space with my hands in the shape of a gun while I hum the *Mission: Impossible* theme. I'm a spinster spy. Although, let's be honest, a spinster spy would most likely find a way to use cats for a weapon — or perhaps sagging breasts would work. You could really whip someone in the face pretty hard with those things if used properly.

I abandon the spy moves and just start dancing around the elevator like a complete fool and singing "Sweet Home Alabama." I'm not really sure how I went from the *Mission: Impossible* theme to "Sweet Home Alabama," but somehow it is a smooth transition.

I'm in the midst of doing a booty-shaking thing with my hand spanking the air when I hear someone's voice clear. I turn around to see the door to the elevator is opened and standing there with a big smirk on his face is none other than... Jared.

Oh dear heaven, please no. Please say I'm dreaming. Please say it's a hologram, and I have entered into some *Mission: Impossible* realm. Oh please, oh please, oh please!

No such luck. I have once again embarrassed myself in front of this impossibly handsome man, and there's no covering it up this time. I am a complete moron. I really should just be put away into a padded cell. It's the only true place I belong... tied up in a white jacket.

I decide to play it cool. "Hey," I say a little breathlessly since my dancing around the elevator has been more exercise than I can take.

"Hey," he says back and his lip twitches like he's about to laugh.

"I didn't know you were back," I say, still slightly breathless, still looking like a complete jackass.

"Just got back an hour ago," he says, still smirking.

"Cool," I say and purse my lips together, shaking my head slightly. *Be cool Julia, be cool.* "I'm just, um, up here to see Mr. Calhoun."

"I know." He lets go of the smirk and smiles slightly at me.

"Oh, you do?" I say, surprised. How would he know? "How do you know that? He said it was 'super-secret?'"

"Well, he's asked me to work on the

'proverbial' super-secret report, too." He uses air quotes when he says "proverbial," doing a pretty decent impression of Mr. Calhoun as well. Quite impressive, actually. "So, shall we?" He motions to Mr. Calhoun's office. "Or do you still want to finish your little song and dance?" He looks at me with that smirk back on his face.

I blush a million shades of red, but raise my head in mock confidence. "No, that was my final performance."

"Are you sure? Because I was really enjoying it," he says, raising his eyebrows and looking way adorable.

I blush another million shades of red. I'm most likely the shade of a beet at this point. "That was my extra-special private dance. No one has ever seen it. You should feel privileged, really." I walk away from him and quickly over to Mr. Calhoun's office.

Did I just pull that off? Did I actually turn something utterly embarrassing into a joke? You have come a long way, Julia Dorning. A long way indeed.

I reach the door to Mr. Calhoun's office without looking back to see if Jared has followed me, but I can hear the rustling of his shirt behind me and I know he is there. My gosh, he smells good.

"Ah, yes, Julia and Jared. Good to see you. Come on in." Mr. Calhoun is sitting at his desk with the phone to his ear. He motions for us to come in and holds up his finger letting us know he's not completely done with his conversation.

Jared and I walk in and take a seat in the chairs facing his desk. We look over at each other and I smile slightly, feeling a little uncomfortable. Jared leans back in the chair with his legs stretched out and hands behind his head.

"Julia," Mr. Calhoun says after he ends his call, "I've asked Jared to work with you on this project. I'm afraid there is more data that needs to be entered, and it may take a while. So, I thought with both of you working together, it would get done faster."

"Mr. Calhoun," I say, feeling a little bit of unforeseen confidence, "can I ask what this is all about? I mean if you don't mind telling me..." I drift off because as soon as I asked, I could see a silent conversation between Mr. Calhoun and Jared happening with their eyes.

"I'll explain it to her," Jared chimes in with a wink at me, and something that seems like a reassuring smile to Mr. Calhoun.

"Good," Mr. Calhoun says as he shuffles some papers around his desk looking for something. "I will need my office tonight, so if you could work with Jared in the conference room, that would be helpful," he says as he finds an interoffice envelope and hands it to Jared.

As we walk over to the conference room, it all of the sudden hits me that I am working on a project with Jared. I am actually working on a project with Jared. Me! Julia Spinster Dorning! I will get to spend time with Jared, all by myself. Just like the article said I should do. I just threw it out to the Universe, and it actually worked. That *Secret* book is gold!

We go into the conference room, which is the first time I have been back here since the "incident." So much has happened since then. I'm wearing makeup, moving out of my parents' basement, becoming pretty close friends with my sister, working on a super-secret project with a freaking hot man... it's pretty incredible how things can change in such a short time. Crazy, really.

Jared sets me up at a laptop near him, and I get to work inputting numbers from some documents he gives me, finishing up the worksheet I was working on yesterday. Some of the formulas are messed up, and I fix them quickly and then write a few of my own that are easier and function much better for the worksheet. In a normal world, this would be pretty stinking boring, but because I am sitting near Jared, inputting numbers has become a glorious task.

I still have no idea what I am doing or why I am here. But now with Jared being put into the mix, I suddenly don't really care as much. Besides, he said he would tell me, and I'm sure he will.

I glance quickly over at Jared, busily typing away on his laptop and wonder what part of this super-secret stuff he is doing. He really is so good looking. I know I've said it before, but seriously — the blue eyes, the dark blonde hair... the chiseled jaw... his incredible smile... oh no, I'm staring. I look away quickly before he notices. Good gravy, I'm like a creepy stalker.

Thank goodness he didn't see. No one should ogle. Ogling is bad... it's probably something spinsters do. Another symptom to add to my list. Really, I could start blaming everything I do on my future spinsterhood. I wonder if maybe there's a clinical doctor-type word for it. Something in Latin. I should find out what spinster is in Latin, and then when I do something stupid, I could tell people that it's due to my impressive-Latin-word-disease. They then would feel sorry for me and not embarrassed for me like I'm sure people normally feel.

"You done yet?" Jared asks, pulling me out of my self-diagnosis.

"Not... quite..." I say and return to entering numbers. "I'm about three-fourths of the way done. Why?"

"That's good enough for now. Let me see what you've got." He stands up and comes over to where I'm sitting. He stands behind me, hands on the back of my chair and leans over me to see the worksheet, his breath on my neck.

Chills run up and down my spine, and I almost want to let out a giggle, I'm so overcome with butterflies in my stomach. Oh please, don't let me do anything embarrassing, like burp all of a sudden... or even worse...

He scans quickly through the worksheet, looking at a few totals and clicking on some of the formulas I had just written.

"Did you change this formula?" He points to one of the formulas I fixed, or thought I fixed. Oh, no! Did I screw it up?

"Um, yeah. But I can change it back." I put my hand on the mouse and go to click on the cell so I can fix it.

"No!" he says, pulling my hand up from the mouse. "I didn't say you needed to change it back. Where did you learn that formula?"

"I just figured it out. You have to do that when your boss doesn't give a lot of direction," I say as I continue to blush and practically barf out butterflies. His breath on my neck, touching my hand... it's really just too much to take.

"Pretty impressive," he says still looking over my shoulder, still breathing on my neck. I might die. At least it would be in a happy way.

He stands up and moves back to his seat. He leans back in his chair and looks at me. At least I think he's looking at me, I'm busily trying to look... well, busy. I really don't want him to see how bad I am blushing right now, and I hope (pray) if I look straight ahead and not at him, he won't be able to tell. I highly doubt it though.

I can feel his eyes on me, and I finally get the nerve to look up. "Yes?" I ask, looking at him quizzically. What would he need to be staring at me so long for? I try to think of some little quip or something witty but nothing is coming to me. Shocking, I know.

He smiles at me slightly but doesn't say anything, clearly deep in thought. I wonder what the heck he's thinking. I look around the room because I'm finding that making eye contact is difficult.

"Tell me about Henry," he says finally breaking the awkward silence and looking back at his computer.

"Nguyen? What do you want to know about him?" I ask, a little shocked, and also a little sad that he was thinking about Mr. Nguyen and not me, as I had hoped.

"Got any gossip on him?" he asks with a slight smile.

What would I say about Mr. Nguyen? I do have gossip on him, but I can't tell Jared because then he'll know I was talking to Brown about this super-secret stuff we are doing, and I was asked repeatedly by Mr. Calhoun not to say anything. I don't want him to find out. I would be fired for sure. I have a mortgage to pay now, I cannot get fired. Plus, if I am ever going to marry Jared and have his babies (a spinster can dream), I need to keep seeing him. I can't do that when we don't work together anymore, now can I?

"Um," I shrug my shoulders stalling, trying to come up with something. "What can I say about Mr. Nguyen? I have worked for him for ten years now, and I can't honestly say I know more about him personally, than I did the day I was hired. He's very private."

Jared ponders that for a second. "What about how he is at work?" he asks, leaning forward and looking at his computer screen, which puts me a little more at ease. I think it's easier to talk to him when he isn't looking at me directly.

"Well, he does his job if that's what you're asking. I mean, I guess he knows what he's doing, but he's not the best boss." I lean back and fold my arms.

"Why do you say that?" He looks up from his screen at me.

"Well, like I said before, he gives poor direction. He never listens to me when I tell him I think something is wrong with a report. He constantly looks at me like I'm a complete idiot, and his long pinky nail seriously creeps me out," I add and shiver at the thought of it.

Jared laughs a little at the last comment. "Yah, what is that all about?" He scrunches his nose a little as he says that.

"I don't know. Brown and I have discussed it many times and have many theories, but short of flat-out asking him, we have no real answers.

I'm sure if I did ask him, he would just give me some annoyed look, and then shoo me out of his presence." I move my hand in a shooing motion to demonstrate how he, in fact, shoos me away. It happens all too often.

"Why do you want to know about Mr. Nguyen, anyway? There really is not much to tell..." I drift off, thinking about how there is something to tell, but I can't. I really can't do that. I do trust Jared, but I don't know how he would respond to me telling Brown about this super-secret crap. As much as I want to share with him, I just need to keep it zipped. So we'll see how long that will last. Clearly I am the vision of secrecy as I totally displayed with Brown.

"Oh, well, I was just curious," he says, looking back down at his screen. "You said he doesn't give much direction, I was just wondering if you knew anything else about him since you work so close to him. Apparently, no one knows about Henry Nguyen."

"Yes, he's a mystery. That's for sure."

Jared moves his attention back to his computer, and I can hear the clicking of his mouse. I decide I better turn back to my work and get it done, although I really don't want to finish it now. Yesterday, I couldn't finish it fast enough, but now that Jared is here... well, it changes everything. Now I just want to go really slow, and then maybe we can continue this on

Monday. How brilliant would that be? But then I would also seem like an imbecile because anyone with half a brain would know I should be able to finish this report. How can I prolong this night?

Now that I think about it, though, I should be acting more like I have plans tonight and need to hurry it up. Honestly, what kind of girl has no plans on a Friday night and can devote extra time to her job? The spinster kind, that's who. It's looking a little obvious I have no plans tonight since Jared has heard no protesting or anything out of my mouth about having to work on a Friday night. He probably already has me pegged for the hermit/spinster type.

Of course, if we're going to go there, then why isn't he openly protesting about being here? He doesn't come off as the recluse type to me. Quite the contrary, actually. He seems like the type of guy who would always have plans. You know, the typical stuff. Watching sports with his guy friends, going to bars to meet women—although we already know he doesn't drink and might be a recovering alcoholic, so the bar option is out.

My stomach makes a rather large growling noise, and I keep typing hoping he didn't hear.

Immediately though, the typing noises coming from his laptop stop and I can feel his eyes on me. Dang it, dang it, dang it.

"You hungry?" he asks, that little smirk back

on his face. It's funny how, just a short time ago, I wanted to slap that smirk off him. Now, I just want to grab it and make out with it.

"Um, yah, I guess I am," I say, looking down toward my stomach, indicating I knew he heard the rumblings. Honestly though, I'm not feeling that hungry. The grumbling was the nervousness and the butterflies. I wonder if I will ever overcome that.

"I'm starving," he says, patting his stomach. "How much work do you have left?"

"I can probably wrap it up in an hour or so," I say, looking back at my screen. Phooey. There goes my evil plan for trying to stretch this out.

"Let's take a break then and get something to eat." He gets up from his chair.

Let's? Him and I? Alone without Brown? This is bound to be a disaster. "Um, okay," I say reluctantly.

"What? I thought you were hungry?" He stands behind my chair and slides me out from the table. He offers his hand to help me up, and I take it. His hand is warm, and I want to keep holding it, but I let go as soon as I'm standing.

"I am hungry. I just thought we needed to get this report done," I say as I grab my purse and follow him out of the conference room. This was unexpected.

"We can do it later." He pushes the down arrow on the elevator. I guess we are leaving? This is all happening so fast.

"Won't Mr. Calhoun care?" I glance over at his office and see the door shut, but the light is on.

"I'm the boss of Mr. Calhoun," he says with a confident smirk on his face.

"Oh, are you *really*?" I say sarcastically. "I'm sure he'd love to know that you are his boss now. I'll just pop in and tell him before we go." I start to walk toward Mr. Calhoun's office, but Jared grabs my arm and pulls me back toward him.

"No, no. He doesn't like to be reminded. It's a touchy subject," he says, still holding my arm and pulling me into the elevator.

Once we're in the elevator, he lets go of my arm, and I can still feel his hand there, warm from his touch. I need to remember every detail of this so I can tell Anna and Brown and we can discuss it thoroughly.

In the elevator, we stand fairly close, and neither of us moves away from each other. I stifle the need to let out a nervous schoolgirl laugh. I must pretend I have some confidence. It's not like I'm going to grab something to eat with a perfect stranger. This is Jared. I've been to lunch with him a few times now. It just feels different because it's not lunch, it's dinner. And Brown isn't here. My buffer, the one who keeps me on a straight path... Oh, this is a terrible idea. I should tell him I need to go and just leave. But, of course, I know I won't. Even if this ends badly—with me spilling food all over myself or even worse, him—I will not pass up the opportunity to spend time with him.

"So, where should we go?" he asks as we go outside, and I shiver a bit from the cool breeze. Well, actually, it's a nice night, so the shivering is all my nervousness coming out. It's actually quite the perfect night. It's not officially summer yet, but it's getting close, and the air has a magnificent scent to it.

"Not sure. What are you in the mood for?" I ask, trying to sound as confident as I can. Like this is just a normal night for me. Only it is *so* not.

We stand outside for a minute, thinking about where we should go, but neither of us offering any ideas.

"Too bad I haven't moved into my new place yet or we could go there, and I could make us something," I say and then immediately freak out. Where did that come from? Holy crap, that was way too presumptuous.

"You got a new place?" he asks, not even flinching at the idea.

"Yah, didn't I tell you?" I thought I had, but maybe I didn't mention it because I didn't want to get into a conversation about where I was moving from.

"No, you didn't. Where is it?"

"Just downtown. In a high-rise off Fourteenth," I say, feeling kind of proud of myself. I am growing up... at the age of thirty-two. Well, better late than never.

"Let's go check it out," he says as he starts walking toward his car.

"But there's nothing there. I thought you were hungry?" I say as I follow him like a little puppy dog.

"So, we will get some take out and eat it there." He unlocks the doors to his car and gets in the driver's seat. I stand by his open door, not sure what to do. "Get in, I'll drive." He reaches across the inside of the car and opens the passenger door for me.

I go around and get into his car. A Range Rover, I might add. Totally decked out. How the heck can he afford this? I know what that HR position paid, and it wasn't enough for a car like this.

I'm feeling a little in a daze right now as we head off to downtown Denver to my new condo in the lower downtown area (or LoDo as we downtown residents call it). I feel like I'm in a dream sequence or something. What are we doing? Are we really going to grab something to eat and go to my condo that has absolutely nothing in it? I mean, I just signed the loan and got the keys two days ago. And now I'm bringing a man there? This is not very spinsterly. My cat was supposed to be the first to have dinner with me in my new place. Not a man. And definitely not a hot one like Jared.

Jared stops at a Chinese place he says has the best take-out and gets us some food to take over to the condo. It smells so yummy, and I realize I really am hungry, which is a good thing. Maybe my having an appetite means I'm finally relaxing.

We park in the garage in my new parking spot (*my* new parking spot!) and take the elevator to the twelfth floor where my new residence is. I love the smell of the new paint and the look of the crown molding in the hallway leading to my condo. I can't believe I am going to live here. It's just so exciting, and also a bit nerve-racking. I did mention I hate change, right? And yet here I am making a whole lot of changes in my life.

We get to my door, and I fidget around in my purse and find my new key that I haven't even put on my key chain yet. I open the door and go inside with Jared right behind me. I flick on the light, and there it is: My. New. Place. There is a living space just as you walk in and off to the right is my new kitchen. It's amazing and beautiful, even though it's smaller than I preferred. Just past the kitchen is the hallway that leads to my room and bathroom. It's a small space, but it's mine. I have been nervous as anything to move here, but as I walk in tonight with Jared in tow, I have to say, it feels like home to me. Even without any of my things.

"So this is it," I say as I set my purse and keys

on the kitchen counter and look around the room.

Jared lets out a little whistle. "Nice place," he says as he nods his approval. He puts the food on the counter and walks around a little, pausing at the large windows facing the west side of the room. It's a full view of downtown and the tall buildings and lights are shining brightly tonight. It was the biggest selling point for me. I wanted something with a great view, after living in a basement for so long.

I walk over to the window where Jared is standing and look out as well. "See that building over there? The one next to the building that's shaped like a mailbox?" he says, pointing in the direction. "That's where I live." He keeps his eyes on the view out the window. "It doesn't have as great of a view as yours, but it's not bad."

I find myself wondering if I will ever see the inside of his place. I wonder what it would look like. A typical bachelor pad? Or would it be all perfectly put together like his perfectly-ironed shirts and pants?

I give Jared a full tour of my new place, which doesn't take long. Afterwards, he grabs a carton of Chinese food and gives me one, and we each grab some chopsticks. We stand by the counter and eat out of the carton for a bit, which is not particularly comfortable. Then Jared, with a mouth full of food, nods his head toward the window for me to follow him and goes over and sits down on the floor. As soon as I sit down, he gets back up and goes over and turns out the lights. So now we're in the dark, sitting on the floor, eating Chinese food, and looking out the windows of my condo at the downtown lights of Denver.

I would say this is the most romantic night of my life ever if I didn't already know it was not meant to be romantic on his part, and if I wasn't a future spinster. I will have to recreate this with my cat.

"So, where are you living now?" he asks, grabbing a large bite of his food with his chopsticks.

Of course he would ask that. Do I lie? I can't tell him where I've been living for the past ten years. Oh gosh, I truly am such a lousy liar.

I smile sheepishly. "Well, if you must know, I am moving out of my parents' basement." I quickly look down at my carton of food and dig around with my chopsticks, fretfully.

"Really?" he says in what seems like a not-very-surprised tone. Of course he's not surprised. As hard as I've tried not to be a complete spinster around him, some of it has had to bleed through.

"Yep. It's true," I say and nod my head. Wow, I sound like such a loser.

"How long were you there?" he asks, not really taken aback like he should be.

"Oh geez, really?" I say out loud, not meaning to. I roll my eyes at myself. Might as well come clean. "I have lived in my parents' basement for the last ten years." I shamefully shake my head as I look out the window, avoiding eye contact.

"*Really?*" He says now sounding surprised. "Ten years? Why were you there for so long?"

"I'm not really sure? It's not as bad as it sounds; there is an actual apartment in their basement, so I wasn't technically living in the same space as my parents." Close enough, though.

"Did you pay rent?" he asks, seeming intrigued.

"No," I say, and take a bite of my food.

"Wow, so you lived rent-free for ten years." He shakes his head in disbelief, and then he laughs a bit to himself. "That's pretty awesome."

"Awesome? Really?" I scrunch my face at him. "I think it was kind of loser-ish, if you ask me."

"That's like a dream for most people. Hell, if my mom had an apartment in her basement, I don't know if she would've ever gotten rid of me," he says and smiles. "Of course, I would have felt it my obligation to stay there since she doesn't have my dad around." Sadness appears in his eyes.

"How long has your dad been gone?" I say, changing the subject away from me and to a topic I have been curious about for a while.

"Since I was a sophomore in college."

"How did he pass?"

"Heart-attack," he says simply, and then looks out the window.

"I'm sorry," is all I can say.

"Yah, me too. It's one of my biggest regrets in life and why I don't drink anymore." He looks down at his food, playing with his chopsticks. "He... um... well, I was at a college party, and I got pretty trashed that night. I don't remember too much, it was that bad. He had a massive heart attack during the night, and my mom tried to call me, but I was so gone I didn't even hear my phone. I didn't get to say goodbye. He died the next morning."

The sadness and regret in his voice nearly makes me burst into tears at this point, so I just look down at my food and keep digging around with my chopsticks, but not ever taking a bite.

"With him gone," he continues, looking down at his food as well, "I've always felt responsible for my mom, you know? I just want to make sure she's happy. I take her on trips every once in a while. She pretends to protest as if she doesn't want to be taken care of, but I know she likes it." I look up to see him looking at me, and our eyes meet for just a moment.

"Anyway, I don't tell many people about my dad," he says, turning his head, looking out the window.

"Yes... well, I don't tell many people I've been living in my parents' basement for the past ten years," I say, trying to lighten the mood. It works; Jared gives me a half smile.

"I'm glad we did this, and I got to see your place," he says as he puts his hand on my knee and squeezes it just briefly.

"Me, too," I squeak out and am eternally grateful the lights aren't on so he can't see me blush a million shades of red.

# CHAPTER 8

"No freaking way," Brown says as we stand outside the building on a smoke break. It's the Monday after I had dinner with Jared, and I'm filling her in on all the gory details.

"Way," I say in my best valley-girl impression.

"So, it was a date then," she says as she smiles big at me.

"No! It so was not a date. I'm embarrassed you would even say that." I look at her like she's an idiot.

"Did he pay for dinner? Did he drive?"

"Um, yes and yes," I say, looking out to the parking lot.

"Then, it was a date," she says emphatically.

"No, it really wasn't. It was just a friendly thing. Really, it was not a date." Was it a date? No, it wasn't. Okay, so I am a bit rusty in that area, but I'm sure it wasn't.

"I'll just have to ask him when I see him." She gives me a little conniving smile.

"You better not!" I say a little too loudly.

"Oh get over yourself, Jules. Of course, I

won't." She takes a long drag from her cigarette. "So, tell me more."

I tell her all about how we sat in the dark, in front of the window, eating our dinner on the floor. I tell her I admitted to him I'd been living with my parents, and he didn't seem to care. I am careful to leave out the part about his dad, knowing how private he is about it. I'm actually surprised at myself since I can't seem to keep anything from Brown. I tell her about the touching of the leg, and she seems quite excited. We discuss that at length.

"So, how did it end?"

"He took me back to the office, and I got in my car and went home," I say, wishing there was more to the ending than that, but there wasn't. It was actually a little anticlimactic.

"Wow, Jules, I think this guy is totally into you." She winks at me.

"No, no. He's just a good friend. That's all," I say, but I'm secretly hoping she's right.

"Jules, I've been friends with guys," she says, pointing her cigarette at me. "And this is definitely more than friends."

I wish she was right, but in my heart I know she's not. Jared and I are just good friends. But I will take it. I can accept that. I can dream though... a spinster can have her dreams.

I head back to my office after our break. It's amazing to me how only just recently, I hated Mondays with a passion. But now I'm excited for Mondays and the weekends actually seem to drag. Today, I am especially excited because we didn't finish our super-secret report on Friday, so I get to spend time with Jared after work again. Also, the monthly budget meeting got moved to today, so I will get to see him there. I heart Mondays. Wow, I don't think I have ever thought that sentence in my entire life.

As I walk back to my desk, I pass by Mr. Nguyen's office. The door is closed, but I can hear voices coming from inside. Actually, it sounds a bit heated. I look around me to see if anyone is watching, then I lean into the door to see if I can hear what is going on. Could this be it? Brown heard he was on his way out, maybe they're letting him go today. I feel a stab of sadness for some crazy reason. I don't know why I feel so bad for him. I really shouldn't, as he has never shown me even an ounce of compassion the entire time I've worked for him. Yet I can't help myself feeling a little sadness. Of course, I'm jumping to conclusions here; they could be just having a meeting.

But wait, I recognize that voice—it's Mr. Calhoun's. And someone else... Jared? Is Jared in there? I can't really make out what they're saying. It's muffled even with my ear to the door.

"I TOLD YOU, I HAVE NO IDEA WHAT YOU ARE TALKING ABOUT!" Whoa, I heard that. That was Mr. Nguyen for sure. I don't think

I've ever heard him raise his voice in such a way. What is going on?

The handle on the door jiggles and I quickly jump back and try to compose myself like I am just walking by. The door opens, and out comes Mr. Calhoun, followed by Jared. They both look at me as they come out the door, Mr. Calhoun looking flustered, and Jared looks composed but sullen. I smile at him, but he doesn't smile back. He just turns and follows Mr. Calhoun down the hall, out of my sight.

What in the heck was that all about? I briefly think of going and asking Mr. Nguyen himself, but I know he will not give me anything. I think about going to see Brown in her office, but I head to my desk instead and get back to work on the report for the budget meeting. I only have thirty minutes, and I need to make copies and get everything in order, including myself. There will be time later to fill Brown in.

Just as I get everything ready and am about to head off to the bathroom to touch up my lip gloss, I get a group e-mail from Mr. Calhoun canceling the budget meeting. I find this quite odd as it's not Mr. Calhoun's meeting to cancel, it's Mr. Nguyen's.

Well, this kind of sucks. I was hoping to see Jared without trying to find some lame excuse to run into him like I usually do.

I guess there's no time like the present to go on a break with Brown. I send her a quick e-mail to which she quickly replies back, and we're outside by the smoking area five minutes later.

"Something crazy is going on," I say quietly to Brown. Even though we're the only ones outside, I don't want to take the chance of being heard.

"Oooh, do tell!" she says, excited for the gossip.

I tell her about what I heard and saw earlier in Mr. Nguyen's office explaining everything in detail. Including the no smile return from Jared, which I am trying desperately not to take personally, but I can't help my spinster self.

"Wow, that *is* crazy," Brown says, and then she takes a long drag from her cigarette, contemplating what I just told her.

"I know, right? I don't know what to think of it. Something fishy is clearly going on there."

"You're going to have to get Jared to talk tonight when you finish up the report," she says, basically taking the words out of my mouth.

"Hopefully he will talk, but I don't know." Although, he loves getting gossip from us, he tends to be a little tight-lipped on his end. It's a bit unfair, really. I mean, he *is* in HR, he should have tons to share. But instead, he just wants to hear info from us and then doesn't offer much in return. Although, the one time he tried he was quickly shot down because we already knew. Maybe he thinks there's no point since we seem to know it all anyway.

184

I promise Brown I will do my best with Jared tonight, and we head back in the building and back to work. I don't really have much to do, which is kind of odd. Mr. Nguyen's office door is shut when I get back upstairs, and there are no voices this time. I think about knocking and asking him for something to do, but then I think otherwise. I don't want to be rudely shooed away like usual, and why would I go and ask for work anyway? If he has something for me to do, he can let me know. This is shaping up to be a crazy Monday, that is for sure.

Promptly at five thirty, I get my stuff and head up to the conference room to finish the report. I am sad that this is my last night. There is no way to extend it any further without making myself look totally inept.

The conference room door is open as I approach it. I can see Jared sitting at the head of the table working on his laptop. I tap lightly on the door, and he looks up at me.

"Hey, what's going on Jules?" he says as he looks back down at his computer screen, no smile either.

"I just came up here to finish the report," I say still hanging in the doorway.

He looks up quickly at me. "Didn't Calhoun get a hold of you?"

"Get a hold of me for what?"

"We don't need you to finish the report. We have it covered," he says, looking back down at his computer.

He's acting so strange, almost cold and aloof. Did Friday night freak him out or something? It's not like anything happened. We just had dinner. But maybe he thinks I am reading into it or something? He probably thinks he's leading me on and doesn't want me to get any ideas. Well, whatever. Two can play this game.

"No, he didn't tell me. Sounds good, though. I have other things I can do tonight," I say as coldly and detached as I can, even though this is a total lie. There's a big black pit in my stomach that's making me feel ill.

He doesn't look up, he just keeps looking at his screen and typing every once in a while. I throw out a "see you later," then turn around and head out the door.

"Julia, wait," he says as I go to leave. "Come in for a second. Sorry, Calhoun has me crazy busy today." He smiles faintly at me.

Relief sweeps over me instantly. He doesn't hate me! He's just been busy. I don't know what I would have done if this thing between us — whatever it is — were to end. I mean, I guess I would go back to being my spinster self, but there would be nothing to look forward to. Work would go back to being just work.

I stay at the door. No need to look

ridiculously needy. "So, what does Calhoun have you doing?" I ask, trying to keep some conversation going.

"It's just a bunch of boring junk," he says as he leans back in his chair, hands in his lap. He pauses for a minute, looking at me. "Hey, I want to ask you something."

"Yah?" I say, my interest piquing.

"Come in, have a seat." He motions to the seat just next to him. I come in and sit down placing my purse in my lap.

He looks at me for a moment like he's deciding whether or not to say something. "Do you like it here?" he asks after what seems like a long moment of that nervous where-to-look-with-my-eyes feeling. "I mean, do you *really* like it here?"

"Um," I say and look around the room, not meeting his gaze. "That's a loaded question. I guess there are parts of it I like." I pause, looking down at my hands, which are nervously twiddling the straps of my purse.

"Really?" He sounds surprised. "What parts?

I think for a second. There really are parts I like, like Brown and Jared. Okay, there are two parts I like. Other than that, there's not much.

"I don't know, I guess some of the people." I smile faintly at him.

A small smile appears at his lips, he knows what I'm trying to say. Does the smile back mean he likes working here because of me too?

After a pause he opens his mouth, "Okay, but what about what you do. Do you like what you actually do here? You told me once before that 'it's a job.' Is that how you really feel?"

I squint my eyes a bit at him. "Now, tell me, Mr. Moody, why would I admit anything to you when you are in HR?" I tease him, my smile brightening as I see him smile.

"Yes, yes, I can see how you could feel a little uneasy about that. How about you just talk to me, as a friend."

And there it is, the dreaded F word. My heart sinks a bit in the realization that this is all we really are... friends. I know I have said I would take it, but the honest truth is I want more. Of course, I do.

I look away, the disappointment might be too easy to read on my face, and I don't want him to see it or pick up on it. "No, I guess there isn't much else I like about my job."

"Have you ever considered changing jobs?" he asks. I can feel his gaze on me, but I don't look back.

"Not really." I look back at him now. "I don't know what I would do. I have a mortgage payment now, so I'm in a position where I actually need this job more than I ever did."

Did he flinch at that? It seems like he did. Now it's his turn to look away, out the window. He looks back at me with resolve in his face. "Can I tell you something, as a friend?"

I could slap that F word right off his face. Stop rubbing it in already. I force out a "sure."

"You're better than this place," he says with a serious tone to his voice. What? My gaze moves quickly to his eyes, which are looking intently at me. That was not what I was expecting. "You are, Julia. You're better than Spectraltech. Don't you feel like you have more to offer yourself — the world — than sitting up in a small office, working for Nguyen?"

I don't know if it's the fact he keeps using the dreaded F word (which really shouldn't have come as a surprise, but it digs deep to hear it) or if I'm just feeling a bit PMS-y or something, but I find myself feeling mad. Who does he think he is? Does he think he knows me or something? He doesn't actually know me at all.

"Why do you care?" I spit out and then immediately want to take it back when his face looks as if I just punched it.

"Why do I care?" he asks like I should know the answer already. But I don't. I have no idea why he cares so much about whether I like my job or not. He shakes his head, frustrated. "I don't know, I guess I just want to see you doing something you want to do, not be stuck here." He looks at me like he's trying to read my expression. "I guess I overstepped. Sorry." He turns his focus back to his computer.

The word "stuck" resonates with me all of a sudden. I always thought I was stuck — I've been leading the same life for the past ten years — but I didn't think anyone else cared to notice that about me. I sit there silently thinking to myself, messing with my purse straps.

"No, you didn't overstep — it's fine," I finally sputter out. "You're right, I guess." I look at him and wait for him to look back at me. "I am... stuck. I guess I'm just not very good at getting... um... un-stuck. The 'proverbial' creature of habit." I smile slightly at him hoping my little proverbial insert lightens the dampened mood.

It works. He smiles back at me and the feeling in the room changes. He leans toward me and reaches for my hand and grabs it. My heart starts to thump in my chest, and I try really hard to slow it because I know this is just a friendly gesture.

"I don't peg you as a creature of habit." He looks down at our hands together, and I silently pray he can't hear my heart thumping in my chest. "I just think you could do better than Spectraltech, that's all." He squeezes my hand, looks up at me, and then quickly let's go. He looks toward his computer in a way that feels guarded, like holding my hand was too much and he shouldn't have done it. I wish he wouldn't have let go, friendly gesture or whatever it was.

"What about you? You could do better than Spectraltech, too." I surprise myself when I say this. Where did this boldness come from?

"No place is really good enough for me," he says, the smirk back in full effect.

"Well, aren't you confidential?" I mimic the smirk back at him. And then suddenly my eyes bug out, realizing my error.

"You meant 'confident,' right?" he says, holding back a little chuckle.

"No. I meant confidential. I stand by it," I say, trying my hardest not to crack a smile, which I fail miserably at. "Can I ask you something?"

"Sure. Shoot," he says, leaning back in his chair.

"What the heck happened in Nguyen's office today?"

Jared puts his hands behind his head and sighs heavily, looking as if he's contemplating. Probably trying to figure out what he can and can't tell me. HR and their secrets.

"Come on, with all the gossip I tell you..." I trail off as I see him smiling slightly at me.

"I'll tell you, but you can't tell Brown, okay?" he says with a serious look on his face.

Yikes. Not tell Brown? She will surely quiz me about it tomorrow, and I know I could/will cave. Maybe it would be better if he didn't tell me.

"Of course, I won't tell her," I say, my gossipy senses taking over my mouth before I can even finish talking sense to myself.

"There's something going on there, Jules. He's hiding something. I haven't figured it out yet, but I think he might be stealing money from the company."

"What? Really?" I stammer out. Oh wow, how the hell am I going to keep this from Brown? I will have to skip all breaks tomorrow. It's just too risky.

"Seriously, don't tell Brown or anyone." He looks at me sternly. Clearly he already doubts telling me this. Probably because he knows my love of gossip and my need to tell Brown everything. I don't blame him.

"Can you think of anything suspicious that you've seen from Nguyen?"

I ponder that question for a moment. "I don't know, I guess so. He's been acting weird for a while now, I mean weirder than normal... and I guess when I've done some of the reports he has me do, I'm feeling, I don't know, a bit of a déjà vu feeling."

"What do you mean?" He turns his body toward me.

"Um, I guess it kind of feels like I've done the same report before; that I'm repeating my work. That probably doesn't make any sense." I look down at my lap again. I don't know how to explain it exactly.

"No, actually, that makes sense." He nods his head, looking down. His hand moves up to rub his temples. "Would you do me a favor?" He puts his hand down and looks up at me directly with his deep blue eyes, making my heart race.

*Just friends, Julia. Just friends.* I have to keep reminding myself.

"Yes, of course," I sputter out.

"Will you send me some of the reports he has you do?"

"Um…" I drift off, not sure what to say. I mean, of course, I will give him the reports, but I also have the feeling of guilt gnawing at me. Why? Why would I feel any remorse for Mr. Nguyen? "Sure, I can do that," I finally say. "Just don't ever let it get back to Nguyen." This is a redundant thing to say because, of course, he wouldn't do that, he's in HR. But I felt the need to say it nonetheless.

"Of course," he says and smiles slightly at me.

I nod my head toward the door. "I'm going to go. You probably have lots of work to do still, and I don't want to keep you any longer." Plus, I need to call Anna immediately so we can discuss him holding my hand, and his incessant usage of the F word. I've also got to figure out my strategy to avoid any and all questions Brown will probably ask me tomorrow.

He doesn't try to stop me from leaving, which is disappointing and relieving all at the same time. I get up from my chair, and head toward the door, turning around to say goodbye before I step out of the room. He smiles at me, and I smile back. I shake my head to myself as I walk to the elevator. I'm not sure how to feel about any of that conversation. Hopefully Anna will be around to help me sort it all out.

I give Anna all the gory details as we sit in our pajamas in the living room of the basement apartment. We're eating fresh brownies that I just made and drinking milk. Anna comes downstairs practically every night and I make us a treat to eat, then we sit and talk about the day's events. I would never tell Anna this, but it has become something I really look forward to and will really miss when I move to my new place

"Wow, that's crazy stuff," she says, totally enthralled in my description of what happened. "He's really giving such mixed signals."

"Right?" I say, and take a big bite of my brownie.

We eat in silence for a bit, chewing over the brownie and the details of my rather odd conversation with Jared.

"Hey, did you ever give that guy my resume?" She asks, clearly not thinking about the conversation as much as I was.

"Yah, I gave it to Mr. Calhoun. I'm not sure he ever saw it, though. The guy is a bit of a disaster. I could ask Jared to make sure he sees it." I love it when I have a good excuse to talk to Jared.

"Okay, cool. I think I'd rather work in that kind of setting, it would be much safer than retail." I nod my head in agreement. Anna working in retail is like letting an alcoholic work as a bartender. Not a good idea.

"Any word from the creditors?" I ask nonchalantly.

"Shhh! Not so loud!" she says in hushed tones, looking toward the stairs like mom and dad are just waiting there, listening to our conversation. I'm pretty sure they have better things to do. "Yes, I've heard from them a ton. Mostly messages, though. I've figured out their M.O., so I know when to answer the phone and when not to," she says with confidence in her voice, which is unfounded. How can you be proud of that?

"It's not going to be long before Mom and Dad figure it out, you know," I say, using my best big-sister-tone.

"Well, I was thinking, maybe I could have my mail forwarded to your new place? That way I wouldn't have to keep an eye on the mailbox here," she says with a pleading look on her face.

"Anna, I don't know…" I fade off knowing this is not a good idea. It feels like a betrayal to my parents.

"Please? It won't be for long. As soon as I get a job, I will start paying everything down, and I bet I could have it all paid off in a year or less."

What kind of job does this college-major-jumper think she's going to get? "Well, I wouldn't be too sure of that. It's tough to find a job out there."

"Well, I'm sure it won't take me too long. Please, Julia? Please?"

She looks so pathetic and desperate, I can't help myself. "Fine. But not forever, okay? And I am not your babysitter. You have to be accountable for your mail—that means coming to pick it up at my place, not me bringing it to you. Okay?"

"Yes, of course." She rolls her eyes at me. "I can't wait to come over and hang at your new swanky condo, anyway. It will be good to get out of this windowless dungeon." She looks around the basement like it's a trap she's stuck in. In many ways, I suppose it is.

When I finally go to bed, my head is swimming with thoughts of the day. From the craziness that ensued regarding Mr. Nguyen, to the conversation leading to the hand-holding with Jared. And to top it all off, and the scariest part of all, how to keep this juicy piece of gossip from Brown. I don't know how I will do it, but I must.

# CHAPTER 9

I have been able to avoid Brown for the better part of the morning, telling her I have too much work to do. She will catch on soon enough because she knows very well I would never use work as an excuse to miss our breaks. Well, rarely ever, that is.

I am actually busy, though. Nguyen has me doing a few reports, and I'm finishing them up and sending them back to him, and then to Jared as well. Feeling a little hesitant about it, but I guess if he is stealing money from Spectraltech, then it is my responsibility to help.

One fairly exciting thing in this spinster's life: I actually have plans tonight. Not the plans I would like to have, but plans. I got an e-mail from my brother Lennon this morning, wondering if we could all get together for dinner. He rarely invites us all out, mostly because he's so busy with work, but I also suspect that his wife Jenny doesn't enjoy going out with us that much. Us Dornings can be a bit loud, and we like to laugh and crack jokes (some of them inappropriate — ahem, Dad) when we're together. Jenny is more of a reserved type. It still amazes me that Lennon married her. She's really nice, but not like us—not the best fit. Maybe that's the reason he picked her.

My computer beeps and there's a message from Brown.

You've been avoiding me all day, Dorning, it's time for a break. I have info on Jared. –B

Must resist. Must resist. Information on Jared? Must resist.

See you in five. –J

Dang her! She got me with info about Jared. How could I resist? It's not possible. Not. Possible. I will just have to remain mum about Nguyen. I will offer my soul to the gods if they can just help me keep my big trap shut.

The breeze that hits me as I open the door and go outside to meet Brown feels marvelous. This is one of those days when I feel like ditching work and driving around town with the top on my car down. Then, I remember I don't have a convertible.

"'Bout time you got here," she says, taking a drag from her half-smoked cigarette.

"What? I told you five minutes," I say, keeping my cool. I can do this. I can do this. I feel like I might erupt at any second and just sputter it all out—*Jared thinks Nguyen is stealing from the company and now he has me sending him the reports I do*—breathe, breathe. Seriously, I didn't have a problem not telling Brown about Jared's dad, so why is this so hard? Because this is gossip. Jared's dad's passing is not gossip, nor should it ever be considered gossip.

"So, what did you find out about Jared?" I normally would have skirted around that, not wanting her to think I am desperate to find out, but this is the best way to keep her away from asking me about things I am not allowed to say. And, also, I'm desperate to find out.

"Well, the info I have is that..." she trails off and takes a drag from her cigarette, keeping me waiting, blowing the smoke away from me. "The truth is, I have no info," she finally spits out, irritation strong in her voice.

What? Did she just say that to trick me into meeting her? Dang her, she's good. "What do you mean, you have no info?" I ask, trying to keep her on the Jared path and not move onto other paths.

"That's what I mean. My info on Jared is that I have no info. He is basically a nobody. There is no information anywhere on the Internet. No address, no Facebook account, Twitter, LinkedIn, nothing." She gives me an exasperated look.

"Why is that so weird? Some people like to stay private."

"Yes, but not in the business world. He should have some sort of track-record, something on-line. A company he used to work for, anything. But there is nothing."

We stand side by side, pondering that for a moment, Brown puffing on her cigarette in frustration. This information doesn't bother me that much, but it really seems to bother Brown. Perhaps because she is known for her ability to dig up information on people.

"I don't know, Jules," she says after a bout of silence, "there's something fishy going on there."

"With Jared?" I scoff. "Oh, please. Yes, he works in HR, they're always the fishy type. So he's secretive, is it really that big of a deal?"

"I think it is, and you should, too. Especially with this thing you two have going." She uses air-quotes when she says 'thing.'

Ah, yes. The *thing*. I want to tell her there really is no thing, at least not what she's insinuating. He used the friend word, more than once even, and so that's the *thing*. And although he's opened up to me about personal stuff he doesn't normally tell people, we do not actually have the type of relationship where I could just march right up to his office and demand answers about his past. I don't even have his cell phone number, or his personal e-mail address. All I have with Jared is work. Every part of our relationship has been based on that, and even though it has seemed to delve into some flirtation, we are just plain work friends. Stupid freaking work friends. That's it.

But if I go into the conversation that happened last night, then I will have to skirt by the Nguyen information, and as we all know, with Brown especially, I cannot keep a secret. So, I'm just going to let Brown think the "thing" between Jared and I is actually a thing.

"I guess I'm not seeing how big of a deal this is," I finally say.

"Jules, we've known this guy for all of what, over two months or so?" I think about that for a second. Has it really been over two months? Doesn't really feel like it. It feels longer.

"Yah, so…"

"So," she interrupts me, "we should've found out more about him by now. It's just… fishy."

"Yah, I guess… maybe..." I trail off. I guess I'm just not getting the importance of this need-to-know information Brown is finding herself so frustrated by.

She blows the smoke from her cigarette out. "So, what else is new? Any gossip?" she asks still sounding frustrated, but finally cluing in that I don't have this same need-to-know desire she does, and so it's a lost cause on me.

This is my cue to leave because I do have gossip. Possibly some of the juiciest gossip we have ever encountered since we started taking smoking breaks together. "Nope. Nothing," I say quickly, looking away from her and out into the parking lot so she can't catch the lie in my eyes. "I guess I better get back to work," I try to say as nonchalantly as I can.

"Yah, me too," Brown says as she puts the cigarette out in the large astray by the door. We walk inside together and head back to our offices.

Did I just pull that off? Am I getting better at lying/keeping secrets? Not sure I should be proud of myself for that, but I kind of am.

I look at the clock, and it's five thirty already, which is just a bit early to meet my family for dinner, but why spend the extra time at work? Besides, today hasn't been the most fun day with all the working and not seeing Jared at all. I mean, what do I come to work for anyway? He may have defined our friendship-ness yesterday, but that doesn't mean I can shut my crush off just like that. It will take me a while to adjust.

I'm surprised to find that going out with my family tonight is something I'm looking forward to. It's been so long since we were all together. Maybe it's my newfound relationship with Anna. Maybe it's finally seeing Lennon after a long while. I don't know what it is, but it's a good feeling.

As I walk out to the parking, lot I look back at

the building, and just as the stalker I have totally become, my eyes move up to the window where the sixth floor conference room sits. I see the light is still on, and so next, as always, my eyes move to the parking lot to look for Jared's car, which is still there.

I have a little time before I have to meet my family, so without really thinking it through, I turn around and head back into the office, onto the elevator, and up to the sixth floor. I'm not really sure what I am doing, and the butterflies in my stomach are making me think this is not the best idea, but I can't help myself. I didn't get to see Jared all day, which is not fair. I just want to say hi really quickly and then leave.

As I step out onto the sixth floor, I consider getting back on the elevator and going back downstairs. I don't just come up to Jared's office without a reason—a work reason. But hey, we are friends. Can't I just come upstairs and say hi to my friend Jared? I push the butterflies out and walk over to the conference room door and knock.

I hear Jared's muffled voice say "come in" and I open the door and walk in. I see him sitting at the head of the conference room table, the light from his laptop screen shining on his face. There are files and boxes strewn all over the table. He doesn't even look up to see who it is; he just stares at his laptop screen.

"Hey!" I say a little too enthusiastically, and a

little high-pitched. Really? Did my "hey" have to squeak out like that? I really am a circus freak sometimes.

He looks up from his laptop and seems surprised to see me. "Hey, what are you still doing here, Jules?" He smiles at me, and I relax a little. I know we're just supposed to be friends, but the sight of him still makes my heart do leaps and skips.

"I was just on my way out, and saw you were still here, so I thought I would come and say hi." The voice in my head adds *"because I am stalking/in love with you"* to the end of that, but I ignore it.

He just nods at me, then he shuts his laptop, leans back in his chair, and looks at me. He looks really tired. His hair is a little tousled, and he has an incredibly sexy five o'clock shadow. I'm finding it hard to stop staring.

"You look tired," I say, not sure if he wants me to stay or leave. I'm feeling butterflies in my stomach as I feel more and more vulnerable and stupid for coming up here, seeing as our last conversation was a little strained and, well, odd.

He stifles a laugh. "You could say that," he says as he leans back putting his hands behind his head and closing his eyes for a moment.

I stand awkwardly by the door thinking maybe I should just say goodbye and leave. Then, out of the blue, he kicks the chair next to him out with his foot and motions for me to take a seat.

He smiles at me as I sit down. "So, what's up?" he asks, his voice sounding tired and there's something else there that seems like maybe sadness? I recognize it from when he told me about his dad. But it's different this time. I'm not really sure.

"Not much. I have to leave in a bit to go meet up with my family for dinner."

"What's the occasion?" he asks, sounding like he is relieved to be able to talk to me and get his mind off whatever he's doing.

"I'm not sure? My brother Lennon invited us." I look down at my hands, feeling his eyes on me, and suddenly I feel even more nervous and now a little self-conscious. "What's new with you?" I ask without looking up.

"Um…" he takes a deep breath, "… too much to talk about, or think about right now." I feel his gaze move away from me, so I look up and see him looking down at his hands, pondering, I guess.

"You okay?" I say with concern in my voice.

He nods his head and looks up at the ceiling. "I'm fine. Just busy."

The tone in the room seems too serious, and I find myself wanting to lighten it. I don't want him to bring up my need to un-stuck myself again.

"It just dawned on me that they still haven't found you a proper office yet, huh?" I say more as a statement than a question.

Jared looks around at his surroundings and only nods his head yes.

"I wouldn't want to leave here, though. I mean look at all this space." I motion to the room with my hand. "You've got a huge desk, nice big windows... I would stay here as long as I could."

He smiles at me and swivels his chair toward me. "Yes, and you never know who I might find under this table." He taps his fingers on the conference room table and gives me his best smirk.

"Yes, you never know who," I say, trying to act cool and praying I don't blush. Ugh, too late. I look back down at my hands, hoping he didn't notice the blushing, which is like hoping you don't have poppy seeds in your teeth after eating a poppy seed muffin. It's just not possible.

I feel his eyes on me, and I try to get over my blushing. I finally look up at him and smile. He smiles back, and then he gets a serious look on his face. This must be my cue to leave, so I stand up from my chair and start to grab my purse so I can go.

"You leaving?" he says, sounding kind of disappointed.

"Yah, I guess I should let you get back to whatever you're doing so you can get done, and go home and get some rest," I say, and smile at him slightly.

As I turn away from him to get my things, all of a sudden I feel him grab a hold of my hand, which catches me off guard, and I turn back around to see him sitting there, staring at me.

"Just… wait a second," he says, and with that he pulls me toward him and in some crazy fast move, right into his lap. What the heck? This was *so* not expected…

"Um…" I say nervously, and slightly breathlessly as I look at him in the eyes, my heart starting to pound in my chest.

He looks at me, our faces just inches from each other. With the hand that is not holding mine, he pushes back some of my hair, which is slightly shielding my eyes, and tucks it behind my ear in a tender way. This, of course, makes me blush, and butterflies are now about to come up from my stomach and out my mouth. There are so many, I feel like I might throw them up.

"Julia…" he says as he looks from my eyes to my mouth, and all of the sudden I realize he is going to kiss me (yes, I realize I'm cluing in a little late here, but this kind of stuff does not happen to spinsters), and I'm not sure what to do. But before I can even think of anything, he leans in toward me and just like that his lips are on mine.

It's soft at first and slow and kind of… awkward. I'm not really sure what I am doing with my hands and neither is he, but then all of a sudden his hands are on either side of my face, cradling it and his lips are hot on mine and the kissing gets intense. I grab fistfuls of his shirt in my hands and pull him toward me.

He moves his hands away from my face and down my back, pulling me in closer to him and I respond by wrapping my arms around his neck, pulling myself into him as well. The kissing gets even steamier.

Many thoughts are going through my head right now like, what the heck is happening? Didn't he just say the dreaded F word? And, oh my gosh, I'm kissing Jared! And please, oh please, let my breath be good.

After what I can only guess was a couple minutes (it felt like seconds), the kissing slows and the intensity starts to lessen. Jared moves his hands back up to my face, cradling it again, kissing me a few more times sweetly and tenderly. Then, he pulls away and looks at me, and he smiles slightly. He tucks the strands of hair back behind my ear again.

I'm not sure what to do or say, and I'm feeling confusion from our conversation yesterday. Do friends kiss friends in Jared's world? Is that really all I am to him? Right now it certainly doesn't seem like it.

One thing I'm sure of is I want more. I want to just ditch my family and make out with Jared all night long, but I know that can't happen. I probably shouldn't ditch my family, and I'm pretty sure Jared will have to finish whatever he was doing before. Plus, I'm not sure where this is all coming from. One thing is for sure, I am *so* glad I came up here. Best. Decision. Ever.

I probably should move off his lap or something, but instead I put my arms around him and hug him tight. He puts his arms around me to reciprocate, nuzzling his head into my neck, and I can feel his five o'clock shadow brush against me, sending shivers down my spine. I never want this moment to end. I would sit in Jared's lap, right here in the conference room where I first laid eyes on him, forever.

Okay, so that last statement was cheesy, but I can't help myself. Suddenly, I feel like I belong here, in Jared's arms, and I haven't felt like I belong anywhere in a very long time.

I'm torn between wanting to stay here and also wanting to pull away because I don't want him to be the one to pull *me* away like I'm some annoying toddler with my arms wrapped around his leg, not letting go. I pull out of the hug, and we look at each other, he leans in and kisses me softly on the lips, and chills run up and down my spine.

My cell phone rings and we both jump, startled by the noise. I jump up out of his lap without thinking it through, and I immediately regret doing it because that means it's the end of the kissing, and I don't know when it will ever happen again. I'm actually having a hard time believing how it could happen at all. Wait, is this just one of those crazy-realistic dreams? I avoid the urge to pinch myself.

I grab my phone out of my purse and see it's Anna calling. I quickly push the end button on my phone, ignoring her call. Leave it to Anna to interrupt the most perfect moment of my life, thus far.

I look at the time on my phone and realize I am now late to meet up with my family, and Anna was probably calling to make sure I'm not dead on the side of the road or something.

"Crap! I'm late!" I say a little too breathlessly and awkwardly. I shove the phone back in my purse and sling it around my shoulder.

Jared stands up from the chair that I will secretly have to steal a piece of at a later time. To, you know, commemorate this less-than-spinster occasion that has just happened in my life. One I will have to promise God that I will live a life of service if it could happen again. Please, *please* let it happen again.

I hate leaving, but then I realize I am leaving on a high note. That's a good thing, right? Brown is always saying how she likes to leave on a high note in any situation. Too much of a good thing can be bad, she says.

So, am I leaving on a high note? I'm the one who ended the kissing—well, technically, it was Anna, but whatever. But it wasn't Jared who had total control of the situation. This is good, right?

I mean, I'm not trying to play those dumb girls' rules, but a girl has to be a little bit mysterious and have the slight upper-hand sometimes, so I've heard. I doubt that's what's happening here, but it's helping me to leave when I really just want to stay.

Jared follows me to the door as I go to leave, ever the gentleman. I turn around as I get near the door and look at him. He smiles at me slightly and grabs my hand in his, just like yesterday, only this time he weaves his fingers through mine. There's intensity in the hand-holding now, like it means something more. I want to ask him what this all means, where this is all coming from. But I can't. I can't ruin any of this by getting all girly right now.

"Julia... before tomorrow, I need to..." my cell phone cuts him off and I try to ignore it so he can finish what he is saying, but he gestures for me to see who it is. I let go of his hand and get the phone out of my purse, and of course, it's Anna. I answer it quickly, let her know I am not dead, and am on my way to the restaurant. Clearly annoyed, she tells me they are all waiting for me. She won't be so annoyed when I tell her why.

"Okay, I guess I better go," I say as I end the call and put the phone back in my purse. "What were you saying before?" I look in his eyes, and I see sadness in them. Oh no! He regrets kissing me already?

"Um… don't worry about it." He shakes his head. "We'll talk about it later." He grabs my hand again, making my worries of him regretting kissing me lessen.

"I guess I better go," I say, not even moving. I just stand there looking at him, and him at me.

I move forward and put my hands around his waist, hugging him again. I hear him sigh in my ear as he hugs me back, nuzzling my neck once more.

Why did this happen tonight? Why, when I have to be somewhere else? Every other night of the week or month or year for that matter, I have nothing else to do. But tonight of all nights! It's probably for the best, though. If I didn't have somewhere to go, I would overstay my welcome like all spinsters do (ahem, parents' basement), and then it would get awkward. No, I just need to leave… leave, while it's still good, while I'm on a high note. Brown will be proud.

I pull back, but he still has his arms around me. This time, it is me that leans in and kisses him. I kiss him as soft and as passionate as I can. He responds like I want him to and kisses me back, then he pushes me back against the door and the kissing escalates as I drop my purse on the floor and my hands move up his back and to the back of his head, running my fingers through his hair and pulling him closer into me. I lose track of caring that I am late to meet up with my family. Who really cares about family

212

right now anyway?

Jared pulls away after a few intense minutes, and both of us are out of breath. "Okay," he says, trying to compose himself. "Aren't you late?"

"Yes, yes. My stupid, stupid family!" I say out loud, which I did not intend to do. Oops.

He laughs at that and then kisses me gently. Not wanting to let go, I reluctantly step back from him and reach down and pick up my purse off the floor. I find myself feeling a little silly how I dropped it so dramatically, caught up in the moment. Like I'm in a movie or something.

He opens the door to the conference room, finalizing my plans to leave—I was still slightly undecided. I walk out of the room and look around to make sure no one is there. It's just him and me.

"Well, I'll see you tomorrow, then," I say, and smile at him. I reach up and smooth down the tousled hair on the back of his head.

He looks away, over toward the elevator. "Yah, tomorrow," he says, echoing me, but clearly thinking about something else. He shakes his head and looks back at me and smiles. He grabs my hand one more time and squeezes it.

I walk awkwardly over to the elevator and push the down button, knowing he is watching me. I turn around, wave at him, and then enter the elevator and press the lobby button. He's still there, hands in his pockets, watching me as the door shuts.

I hold myself back from screaming in the elevator because that's what I really want to do. Jump up and down and scream like I'm fifteen. But I wait until I'm in the car and have driven away from the parking lot before I let what just happened hit me. Then, I let out a big scream of excitement and giddiness.

What just happened? My head is reeling. Jared just kissed me. I kissed him back. Yesterday, we were just friends; today, we are kissing. I don't want to read into it, I don't want to over-think it. I will save that for later. For now, I just need to bask in this feeling. This feeling of... whatever it is, I'm not sure, but it's the best feeling in the world.

Immediately, I grab my cell phone and call Brown. I have about a ten minute drive until I get to the restaurant to meet my family and that is hardly long enough for me to describe everything in detail, but I will do my best.

When I arrive at the restaurant, everyone is already seated, and drinks have been ordered. I feel giddy and delirious and about to pop. Brown didn't answer the phone, and I need to tell someone about what just happened.

I sit in the open seat next to Anna and apologize to everyone for being late.

"Why are you smiling like an idiot?" Anna asks quietly in my ear. "You look high."

"What? Oh sorry," I say, trying to wipe the smile off my face, but I can't. "I'm just... I just..." I can't even tell her, I'm so giddy.

"Spit it out!" She punches me lightly in the arm. Everyone else is having their own conversations, not paying attention to us.

"Um, so I went upstairs to Jared's office before coming here..."

"So, that's why you were late," she rolls her eyes, disapproving.

"Yes. But it's better than just that..." I trail off, and smile at her.

"What are you saying? Wait? Did he?" Her eyes bug out of her head.

"He kissed me!" I squeal out. She lets out a high-pitched little scream, and grabs my arms and shakes them in total Oprah fashion.

"Are you serious??" She's smiling like a silly schoolgirl now, too.

All I can do is smile back at her and shake my head yes. It's so fun to have Anna to tell this stuff to, and she reacts just like I need her to.

We both turn at the same time to see our family looking at us like we are a couple of elementary school kids.

I clear my throat. "Sorry, I just had some exciting work news I had to tell Anna about."

"Well, share it with the rest of the family then," my dad says, looking very interested in this piece of news.

I'm totally not going to tell the rest of my family what just happened. First of all, they have no idea who Jared is. The only person I've been sharing that information with is Anna. Secondly, this is not a dinner-topic discussion. I can just picture it: *"Mom, Dad, Lennon, Jenny... I totally just made out with my coworker in the upstairs conference room of our office building! Squeeeeee!"* Thirdly, my dad and brother, being men, would have no idea why I would be so giddy about this and they will totally rain on my parade.

"It's nothing really. I'll tell you later," I say, and look at Anna who smiles back at me.

"Well, I have something to announce," Lennon says, and we all direct our attention to him and away from me, thank goodness. "I invited you all to come to dinner to tell you that..." he trails off, looking at Jenny who she smiles brightly at him. "Well, Jenny and I— we're going to have a baby."

The table erupts with excitement. My mother starts to cry, my dad pats him on the shoulder, beaming. Both Anna and I proclaim how thrilled we are by gushing and asking a ton of questions they can't seem to answer fast enough. This is very exciting news for the Dorning family. Very exciting news, indeed.

Normally, information like this would've sent me into a tailspin of overeating and self-loathing/depression. I am the oldest child in the

Dorning family and, therefore, *I* should be the first one to have a baby. Isn't that the rule? Isn't the oldest supposed to do everything first? But we haven't followed those rules in this family at all, clearly.

Lennon obviously got married before I did since I am not... well, married. That was devastating at the time. It was made worse by the fact that at the wedding, all the older relatives kept coming up to me and saying what they thought were encouraging things to me like "Your turn is next!" or "I betcha we'll be back here for your wedding soon!" or "That special someone is waiting just around the corner!" I finally got so fed up that, in the wedding line (Anna and I were bridesmaids), I told Jenny's old and frail grandmother I would not be "finding a man" anytime soon because I was a lesbian. She was exasperated, Jenny was mortified. I suspect that she still holds a little grudge toward me because of that. I couldn't help myself though.

So yes, normally this kind of information would drive me to drink/eat my weight in food, but today? I don't think Lennon announcing they already had a child who is now fully grown and married and will be having a baby, making Lennon a grandpa and me a great Aunt before I even had a chance to have children of my own... I don't think that would even dampen my mood.

The rest of the night is filled with talk of babies and sexes and names and all sorts of baby-fun plans. Before the night is over, Anna and I have volunteered to throw Jenny a baby shower and I have declared myself this baby's favorite aunt. Because I totally will be.

After dinner, Anna meets me down in the basement apartment so I can fill her in on all the details of what happened between me and Jared in that glorious sixth floor conference room.

"So, he just pulled you onto his lap?" she asks, eyes wide and mesmerized by the info.

"Yep. It was like some smooth ninja trick," I say, still having a hard time suppressing the giddy smile.

"So, how was it?"

"The kissing?"

"No, your dinner. Yes, of course I was asking about the kissing, you idiot." She rolls her eyes at me.

"It was a.maz.ing. Seriously, the best."

"Really? It's been a long time since I've been good and kissed." She sighs and closes her eyes leaning back against the couch. How fun it is to have Anna living vicariously through me. Up until this moment, I can't say anyone would have wanted to live vicariously through any part of my life.

Anna opens her eyes and looks at me. "So, what do you think it all means?"

"I have no idea." I slouch back in my seat. I

know I will have to think this through and analyze it all, but I don't really want to right now.

"Well, don't get all girly on him and start asking too many questions. Just see what happens tomorrow, let it play out."

"Yah, that's a good idea," I say, pushing out the uneasy feeling that tries to slip in. What *will* tomorrow be like?

I shake off the path my mind is trying to take me and lean my head back on the couch and close my eyes, replaying every kiss, every touch. I wonder what he's thinking about right now. Is he thinking about me, too? I'm sure he's not replaying everything in his head, doesn't seem like a guy thing to do. But maybe I've crossed his mind, and he's smiled to himself.

As I go to bed, I'm still feeling butterflies and excitement, finding it hard to believe it all happened. So much has occurred in my life in the past couple of months. I look around at my half-packed room. This weekend I will be moving to my new condo, I'm wearing makeup, dressing differently, making out with hot men — well, just one hot man. I'm so much less of a spinster than ever. It feels good.

# CHAPTER 10

It's the next morning, and I pop out of bed quickly, excited to go to work. I'm so eager to see Jared, and also feeling a little apprehensive about it. I've put off allowing my mind to go there, but I can't help myself anymore. What if overnight he has decided kissing me was a complete mistake and now regrets it? What if things are awkward between us? What if he completely avoids me? I don't know what to expect or how to act in these situations, it's been so long.

Things were somewhat strained between Brian the troll and me after our little tryst in that same conference room so long ago. A few awkward hellos in the hall, avoidance in the break room for a while. But that was different. We were at a party, we were both being stupid. It didn't mean anything. Things are different with Jared, the kissing meant something. It had to.

I get ready and take time to make sure my makeup looks especially good, and I pick out something to wear that I know flatters and makes me feel confident. Today will be a good day, maybe even great.

When I arrive at work, the butterflies are running rampant in my stomach. I park my car and, as always, look for Jared's. I don't see his car, so he must be running late. With him not at the office yet, it will be that much longer until I see him, until I might be able to determine what he is feeling today. That actually makes me relax a little, and the butterflies die down.

The office building is particularly quiet this morning as I walk through the hall and to my office. Mr. Nguyen's office door is closed, and there is no light coming from underneath the door. Mr. Nguyen late to work? What is this world coming to? All the better for me, though. Now I can just sit at my desk and dream—daydream about last night.

I log on to my computer and see an e-mail from Mr. Calhoun calling for an all-hands meeting this morning at nine. Strange, I don't remember hearing any talk of an all-hands meeting coming up.

My door swings open, and in walks Brown, no knock. She plops herself down in the chair in front of my desk. She has a strange look on her face, one I've never seen Brown have. Stress maybe? Worry?

"Have you checked your e-mail?" she asks, eyebrows creased.

"Yah, I just saw the e-mail from Calhoun.

What's that all about?" I ask, a slight chill prickling up my spine. Without Brown's usual sense of confidence and poise, I'm suddenly feeling a bit uneasy.

"An all-hands meeting out of the blue? It can only be one thing. Layoffs, Jules." She looks at me and purses her lips together.

"Layoffs? Oh geez, Brown. I think you've lost your mind."

"No Jules, I've wondered if this was coming. I didn't say anything because I didn't want to scare you, but I have suspected this was going to happen." She looks out the window, shaking her head dubiously.

"Even if there are layoffs, why do we have to worry? There is no way you would get laid off, they need your good looks in Sales," I joke, but she doesn't laugh. "And I am the only assistant to Mr. Nguyen. Who would take my place?" Even though I feel confident about what I am telling her, a bristle of uneasiness goes down my spine.

"There are no guarantees at any job. Who knows? Maybe they didn't like how many breaks we took during the day." She shrugs her shoulders.

"We work hard, though. Harder than most people at this company." This is sadly a true statement. Spectraltech is full of lazy employees.

"I don't know, Jules, guess we'll find out." Brown gets up from her chair and heads out the door, leaving me there to ponder.

I try to keep myself busy for the next thirty minutes, clicking refresh on my e-mail, hoping for something from Jared—anything. If I heard from him, I would feel better. I would feel less anxious about everything. But no such luck. I thought about moseying around the office for a bit, just to see if he has come in yet or not, but I thought it would be better just to stay put in my office.

At five minutes to nine, I refresh my lip gloss and head to the large conference room on the bottom floor of the building. I'm sure I will finally see Jared now as this meeting was called by Mr. Calhoun, and he will definitely be doing some part of it.

The atmosphere is ominous as we all enter the conference room. Word must have spread, and everyone is feeling apprehensive about what this meeting might mean. There is basically standing room only; too many people and not enough chairs.

After we all file in and try to make room for one another, Mr. Calhoun enters last and tries to maneuver his way to the front. He really should've thought this through better. All of us in this conference room, and his big rear trying to force his way to the front? Not the greatest idea.

I look around for Jared, still no sign of him. My heart sinks. If I could just see him, see him smile at me or something, I would feel better about everything.

Mr. Calhoun clears his throat. "Attention, attention everyone. We have some important things to discuss in this meeting, so I need everyone to be quiet and listen. I know this is not the most comfortable setting for us to meet so I will make my comments and announcements quickly." He looks down at some papers he has brought with him, and then clears his throat again. "Many of you have suspected because of the down-turn in profits over the last four quarters, and because of this ever-changing 'proverbial' economy that, at Spectraltech, we, too, would somehow be affected."

You could hear a pin drop at this point; everyone is on edge and giving each other nervous glances.

"We have been able to stay afloat for some time now, but I'm here today to tell you that, unfortunately, this is true. We are now feeling the effects of this economy."

A gasp filters throughout the room as we all let this information set in.

"So, what does that mean?" Someone yells from behind me and others start to chime in, asking the same thing.

"Shhh, everyone. Please. Just let me talk, and all will be revealed. Please be quiet everyone." Mr. Calhoun's face reddens as he tries to get everyone to return their attention back to him.

He clears his throat and looks down at his papers. "It is with much regret I must inform you today, we will be laying off thirty percent of you."

A different kind of gasp filters throughout the crowd, and everyone looks at each other wondering who it's going to be.

"Unfortunately, we do not have the ability to make this a long goodbye. The layoffs are happening today." More chatter fills the room, now everyone is feeling a bit on the frantic side. I'm feeling flustered, even though I'm confident my job is solid.

"Listen everyone. I know this is difficult, but I have more information to give you." Mr. Calhoun waits for a moment as the chatter subsides and the focus returns to him.

"If you are one of the ones who will be laid off, you will have a blue envelope on your desk. Inside the envelope you will find a letter detailing your severance, which, unfortunately could not be much, but it is something. You will also find information detailing your COBRA health-insurance plan should you need insurance coverage in the interim."

People start to exit the room even before Mr. Calhoun can finish, too anxious to find out if they are part of the thirty percent. I keep looking around the room for Jared, hoping he might have snuck in the back or something. He's nowhere to be found.

"Listen up everyone, please!" Mr. Calhoun calls out to the crowd, who he has now clearly lost the attention of. "I hope you know we value you all as employees, as part of the Spectraltech family, and we have tried everything in our power to ensure this not happen, but unfortunately, we just could not sustain any longer."

Everyone is leaving and going back to their desks, ignoring Mr. Calhoun's last words. Even I find myself feeling like I need to go back to my office, just to make sure.

We filter out of the conference room and head back to our offices. I run into Brown as I'm trying to make my way through the crowd.

"You're good, Jules. You're good. I am, too," she says in my ear.

"What do you mean?" I look at her, perplexed.

"I ditched out of the meeting early. I had to make sure. Both of our desks are clear."

Relief washes over me instantly, and the weight that I didn't think I was actually carrying lifts off my shoulders. I don't know what I would do if I were laid off. I just bought my new place. I can't afford to lose my job now.

Brown winks at me. "You okay?" she asks, seeing the tension drain from my face.

"Yah... yes. That was just crazy."

"See? I told you what was going on. You

should always believe me. I know everything." She smiles confidently at me. "I would say we should take a break, but under the circumstances…" she trails off.

"Um, yah, no we should probably just go back to work." The crowd thins around us. "Hey, did you ever see Mr. Nguyen in there? Or Jared?"

Brown shakes her head no. "Haven't seen Nguyen. Although, I wasn't really looking for him," she says, looking around to see if anyone is listening to her besides me. We don't usually gossip in the hallways, if you can call this gossip. "Anyway, I'm sure Jared was busy doing stuff for Calhoun. Maybe he had to hand out the letters." Of course, that was what he was doing! That makes perfect sense. Poor guy, that must've been hard for him.

"Hey, you called me last night—what was going on?"

"Oh, that. Yah, I just called to tell you Jared kissed me," I say with as nonchalant a facial expression as I can, but then, despite myself, I smile.

"What? Are you serious?" Her eyes bug out of her head.

"Yep," I say, the giddiness returning. But then I stop myself quickly. Right now people are finding out they are losing their jobs, their lives turning upside down. It's not the best time to be acting like a silly teenager in the hallway.

"I need details," Brown says, shock still on her face. "Let's go back to your office."

The walk back to my office is a gloomy one. Mixed emotions everywhere. Some with the look of relief on their faces, some with the look of total shock, some people even crying. What a sad day at Spectraltech. One I am sure I will not to forget for a long while.

I glance over at Martha's desk and see her smiling slightly. Her job must be safe, although of all the employees here, her job should have been the first to go. I guess her relationship with Mr. Calhoun saved her? That is disturbing and ethically wrong on so many levels, if that is the case. Martha's job is totally redundant. Everyone knows that. Brown and I will have to discuss.

We reach my office and close the door behind us. "Fill me in, Jules! He kissed you? I need to know everything," Brown says immediately as the door shuts.

"Okay, okay! I'll tell you... I..." I let out a tiny gasp as I pull back my chair that was neatly tucked under my desk. Sitting right there, hidden from someone that might just peek in my office, is a crisp, blue envelope.

I pull it out and show it to Brown.

"No!" she says loudly. "No, Jules. That can't be right, it has to be a mistake."

Slowly, I open the envelope and pull out the letter, skimming it quickly and seeing with my eyes that I am, in fact, being let go from

Spectraltech.

I feel like the wind just got sucked out of me. What a fool I was. Here I was happily coming back to the office, getting ready to tell Brown about what happened with Jared yesterday, and all at once the rug was just ripped out from under me.

"Julia? Are you okay?" Brown's looking at me like I might faint. I just might.

I clumsily take a seat at the desk and just stare at the letter. Wishing it away, not believing this is happening to me.

"I... I'm not sure..." I trail off, looking at Brown.

Brown stands up and moves over to me, putting a hand on my shoulder. "Jules? You're going to be okay, alright? You are. It's just a set-back. You will be fine."

Tears well in my eyes as the reality sets in. "A set-back? This is total devastation!" I say, louder than I meant to. "What am I going to do, Brown? I just bought a place, I'm supposed to be moving there this weekend. Nearly all my savings went toward it. This is a nightmare!" I bury my face in my hands and try my hardest to not completely blubber like I want to.

I've been laid off. I've actually lost my job. How could this happen? How is this even possible? Just a moment ago, I was traipsing happily down the hallway to my office, feeling confident about work, thinking about Jared.

Now, my whole world has been turned upside down.

I worked, I did my job. That was more than Martha can say. That's more than many people at this company can say. So, why me? I am the only person who works for Mr. Nguyen. Who is going to do my job now?

And what will I do with myself? I don't even have a current resume.

"I don't understand, Brown. I worked, I did what I was asked to." I look down at the stupid blue envelope.

"Just because you do your job, doesn't always keep you safe from layoffs, Jules. Sometimes positions just go away." She takes her hand off my shoulder and goes back to take a seat at the chair in front of my desk.

Jared pops into my head and I decide I don't care about any inhibitions I might have, I am going to find him. He's in HR, maybe he can give me some answers or talk some sense into someone? Yes, I must find Jared.

"I'm going upstairs." I stand up and head out the door.

"What are you going to do?" Brown says, looking concerned like I might go postal or something. She follows me out to the hall.

"I'm gonna go find Jared," I say as I walk toward the elevator, leaving Brown standing in the hall. She doesn't try to follow me, and I'm glad she doesn't. I hate to admit it, but part of me really hates the fact that I just got canned, and here is Brown, still with a job, still in her perfect pretty-princess life. I know it's rude and awful to think, but I can't help myself.

I get off the elevator at the sixth floor and go over to the conference room, and the door is locked. Despite the fact that I can't see any light coming from underneath the door, I knock anyway. Nothing.

"Julia?" Mr. Calhoun peaks out of his office. "Can I help you with something?" There is such sadness in his eyes that for a second, I forget why I'm here.

"I'm trying to find Jared Moody," I say with as much resolve as I can muster, remembering my reason for coming up here.

"Jared?" He repeats and looks at me like I've lost my mind. Maybe I have.

"Yes. Jared," I repeat.

"Well, he's not here. He's, uh, gone... part of the layoffs. I let him go this morning before the meeting," he says looking past me and down the hall. I turn my head to see what he's looking at. No one is there.

"He's gone?" My eyes dart around, confused.

"Yes," he says flatly. He looks down at his hands resting on his belly and twiddles his thumbs.

"Can I ask you something, Mr. Calhoun?"

"Yes, of course. Anything," he says and smiles slightly at me.

"Why me? Why did I get laid off?" I say timidly, wishing I could scream it at him, but I can't find it in me.

"Well, it wasn't my decision to make. For what it's worth, Julia, I want you to know I fought hard to keep you here at Spectraltech. But the 'proverbial' powers that be made all the decisions."

"Okay, well, thank you, Mr. Calhoun," I say, defeated. I'm pretty sure the only reason he wanted to save my job was for my baked goods.

"Take care of yourself, Julia," he says as I turn to go to the elevator and back to my office, or what used to be my office.

As I get on the elevator, I turn and give him a small thin smile. The best I can do under the circumstances.

It doesn't take me long to clean out my desk and gather all my things to take with me. After ten years of working here, it's surprising how little I have.

I'm feeling kind of like a robot. Like I'm not really part of my body, and I'm in some sort of dream sequence.

How could this be happening? I've lost my job. I am no longer gainfully employed. And to make matters horribly worse, I've lost contact with Jared. I have no contact information on him other than work. We never exchanged personal numbers or e-mail addresses. Now we're both jobless, and I have no way of getting ahold of him to see how he's doing, to see how he's feeling—about the job, about last night, about everything.

Why did he just leave? Why couldn't he hang around for the meeting? Did he know I was getting laid off, too? Didn't he want to talk to me and see how I was doing?

So many questions and thoughts keep running through my head. I'm feeling delirious with everything.

Before I shut down my computer for the last time at Spectraltech, I decide to send out an e-mail to a few of the people I would like to say goodbye to. As soon as I open my inbox, right there at the top is a message from Jared, date stamp says it arrived ten minutes ago.

Decided to take my mom on a trip. Will be back in two weeks. Call me then –J

My heart skips a beat. An e-mail from Jared and at the bottom he has put his cell number. He didn't just leave me after all. I smile to myself. A silver lining. I lost my job, but I didn't lose contact with Jared.

I think Brown was right; I am going to be okay.

# CHAPTER 11

I'm sure I've heard it before, but I really should've had a plan B. Just in case something like this ever happens. You always think to yourself, "Oh yes, that's a good idea... for other people. That kind of stuff will never happen to me." But here I am, no plan B. I have no job, and now I own a new condo filled with my belongings and my new furniture I purchased back when I was footloose and fancy-free. Ah, the good ole days, when I had a job... which was just two days ago. I do enjoy reminiscing about it, though.

I've been told moving is one of the worst experiences in life, and I would say that as far as moves go, this one hasn't been as bad as I thought it would be. Even though, right now, as I sit on the floor with Charlie purring comfortably in my lap, and look at the sea of junk I now get the opportunity to go through and find places to put it all, I'm still enjoying it. I guess because, for the first time in my life, I am on my own in my very own place. I'm free of the shackles of my parents' basement apartment.

Although I never thought of it that way, it really was.

It's all very new and exhilarating. If only the gnawing feeling of no job didn't keep reappearing in my head, then it would be a perfect move.

Although I do not have a plan B, I do have a plan. For the rest of the weekend I will settle into my new place and come Monday, I will start looking for a job. I have ten years of experience and a degree that had nothing to do with said experience, but I'm feeling confident there will be something out there for me.

It's sad how one simple e-mail from Jared lifted my spirits enough to make me not go into a bout of self-despair/self-loathing. But at least I have that. At least there is still Jared, and the thought of talking to him again. If I lost my job *and* Jared, I think... well, I don't really want to think about it. And let's be honest here, I don't actually have Jared, but the possibility of something — anything — that's enough for me right now.

I hear a knock at my door, startling Charlie who jumps out of my lap. I get up from the floor to find out who it is.

"Hello, dear!" my mother says cheerfully as she and my dad come through the door carrying a few odds and ends I must have left in the basement, along with a fresh bouquet of flowers. "These are for you," she says as she hands me the flowers, "a little something to brighten up your new place."

"Thanks, Mom," I say as I hug her.

"Well, honey, we are just so proud of you." She smiles brightly at me.

"Yes, your jobless daughter has now moved out of your basement. You should be proud," I deadpan.

"Oh, you will find a job soon, I'm certain of it." My mom has always been a glass-half-full kind of gal.

"Well, this is a tough economy," my dad throws out, and my mom darts him an evil glare, "but I'm sure you will do just fine." He adds with a wink.

I smile half-heartedly back. "Thanks for your vote of confidence."

We small talk about the condo, and I fill them in on my plan to start looking for a job on Monday. They agree that I should take a few days to relax, unpack, and then get back to the daily grind. I hope it is that simple.

"We have some good news!" my mom announces during a lull in the conversation. "You tell her, Raymond," she nudges my dad in the shoulder.

"What news?" He looks at her puzzled.

"About Anna," she says, giving him an incensed look.

"Oh right, that." He shakes his head. "Your mother is just excited that I was able to give

Anna a job answering phones at the firm." He half smiles. "But you just say the word and the job is yours, Julie-bear," he says and winks at me. It's hard to believe I am in my thirties and my dad will still sometimes refer to me as "Julie-bear." I can't lie, I still love it.

"Thanks, Dad, but answering phones is a little beneath my skill-set. But I will definitely keep that in mind," I say and wink back. "Anyway, I think Anna needs the job more than I do with all the debt she has." I say without thinking.

"What debt?" my mother quickly asks, confused.

Oh crap, oh crap, oh crap. What the hell did I just do? How can I spin this? How can I make this better? Why am I constantly putting my foot in my mouth? Must lie, must lie, must lie... But there is no lie to tell. Anna shouldn't have any debt because my parents have been paying for everything for her for years now.

"Um, well, I'm not really sure... I could be wrong..." I sputter out, keeping my eye contact away from theirs.

They look at each other and then both back at me. They know I'm a horrible liar, they raised me that way. Damn them and their integrity.

This is not good for Anna. Not good at all. What do I say here? How do I smooth things over for her? She is going to kill me. Maybe they'll just not say anything to her. She is an adult, maybe they'll just let her take care of herself and not butt in. Yes, just like unicorns are real and pigs fly. There is no way they will let this one go. Anna will hate me for sure.

"Do you know anything about this, Ray?" She looks at my dad for answers.

"I've never heard anything about it." He looks at her and shrugs.

I might throw up. I'm sick to my stomach. "Just don't worry about it. I don't think it's that big of a deal. I'm probably wrong." I give them a fake smile, dying inside.

My dad looks at his watch. "We better get going, Katherine," he says as he gets up and starts to head for the door, his mind obviously preoccupied with the information I just unthinkingly gave him. I really hate me right now.

"Yes, yes," my mother shakes her head out of the sudden trance she was under. "We have dinner plans with friends." She smiles slightly at me.

"Okay," is all I have to say.

They both smile at me as best they can and say a quick goodbye. They are out the door before I can even think of something to say — anything to say — that might make them forget what I just told them about Anna. It was a lost cause though, it's already out there and can't be taken back.

I should probably call Anna and give her a heads up. I don't know if I can do that, though. I don't know if I can handle the anger she'll unleash from the other end of the phone. I think maybe I should sleep on it and try to come up with a good way to tell her. I don't think there is a good way, but I will try to find one.

The next morning I wake up to my phone ringing. Whoever it is, I will kill them. Who calls people at eight in the morning on a Saturday?

Brown, that's who.

"Hey, what's up?" I try to say in less sleepy tones, but I'm pretty sure I failed.

"You awake?" she asks, intensity to her voice.

"I am now," I say flatly. "What's going on? Why are you calling me so early on a Saturday?"

"I wanted to call you earlier, but decided you were probably sleeping, so I went for a run instead." Even through the phone I can tell she sounds fidgety, unsettled.

"Well, I was still sleeping, and I would like to go back to sleep. So, tell me why you're calling," I say yawning, my head falling back on my pillow. I was having the best dream, and yes, of course, it included Jared. And no, it was not one of *those* dreams. Just a good old-fashioned sappy, romantic dream. Sigh.

"Julia, I have gossip," she says, but not in her sing-song voice she usually uses when she's excited to tell me something.

"Okay, tell me," I say, now fully awake and interested. Why is she being so serious?

"Well, first of all, Martha and Calhoun—totally true."

"What? Oh sick!" I say loudly. "I mean, I guess we knew, but to have it confirmed? Yuck."

"I know. It's disgusting. Anyway, the reason I found out this information is because a bunch of us went out last night after work. To sort of celebrate our... still having... jobs." She says the last part slowly, like she's trying to ease the sting of the fact that I wasn't there to celebrate. "Sorry," she adds quickly.

"It's fine," I sigh. "Go on."

"Okay, so anyway, Martha was there and, of course, Mr. Calhoun wasn't. The reason I found out about her and Calhoun was because Martha got stupid trashed. Like, totally drunk off her butt, and she told me some other things. Things I'm positive she wasn't supposed to tell me."

"Go on?" My interest piqued.

"Well, first of all, as it turns out, Mr. Nguyen was totally stealing money from the company."

"Yah, I'd heard something like that," I say before I can stop myself.

"What? You heard and didn't tell me?" she asks, sounding extra annoyed.

"Yes, sorry. I overheard someone talking about it. Anyway, that's not important. How did they figure it out?" I say trying to get her past my mini-betrayal, and trying not to reveal my source, although at this point, I suppose it doesn't really matter.

"I'm not sure of the details exactly; Martha only gave me bits and pieces. What I was able to put together was that the daily reports he had you doing were bogus reports. The reports he was sending out to the other VPs and the Board were reports he did himself, fudging the numbers just slightly so he could take some off the top. Again, I'm just putting two and two together from what Martha slurred out."

"Whoa, that's crazy! I knew there was something going on with the daily reports! How long had he been doing it?" I try to think back to when I had first noticed that the reports seemed weird to me.

"I'm guessing like six months or something. It wasn't very long. He wasn't able to get that much money. Only like several thousand."

"Wow, Mr. Nguyen was really stealing from the company..." I trail off, thinking of the times he blew me off when I had questions about the reports. He didn't need to give me answers, they were bogus. At least he had the decency not to implicate me in anything. He just had me doing bum reports. Six months' worth. I guess Jared was right after all. I'm sure he will totally gloat about that.

Just thinking about Jared makes my stomach do a couple of flips, and the butterflies invade. It hasn't even been a week since I last saw him, since we kissed. Yet it seems like so long ago. So much has happened. I really wish he didn't just jet off like he did. I hate having to wait so long to talk to him again. I have been debating whether to call and leave a message giving him my number so it will be there when he gets back, but I don't want to seem desperate, so I'll wait.

"Jules, there's more," she says, her tone lowers, interrupting my thoughts of Jared. "It's about the layoffs."

"Yah?" I say, coming back to the conversation. "What about the layoffs?"

"Well, it turns out it wasn't entirely done by the Board of Directors and the VPs as was speculated. There was actually someone inside the company who was doing the snooping to find out which jobs were necessary and which weren't..." she trails off going quiet for a second.

"Oh, *really*? I bet it was Martha. That's probably how she and Calhoun hooked up in the first place because she was doing all his dirty work for him. She always was a little snoopy. Plus, she totally hated me so that would explain why I lost my job." I nod my head to myself. "Although, that would've required Martha to actually work."

"It wasn't Martha," Brown replies, not laughing at my Martha comment like she usually would.

"Well, then who was it?" There really isn't

anyone else I can think of.

"Jules, it was Jared."

"What? What are you talking about? That doesn't even make any sense." My mind starts to race, my heart pounding. How could this be true? It's not true, it doesn't make sense. Brown must be confused.

"It was Jared. Martha told me. She said something about the Board of Directors hiring him to do consulting, to help them downsize. I didn't believe her at first. I was sure she got her information mixed up. But then I did some more digging around about Jared on the Internet last night. I was going down the wrong avenues before, but with this new information from Martha I tried a different angle, and I finally found something. A URL name that was purchased by a J.D. Moody five years ago. I looked up the web address, and it's for a consulting firm. I think he's a consultant that they fake-hired to do reorganizations."

"What? How is that even possible? How could he even pull that off? Come on, Brown, it doesn't make sense," I say, not intending the angry tone in my voice.

"Think about it, Jules. Just think about it for a while. It makes sense. He was elusive about his past, about what he did for the company. We just assumed what he did. We really had no idea."

I'm silent. It can't be true. It just can't. I don't

want to believe it. But even as I deny it in my head, parts of conversations we had, things he said to me start to come back to memory. The puzzle pieces start to come together.

Suddenly, my stomach starts to turn. My room feels cold and the walls too close to me. No. No, I don't want to accept it. I can't.

"Are you there, Jules?" Brown asks quietly.

"I'm here," I say, barely audible.

"I know it's hard to believe. I didn't want to believe it either. But it's true, Jules. It is."

"I just can't... I just don't know what to think," I squeak out.

"It's worse, Jules."

"How? How could it be worse?" My head is swimming now. My rational and emotional sides are struggling to make sense of it all.

She inhales loudly. "Who did he get so much of his information from?" She pauses, waiting for it to sink in, to hit me. "From us, Jules. He got his info from us. He used us."

"Oh my gosh, Brown. Oh my gosh..." I trail off, sickness welling in my stomach.

"We told him everything about everyone, and he used that information, of course he did."

"This can't be true, it just can't," I say quietly, dramatically. I can't help myself.

"It's true, Jules. It's all true. If I saw him right now, I'd punch him in the face," she says, anger running thick through her voice.

I don't even know what I feel. Anger would

be better than what I'm feeling. It's a harrowing mixture of emotions. My internal struggle of realization and not wanting to believe make it hard for me to sort anything out.

"People lost their jobs because of us." The notion comes out of my mouth before I've even had a chance to internalize it. And suddenly an even more horrible feeling comes over me. How honest were we when we gave him company information? Did Brown or I ever exaggerate anything? Did he ever take as gospel something that we were just speculating on? What if information we gave him wasn't entirely true, but it got someone fired anyway? My breathing speeds up, panic taking over.

"No, they lost their jobs because of *him.*" Brown practically spits out the last word. "We may have given him information to make his job easier, but he would have found out anyway. Don't do that to yourself." She sounds like she's trying to convince herself as well.

I breathe deeply, fighting off the panic as best I can.

"You okay?" she asks after she hears my breathing.

"It's just a lot to take in," I say between breaths.

"It all makes sense though, Jules. It all fits together. The only thing I can't figure out is why you got laid off. I mean, it was obvious you didn't like your job, but you did your work. If they knew Nguyen was gone, then why weren't you kept around to at least keep that department afloat?"

"I don't know, Brown... I don't know." But even as I say it, Mr. Calhoun's last words filter through my head: *"For what it's worth, I fought hard to keep you here at Spectraltech. But the powers that be made all the decisions."* The powers that be—was he talking about Jared? Did he insist I be let go even after Calhoun fought for my job? Why would he do that?

The sick feeling in my stomach is almost overwhelming. "I've gotta go, Brown. I'll call you later," I nearly whisper into the phone, then quickly end the call.

The tears come fast and quick. Conversations I had with Jared run through my head. Some things make more sense now, and some make less. I feel weird, almost numb, my head still swimming with all of it.

My life has taken a quick unchangeable nosedive. Things were starting to look up, starting to happen for me. I had a life. More of a life than I ever had. And now it's all gone, and I'm alone. Alone and jobless with only a cat to snuggle with me right now as I cry. I have never felt more like a spinster.

# CHAPTER 12

Hurt.
Betrayal.
Loss.
Dove Chocolate.
These are the things I am experiencing right now. The chocolate is supposed to cover up the other feelings, but it's doing a poor job. And when I opened it to read the usually uplifting note on the inside of the wrapper, mine said "Build a bridge and get over it! By- Lori in Fenton, MO." What kind of uplifting crap is that? Why don't you come live my life, Lori in Fenton, Missouri? See how you feel. Maybe you won't be so willing to build that damn bridge.

Here's what we now know about Jared. He's an a-hole. That pretty much wraps it up. It's actually been a week since I found out about what really happened and I have to say, it was a bigger blow than losing my job. Although the two are connected, I seem to be separating them in my head.

To top it off, word got back to Anna for my huge foot-in-mouth-blunder with my parents,

247

and she was livid. She couldn't believe I would betray her like that and went on and on about how she trusted me. I just kept telling her I was sorry, and that it was a stupid accident, but she wouldn't hear it. She eventually hung up on me. I sent her a text saying how sorry I was, but she never replied back. So now I don't even have Anna to talk to about Jared and everything that has happened. I've completely ruined everything with my big fat mouth.

I really need Anna right now to help me sort things out, to sort my brain out. I need someone to bounce everything off of so I can make sense of it all. As it stands, I just keep replaying everything in my head, trying to sort out the real from the fake. And it's hard — too hard for me to do alone.

I don't really know what I'm feeling about Jared. It's a mixture of emotions. I find myself wondering if maybe everything that happened between us was all just acting on his part. Maybe all of his actions were just to get information from me. I don't want to believe that, but what other explanation is there?

I tried talking to Brown, but she just doesn't understand. She always ends up going off on a tirade about how he won't get away with this, how we're going to find out where he lives and put sugar in his gas tank, or some other vandalizing thing to get even. While that does sound appealing, it's not really helpful. She's just not analytically going to break this all down with me, like I need her to, like Anna would've done for me.

The totally pathetic part of all of this is I don't feel angry. I know I should, but the truth is I feel utterly heartbroken instead. Go ahead and gag at that, but it's the only way to say what I'm honestly feeling. My heart is broken and it's the kind of broken that feels irreparable. I know it's dramatic and maybe untrue. But so far, it feels true.

So, with only myself to try and sort things out, I did what I always do, I avoided. At first, I just laid around and slept or tried to find something funny on TV to cheer me up (never worked).

On Monday, when I was supposed to be looking for a job according to my "plan," I decided to forget it and bake. Taking a chapter from *Grey's Anatomy* when Izzy baked her feelings away after the handsome and wonderful Denny Duquette died (heartbreaking). I went to the store and bought a ridiculous amount of supplies which probably wasn't the most prudent thing for me to be doing at this time, but I did it anyway. I needed something to do, something to get my mind off things, and baking was it.

And, boy, did I bake. I made cupcakes, three different flavors. Vanilla, chocolate, and red velvet. I was meticulous with the frosting;

piping it on with the perfect tip, and then I added sprinkles, and edible pearls, and Art Deco designs out of chocolate to put on top.

Then, I made choux dough so I could make creampuffs. Instead of filling them with the traditional sweet cream, I used custard. I tried a new recipe for custard, and it was difficult, but once I got it right, it was some of the best I've ever made. Did you know if you don't accustom the eggs properly to the heat that they will actually scramble, leaving you with a gooey, doughy, clumpy mess? Well, I do. I learned it the hard way the first time I made custard. I didn't make that mistake this time. It was the most perfect custard I have ever made. So, I piped the perfect custard into my puffs and dipped some in chocolate and left some plain. They were amazing. Some of my best work, really.

Next, I made sugar cookies. I cut them in whimsical shapes and frosted them all with my best butter cream frosting, in different bright colors. Yellows, reds, blues, pinks. The colors made me happy, even if temporarily.

And that was just the first day. It worked, though. I baked away Jared and Spectraltech and Anna. All the things that have gone so horribly wrong in my life. It felt good to be creative and do something I love. Good, not great. But good was enough.

After the first day of baking, I ran out of room

in my kitchen, so I went to the restaurant supply store and I bought some cardboard display boxes, and filled them full of all my creations. Then, I took them over to my mom and dad's and also dropped some off to Brown for her to take to the nerds at Spectraltech. I didn't have the nerve to drop it off myself.

The next day, I tackled cheesecakes and tarts. I made three different kinds of cheesecake. A berry lemon, a layered chocolate mousse, and a vanilla bean. They looked magnificent. Especially the chocolate mousse cheesecake. It was so pretty I almost didn't want to give it to anyone, knowing they'll eat it and ruin my masterpiece. But if I kept it, I would eventually eat it, and that would have been bad for many reasons, mainly my thighs.

The tarts were a little more tedious, in my opinion. I didn't have enough small-sized muffin pans, so it was a struggle having to cook the shells in such small batches, but I did it anyway. I made the custard again—the one I used for the cream-puffs. Then, I painstakingly placed different types of fruit on the top of each tart. I glazed them with apricot marmalade, which gave them a perfect sheen. I should have taken pictures, I could have entered them into a contest, they were that perfect.

Once again, I ran into the counter space problem, so I filled up more boxes and then dropped them off to my parents and again to

Brown. My dad was particularly excited because he had taken the first day's goods to work with him and they were received with rave reviews, so he was eager to bring more.

The next day I tackled French pastries. First, I made napoleons. Did you know that in French they are called mille-feuilles, or thousand leaves? Why do I know this? I have no idea. I read it once and it stuck with me. I decided to make my own puff pastry instead of using the store bought. It was quite tedious but well worth it. The coloring of the baked pastry was the perfect shade of light brown. I've never gotten store-bought to cook that beautifully. I then layered some with just custard, and some I added sliced strawberries in between layers. I used almond flavoring in the glaze, and then drizzled it with melted chocolate. They were complete works of art.

Then, since I had already made the puff pastry, I tried out Pithiviers. Fan-freaking-tastic. Seriously, I highly recommend them. I've always wanted to make them since I'd tried them at a French patisserie that I went to when I was in my teens. The flavors stuck with me for so long, they were that good.

I kept up the baking the rest of the week, like a mad woman. I also kept up with the nightly deliveries to Brown and my parents. As the week wore on, the greetings I received when I delivered the goods went from total delight to utter concern. My dad did a pretty decent job of not looking too concerned, but it was clearly written all over my mother's face. And also, she literally said, "I'm concerned." Whatever. She doesn't understand. No one does.

I really shouldn't have been surprised when Friday evening I heard a knock on my door. I was working on my third attempt at making a chocolate soufflé (they kept falling during the baking process), and I was getting frustrated. I peeked out my peephole, and there was my family standing outside my door. Everyone except Anna, that is.

They'd come over to have an intervention — a baking one. Apparently, I'd been scaring them with my obsessive-compulsive need to bake things. My mom told me she thought I was having some early mid-life crisis and that she wanted me to get some therapy. Jenny didn't have much to say, but Lennon made up for it by semi-lecturing me about getting my resume in order, and how I need to get myself out there rather than sitting in here baking all day. He made me set some goals for the following week and wanted me to report back to him (whatever).

My dad was dragged along for the ride on this one; my mom insisted he come with. He didn't have much to say at first, but then he told me some of the other partners in the firm were taking the baked goods home to their wives and families. It turns out one of them, Richard, has a wife who owns a little bakery down on Sixteenth Street. She was so taken with my creations that she wants me to come in and talk to her about working at the bakery. The hitch being that the pay is total crap. He didn't think I'd be interested, but after seeing me in the state I was (still am), he must have had a second thought.

I said no at first. I needed to focus on finding a real job. Not a job to appease me while I looked for one. But then I started to think about it. Why couldn't I work there in the interim, while I'm looking for my "real" job? I would be able to keep up with this obsessive baking thing I have going on right now, and isn't it good to have a little money coming in? Regardless if it's not that much. Anything can help at this point. So, I told my dad I would meet with her.

My dad gave her husband my contact information that night, and I got a call this morning. Her name is Beth, and I'm going to meet her at the bakery on Monday morning to talk about working there. I can't say I'm excited to meet with her or to be working there, but I do feel like it's something I should do whether I'm excited or not.

Tonight, I'm having drinks with Brown. She forced me, told me we needed to hang out and talk. I don't really want to go, but if I stay home another night without baking (I stopped after the intervention — it *was* getting ridiculous), well,

I think I might lose my sanity, what's left of it anyway. Without the distraction, I keep replaying the events of the layoff and my hatred for Jared in my mind. So, I will be going out for drinks with Brown, half-grudgingly.

We are meeting at a place off of Fifteenth which is only two blocks away from my condo. At eight o'clock, which is the time I'm actually supposed to be there, I drag myself out and walk the two blocks over to meet Brown.

"Hey, Jules!" she says brightly as I approach the bar and take a seat.

"Hey," I say flatly.

"Wow, you really went all out tonight." She looks me up and down, pursing her lips in disapproval. I'm wearing yoga pants and a hooded sweatshirt, no makeup, and my hair is pulled up in a bun on top of my head.

"Yes, well, I told you I didn't want to go out tonight. So, what you see is what you get," I say, sticking my tongue out at her like a two-year-old.

"Well, I'm glad you're here, even if you look like you haven't showered in days." I haven't, but I'm not going to admit that to Brown.

"So, what's been going on? Still baking?" she asks as the bartender comes over and asks me if I want anything. I order a soda, nothing else sounds good.

"No, I had to stop. My family came over and had a 'baking intervention' of sorts. They cut me off." I stuff my hands in the pockets of my sweatshirt, glowering.

She laughs a little at that. "I thought it was getting a little ridiculous. But the nerds, they loved it. They miss you, you know. Especially Brian."

"Whatever." I roll my eyes at her as she gives me a little smirk.

"Oh, come on, Jules, lighten up," she says as the bartender brings me my soda and I take a sip from the straw, the cold bubbles tingle my throat as they go down.

"Why should I lighten up," I say after a few seconds of drinking. "I have nothing to lighten up for."

"Wow, you are a ball of fun. So, what about the job search? How is that?" she asks, taking a drink of whatever she is drinking. It's some fancy cocktail like a Cosmo or something. So fitting for Brown.

"I haven't really looked yet. I still need to figure out my resume. I have an interview on Monday, though." I throw this out there so I don't sound like a complete loser.

"Oh really? Where?"

"Well, it's not a real job, it's just with a bakery down on Sixteenth. Just something to pass the time while I look for something else."

"That sounds fun! Good for you, Jules," she says, with her condescending tone that isn't meant to be condescending I'm sure, but it's annoying nonetheless.

"So, what's new at Spectraltech?" I say, not really wanting to know, but I don't feel like talking about me.

"Not much, just adjusting to all the positions now gone. They have a junior sales assistant with an accounting background doing Nguyen's job until they find someone to fill that position." It's so weird there is a Spectraltech without Henry Nguyen. He's practically been there from the beginning. But, of course, stealing money will pretty much secure job loss. I've never heard of it working the other way.

We sit in silence, drinking our drinks. There's a certain awkwardness happening. I'm not sure if it's because Brown and I rarely ever go out together outside of work, or if I have some pent-up anger toward her and her Barbie-doll life. Probably a little of both. It's not her fault everything seems to work out in her favor. I need to let it go, it's just a little hard.

"Okay, let's talk about Jared." She says the name I really did not want to hear tonight.

"No, thank you," I say and wave the bartender over to get me a refill. He acknowledges me and then goes back to his higher paying customer at the other end of the bar. Rude.

"Come on, Jules. We need to talk about it. *You* need to talk about it. Obviously, it has affected you — you were less depressed about losing your job." She looks my face over, looking for some sort of reaction.

"Fine. What do you want to talk about?" I need to talk about it, to figure it out. But not with Brown. I've tried that, and it hasn't helped.

"So, what happened? You didn't get to tell me about the kissing." She gives me a little smile, one she used to give me when we were talking office gossip.

"There's not much to tell. I went up to his office the day before the layoffs, and we kissed." The thought of that day still sends a little chill down my spine, despite what I now know about the situation.

"Was it just a little kiss, like a peck?" She takes a sip of her drink, full attention on me.

"No, it was a full-on make-out session," I say and sigh to myself. I would love to go back to that night. Back to when I didn't know Jared was a back-stabbing a-hole.

"Really?" Her eyes widen. "That's interesting."

"Why is that interesting?"

"It just is. No particular reason. Didn't he give you any indication of the layoffs?" The bartender finally makes his way toward us and brings me my refill.

"Not really. He seemed stressed and tired, but that was it. He didn't tell me anything. But then again, what could he tell me?"

"True." She nods her head and purses her

lips, contemplating.

"I don't know... I guess it's hard because I thought he actually cared about me. He really seemed like he did. It was the first time since I can remember that I felt... I don't know, special?" I shake my head to myself, annoyed at how cheesy that sounds: Special. There's no other word though, is there? "But clearly he's just one of those guys who get their jollies by preying on the weak and spinsterly," I say and look down at my lap.

"Spinsterly?" She chuckles slightly at that. "Why in the world would you think you're spinsterly?"

"Because that's what I am. A spinster." I feel like adding a "duh" there, but I hold myself back. I've never actually said it out loud to anyone, and I expected she would nod her head in agreement rather than question it. "Up until about a week ago, I lived in my parents' basement. I have a cat, no boyfriend, or prospect of one, and now no job. I'm a spinster, or at least on my way to becoming one." I sip my soda, sulking.

"You're crazy." She rolls her eyes at me. "You are not a spinster, Jules. Don't you think you're being a little overly dramatic?"

"Whatever," I say, blowing her off. What would a blonde-prom-queen know about it anyway? "Look, I'm exhausted. I have more unpacking I've been putting off to do tomorrow, so I think I better go home and sleep."

"Okay." She smiles thinly at me, not trying to talk me out of leaving. I'm not really fun to hang out with, so why would she?

I throw some money down on the bar and get up to go. "I'll see you later." I try to muster a smile, but it's hard.

"Jules, for what it's worth, I do think he cared about you. I don't think he was just acting."

"I wish I believed that," I say quietly and give her a small wave as I turn and walked out of the bar.

# CHAPTER 13

I'm not sure what I was picturing when my dad told me about Beth's bakery (aptly called "Beth's Bakery"). Something simple, perhaps? But what I see when I arrive is totally unexpected. It's definitely more of an upscale bakery. Brick wall interiors, leather couches and chairs in the corners. Small two- and four-person tables with high-back, brightly colored fabric chairs scattered around the room. The ceiling is unfinished, with spotlights hanging neatly below piping. It has the smell of freshly roasted coffee and the quaint scent of baking pastry with lingering remnants of almond.

I like it already. Strike that. I think I might love it already.

There are a few people still strewn around, reading newspapers in the corner chairs, or working on computers at the tables. Someone who must work here is busy bustling around, cleaning up tables from what looks like a pretty busy morning rush.

I approach the display counter, which has been rather picked over, wishing I had got here earlier to see all of the goods displayed.

A blonde woman, probably in her fifties comes out of the door behind the counter.

"Are you Beth?" I ask, feeling unsure of myself. I hate meeting people for the first time, it's always so awkward.

"Yes, you must be Julia," she says, smiling as she holds out her hand to shake mine. Her hand has a slightly rough and weathered feel to it, like the feeling of hard work. Mine, I'm sure feels dull and frail, like someone who has sat on their butt using a computer for the past ten years. "Come, have a seat." She gestures over to an open table close to the front door.

"So, tell me about yourself," she says as we both take a seat.

"Well, there's not much to tell," I say and shrug. "I've just been laid off recently, and so now I'm thinking I want to do something different." I fib a little. I don't want her to know I'm just planning on doing this temporarily. I may have only worked for one company since I've been out of college, but everyone knows if you tell a potential future employer you only want to work there until something better comes along, they probably won't hire you.

"I have to say, I've had some of your creations, and they are pretty amazing." She smiles brightly at me.

"Thank you. I would've loved to try some of yours, but I see they're pretty much gone." I nod over at the nearly empty counter display.

"Yes, we have a pretty busy morning crowd. Lots of regulars." She looks around the room and then back at me. "So, did you go to culinary school?"

"Nope, just self-taught," I say and then quickly add, "I hope that's okay?"

"Of course. I'm self-taught, too," She adds with a wink. "Well, there's no sense in dragging this out. Of course, I would love for you to come work for me if you'd like to," she says and smiles in a motherly way. "The pay is twelve dollars an hour, and you can start tomorrow if you like."

I gulp a little at the pay. My dad said it wasn't very good, but I had no idea it would be that little. I don't even want to think about what I was actually making an hour at Spectraltech. More than twice that much? I will seriously have to get my butt in gear to find another job. But at least I'll have *some* money coming in until I can find one.

"Sure, I would love to." I give her a smile.

"Wonderful. Let me give you a tour." She gets up from her chair, and I follow suit. She takes me to the back of the bakery, into the kitchen. When I see it, I want to cry. It's so amazing. With long metal tables to roll out dough, and tools and gadgets I have only dreamed of hanging on hooks on the walls. Against the wall are the most beautiful ovens where you can cook trays and trays of cupcakes at the same time. I think my favorite thing I see is the industrial sized KitchenAid. I kind of just want to cuddle up and live inside it. This job, temporary as it is, has some fabulous perks. I'm starting to see that now.

So, I am to start tomorrow... at five in the morning. I tried really hard not to let my eyes bug out when she said that, but I think I was only half-able to because she laughed at my reaction. I'm not sure why it came as such a surprise. Of course, if you are to have a bakery — a functioning one — you would have to be up earlier than the roosters in order to be ready for the day on time. But it was still a shock. One of the very small silver linings to being laid off was being able to sleep in. At least I didn't have too long to get used to it.

On the walk back to my place, I send a quick text to my parents telling them that I took the job with Beth. I'm actually feeling kind of excited about it. I mean, not the fact that I will be making less than half of my Spectraltech pay, but the fact that I actually get do something I love to do, even if it is only temporary.

Wishing I could talk to Anna and tell her about everything, I decide to send her a text.

Do you still hate me?

I hit send and then wait. But as usual, no

reply. Even a simple "yes" would be better than complete silence. I just wish we could talk and get this all worked out and go back to being us. Me and Anna. I miss it.

It's officially summer here in the Mile High City, and the slight breeze feels good alongside the heat from the sun. Having something to do tomorrow, rather than sitting in my place dwelling on recent events, is lifting my spirits a bit. It's better to avoid feelings rather than actually feel them. I'm good at avoiding. I've been doing it for years.

Now, on to find something to help me avoid the rest of the day.

Four in the morning came remarkably fast, even though I went to bed at eight. I want to say I went to bed early because I am just a good reliable employee, but that wasn't the case. I didn't have many options to keep me occupied last night, so, sleep it was.

Even though I'm feeling something like a mix of grogginess and apprehension, I'm still finding myself a little excited to see what the day's events will entail. I'm going to spend the day doing something I love and get paid for it. This must be what people feel like when they love their jobs. Having never loved a job before, it's kind of exciting.

The cool morning air wakes me up from my grogginess, and I feel a little skip in my step as I head over to Beth's Bakery. The brief memory of the last time I went to work with a skip to my step crosses my mind. It was when Jared was there.

Jared. The name makes me feel all kinds of emotions. Hollow, sad, stupid, crazy, betrayed. If I saw him today, what would I say to him? Surely he's still traveling with his mom, having no idea that Brown and I know about everything. He will never know because there will be no reason to tell him. He gave me his number, and I won't be calling. I don't know if he even wanted me to call. He was probably feeling guilty for using me, and after having kissed me, he thought he would throw that out there. And if I didn't call, then at least he tried, and he didn't have to feel bad about himself. So, he will probably get everything he wants then.

I try to push him out of my mind, but then Anna comes into my head. Yesterday's avoiding is now catching up with me. That's the thing about avoiding things, they come back to haunt you.

I just wish Anna would talk to me. If we could talk, then I could tell her the whole story, make her see it was just an accident. It's even strange to me that I care really. I mean, just a short while ago, I found her to be an annoying little brat and more of a nuisance than a sister.

266

Things have changed though. Anna and I are more than sisters now, we are friends. Well, at least we were.

My life sucks. Seriously, it does.

My bout of self-pity ends quickly as I open the door to the bakery and the waft of yeasty-bread baking in my dream ovens come out in full force. One of the best smells in the world, in my opinion. And just like that, all the depressing thoughts I had on my walk here easily go back to being avoided.

Banging of pans, mixers, and chatter come from the kitchen. I walk toward the door, the apprehension back. Why do I hate change so much? I should really get some therapy.

"Hello?" I say hesitantly as I walk in the kitchen.

"Julia! Welcome!" Beth says, a little too brightly for five o'clock in the morning. She must be a morning person. I suppose I will have to learn to be one too if I'm going to work here.

She gestures for me to come over to where she is. "Gals, I want you to meet Julia. She is the one I was telling you about—the one who made the creampuffs." At Beth's comment, the two other women in the kitchen smile brightly and make comments, talking over each other about how they are so excited to try my creations, and they've heard so many good things about me.

Beth introduces them. Patti, a brunette with big hair and a thick southern accent is probably in her late fifties, and Debbie, a redhead with freckles, looks like she might be in her late forties. They both welcome me repeatedly as if they are trying to one-up each other with their welcoming (it gets a little awkward).

"Come to my office for a sec," Beth says, leading me to the back of the bakery and into her cluttered office. "We need to do some paperwork and get you all set up with your uniform." The uniform being a black t-shirt with Beth's Bakery logo on it and jeans. On the back of the shirt, it says, "You are what you eat, so eat something sweet." How freaking cute is that? And jeans and a t-shirt at work? I could get used to this.

After filling out paper work, Beth takes me to the kitchen and has me start working on recreating my creampuffs, they will be the special today. I hope they turn out the way she remembered.

I get right to work making the choux dough. It takes me a bit to get acclimated with the kitchen, nothing is where I would put it. The ladies are super helpful and kind. It's such a different feeling here. No politics. Nothing to gossip about, at least not work-related. Patti and Debbie seem to have a lot to talk about. I don't offer much as I quietly work.

The morning goes quickly. It feels like it's only been minutes when Beth announces that it's opening time. We clean ourselves up and head out to the front of the bakery and get everything ready for the morning crowd. Doors open at seven-thirty, and there are already a few people gathering outside waiting for Beth to open. Regulars, so I am told. Apparently, every morning there are always a few people waiting outside patiently to get their morning coffee and whatever pastries and baked goods Beth and the girls have created that day.

Today, there are scones: lemon-blueberry, almond, and orange-cranberry. I want to eat them all myself, they look so good. There are also bagels, assorted muffins, and croissants. This is just for the breakfast rush. For the lunch rush, we do sandwiches and different salads, plus yummy desserts.

While Beth and Debbie work the front of the bakery, Patti and I work in the kitchen making toffee bars, different kinds of cookies I'm told are the size of your face, and, of course, the cream puffs. Patti focuses on the toffee bars and the cookies while I keep working on the cream puffs. It's hard to believe these women can create as much as they do; they are all so fast and efficient. I have much to learn.

I work hard on finishing the creampuffs before the lunch rush. I had to remake the custard three times after scalding it twice. I'm not used to the gas burners yet. They turn out perfect, despite my few setbacks. I leave half plain and dip the other half in chocolate. Patti and I sample one of each, and she gushes over them.

As it turns out, the cream puffs are a hit in the front of the bakery as well. In fact, they sold out, which was quite exciting. People paying money for my creations. It made me feel good… special, even.

I never got the chance to work in the front of the bakery and, to be honest, I kind of liked it that way. Working in the front would take me away from the kitchen. And the kitchen is totally where I belong.

After clean-up and prep for the next day, we close the doors at three in the afternoon. That was it. My first day at the bakery and I'm done at three in the afternoon with all this time on my hands. If I had any kind of social life, this would be the perfect job. Except for the getting up ridiculously early part… that would not be so good.

As I walk back to my place I feel, I don't know, kind of fulfilled? Like this is the job. *The* job that I was always meant to do. It's the perfect fit for me. Why can't the pay be any better? Even after I find another job, I wonder if Beth will let me come in at nights and work for her. It's hard to believe I would even be thinking about this only after my first day, but it's how I feel. I belong here. It's nice to feel like I belong somewhere.

# CHAPTER 14

I've been at the bakery for a whole week now, and I love it. I mean, I really, really love it. Like I would marry it if it were legal to marry a bakery. It's depressing we close so early; I would stay even later if I could. And that is a sentence I would have never said at Spectraltech. Ever.

I've learned so much already. Beth, Patti, and Debbie are overflowing with information and love to share their knowledge. I have been like a sponge, learning anything and everything I can about the bakery business. I now can make the most perfect melt-in-your-mouth croissants. They're a super big pain in the butt, but they are incredible. I thought the recipe I was using was good. Beth's recipe puts that one to shame. The technique also has a lot to do with it, and to have all the necessary tools at my disposal makes me want to cry happy tears. I heart this bakery and this job. I hate how it's only temporary. I never want to go back to sitting at a desk again. But to live, I must.

I figured it out, and with the pay from the bakery and my severance, I can stretch it out for a couple months before I have to go back to real work, sitting at a stupid desk. I've been looking here and there, but not too seriously. I did finally update my resume, and that was a step in the right direction, I suppose. Well, that's what Lennon said anyway when he was checking up on me.

As far as jobs go, there's not much out there. That's the sad truth. The job market sucks right now. I may be slightly using that as my excuse for not diligently looking though, especially when my dad asks me for an update about how my job search is going.

Anna is still ignoring me. The longer we go without talking, the more I'm starting to question why I even considered her a friend. I mean, this is ridiculous. I didn't ruin her life. She may think that, but she ruined her own life. The truth would have come out eventually. If anything, I helped her. I sped up the process. My parents won't talk to me about it, they're so tight-lipped. They keep telling me I need to talk to Anna. I tell them I've tried, but she won't respond. Whatever, I can move on and find myself another sister. Well, someone to take her place anyway.

I just finished work and am now walking back to my place. Today was actually a tiny bit stressful. The first time I've felt a smidgeon of real stress at the bakery. We had an exceptionally large rush during lunch, and I even had to come out of the kitchen and help. I had no idea what I was doing, but the girls were patient with me, and even though I messed up a couple orders, I think I did pretty well. Still, working the front is not my favorite thing.

My phone rings and I look to see who it is. Brown. She probably has some gossip for me. Occasionally, when the timing works out, she calls me from a smoke break so she can update me on whatever is going on at Spectraltech. I still enjoy hearing the gossip, even if I'm no longer a part of it all.

"Hey, Brown," I say as I press answer and put the phone up to my ear.

"Hey nerd, we need to talk," she says quickly and rushed.

"Sure, I'm just walking home. What's up?"

"No, I mean in person. What are you doing tonight?"

"Um, nothing? What else would I be doing?"

"Okay, good. Meet me at that bar on Fifteenth at seven, okay?"

"Okay," I say slowly and reluctantly, "what's this all about?"

"Can't talk right now, just meet me later," she says and then hangs up.

What the heck was that all about? Suddenly my nerves get the best of me. Why couldn't she just tell me on the phone? What if something happened at Spectraltech? What if they think Brown and I took too many breaks and now they want to sue us for our salaries or something? What if I am being implicated in Mr. Nguyen's junk, whatever that may be? My heart pounds a little in my chest with worry.

See? This is why you work in a bakery and not an office. No office politics, no backstabbing, or using people to get what you want. It's all just what it is—honest work. I do not miss working in an office at all. I can't believe that soon I'll have to go back to it.

At seven on the dot, I arrive at the bar on Fifteenth and Brown is already there, waiting for me. She's on the phone, so she motions for me to take the seat next to her. I flag the bartender and order a soda while I wait for her to finish her conversation.

I try not to eavesdrop, but I can't help but catch bits and pieces of her phone call. Since I can only hear her side, it's kind of hard to piece together what she's talking about. So far I've heard the words, "nothing officially planned yet, "super excited," "can't believe it." Well, whatever it is, it's not about Spectraltech. Those are not sentences one would use when talking about that place.

"Hey, Jules," she says as she finally ends her call. She has a huge smile on her face. Actually, it's a bit odd for Brown to be smiling this big.

She kind of looks ridiculous. I can't help but smile back at her, it's contagious.

"What's going on?" I ask, giggling slightly at her grin.

"Oh nothing, just talking to my mom," she says, still smiling and doing something weird with her hand. She keeps kind of waving it around, but not in my face. More like lower by the bar so I can see her…

"You're engaged?" I say loudly and more in the form of a question than I intended.

"Yep!" She does little bounces in her seat. She is down-right giddy, and this is totally weird for Brown. She doesn't get giddy about much. Minus some good, juicy gossip.

"You're engaged!" I say with more excitement this time. And then I too join in on the bouncing in the seat. "When? When did Matt propose?" I grab her hand to look at the ring.

"Last night. It was amazing! Totally out of the blue, I had no idea."

"Liar!" I say after I see her smirk at me. The same smirk she gives when holding back juicy information.

"Oh okay, I kind of knew. But still, it was slightly surprising. Can you believe it? I'm getting married!" She bounces again in her seat like a little girl.

"So, when? When is it happening?"

"Don't know yet, but Jules?" She grabs my hand in hers, "I want you to be one of my bridesmaids."

"Really?" My eyes tear up just a bit at that. I'm actually a little shocked they do. But it makes me realize I am so grateful for Brown's friendship. After recent events, she's the only friend I have really.

"Yes, of course! You must be there." She winks at me.

"So, why couldn't you tell me this over the phone today?" I wonder why she had to do it in person. I mean, I know she wants to show off the ring, but she seemed a little too serious, not giddy like she is now.

"Well, I wanted to show you the ring of course, but that's not the real reason I called you to meet. Jared called me today." She looks me in the eyes, looking for a reaction.

My heart does a little flutter when I hear his name, which is so rude of my heart because, clearly, I hate Jared. My mind is made up about that. Apparently, my heart has not gotten the memo.

"What did *he* want?" I ask, the engagement giddiness suddenly gone.

"Well, at first I didn't give him a chance to say. When I answered the phone, I was really shocked to hear his voice on the other line. Like, why the hell is *he* calling? He's got some nerve, you know? But then I remembered he had no idea we know about him. So, at first, I played coy, not letting on."

"So, why did he call?" I ask anxiously.

"Well, he called... looking for you, actually." She searches my face again.

"For me? Why?" I shake my head at this information, it's confusing.

"He said he wanted to talk to you, but never got your number. He thought you would've called him by now because I guess he gave you his?" She gives me the look that she uses when I've neglected to share information with her.

I roll my eyes. "Yes, he sent me an e-mail right before I left Spectraltech, telling me he was going on vacation but to call him in two weeks when he got back." I give her a look that says "Are you happy now?"

Satisfied, she goes on. "So anyway, at this point, I asked him why he thought you would even want to talk to him after what he did." She pauses to take a sip of her drink.

"Go on..." I say, my interest at a fever-pitch.

"He seemed confused at first, obviously, but then I just laid into him. I told him we know who he is and what he does for a living. That he used us for information and that he's a liar, and he totally betrayed us. Then, I think I threw in a 'rot in hell' and I hung up on him."

My eyes are bugging out of my head at this point. I'm so glad Brown was the first to talk to him. If it had been me, I would have sheepishly said something like "You're a big meany-pants," or something ridiculous like that. I'm not very

277

good with confrontation. I get all tongue-tied, and it's not pretty. Brown, on the other hand, says exactly what she means. I wish I had that skill.

"So, that was it?" I ask still reeling that he called her, still not believing he was asking about me. Why would he be asking for me?

"No. He called back." She takes another sip of her drink.

I slap her lightly on the arm with the back of my hand. "He did? Tell me what he said!" I say a little too loudly.

"Well, first he was pretty pissed I hung up on him, and didn't give him a chance to explain. I told him there was nothing he could say, nothing would change what he did. So, he didn't try to explain. Then, he tried to find out who told me, but I wouldn't tell him. Then, he started asking more questions about you."

"About me?" I furrow my brow. "Like what?"

"He asked how you were doing, if you were okay. I told him you were doing fine, no thanks to him. He told me he really wanted to talk to you, to explain. But I told him you wouldn't want to speak to him. He wouldn't let up, but I never gave in, obviously. He then asked me to pass on a message to you and tell you to please call him. So, I'm passing the message on to you." She cocks her head slightly to the side as she looks at me.

We sit in silence for a moment as I take in all

she just told me. My heart is racing, and my head is reeling. Why would he want to talk to me? I don't get it. Part of me wants to call him, to say something to him about how horribly used he made me feel. The other more rational part just wants to let it go. Be done with it.

"You're not going to call him, are you?" She asks, most likely responding to the conflicting look on my face.

"No! Of course not..." I trail off, shaking my head. "I just don't understand why he wants to talk to me."

"I don't know. Maybe he just wants to see how you were doing after everything." She looks down at her ring, the diamond sparkling brightly as it reflects off one of the pendant lights hanging above us.

"Yah, well, he doesn't get to know how I'm doing," I say, sitting up straight in my chair, feeling defiant. "I won't give him the satisfaction."

Brown smiles slightly at me. "You want to call him, don't you?"

"No! Of course, I don't. I don't have anything to say to him. And he can't say anything to me to make up for everything that happened," I say, feeling defensive.

"Well," she pauses as she reaches into the pocket of her suit jacket and gets out a pink piece of paper, "I said I would give you the message, so here it is." She slides it across the bar to where I'm sitting.

I stare at the paper for a moment. A message from Jared, for me. For some reason, it feels even more real on paper instead of just from Brown's mouth. My heart betrays me yet again as it flutters at the thought of talking to him. Even if it is to rip him a new one. My brain, however, reminds me that even if I could muster up enough confidence to tell him off, what good would it actually do? I doubt it would make me feel better.

I pick up the pink piece of paper, rip it into pieces, and then put it in my empty glass. *That* is what his message means to me.

"That's my girl," Brown says smiling. "He doesn't deserve the chance to talk to you."

"You're right. He doesn't," I say flatly, coldly.

Brown grabs her purse off the bar and stands up. "Well, I better go. I've got wedding plans to start," she says, giddiness creeping back into her voice.

"I better get going myself. I have to be up at four in the morning," I say, making a sour face. The mornings are still rough for me.

"Ew, I had no idea you had to get up that early." She makes a sour face back.

"Yes, it's what we bakers do," I say and smile slightly. I'm a baker. I like calling myself that.

"Well, good luck with all that. Call you tomorrow." She gives me a half hug and then heads toward the door, purse swinging in her hand.

I sit at the bar for a minute, staring at the ripped up pink paper in my drink glass. The truth is I don't even need the message, his number is still saved in my phone. I could still call him if I wanted to and tell him what I honestly think about him.

I pull my phone out of my purse and scan down my contacts until I see his name: Jared Moody. Then, I click the edit contact button and press delete.

There. Now Jared is out of my life for good.

# CHAPTER 15

So, I just lied to my dad once again. I'm getting pretty good at this lying thing. Which is a bad thing, right? It is, I know it is. But he called tonight as he has been doing practically every night for the past three weeks (since I started working at the bakery), to see how my job search is going. And well, to put it simply, it's not.

I'm just so busy at the bakery, and then when I get home I'm so exhausted. The last thing I want to do is look for a job. The bakery is closed on the weekends (not enough business to stay open), so I always think I will focus on it then. But then it's the weekend, and I have other things I need to do.

The truth is I don't want to work at a real job again. I can't. Now that I have tasted what it's like to actually enjoy my job, I can't go back. I have to stay at the bakery. I did the numbers, and if I sell my car, which I don't actually need right now since I walk everywhere, and if I'm extremely careful about not going out to eat, or shopping for clothes, I could survive... barely. I also could get a job on the weekends to supplement. That would mean no social life at all, but who am I kidding? I haven't had a social life in over ten years, why start now.

My dad knows where I am going with this, he's no dummy. He knows that the longer it takes me to find another job like I had at Spectraltech, the more I will be sucked into the baking world and never come out. So, he has taken it upon himself to make sure this doesn't happen by calling nearly every night, gauging my job hunt desire/success.

So, I told him, as I do every night he calls, that I have been looking, and there isn't much. But something will come up soon, I'm sure of it. Soon, I'm sure, he will sick Lennon on me (who laid off me once my resume was updated to his standards).

It's slightly true, the times I have looked, there just isn't much out there. I feel bad for the people in the same boat as me, but have families to provide for. I only have Charlie and myself.

Yep, it's just me and my cat. My spinsterly life in the making. I've actually been trying not to refer to myself as a spinster lately. I've been trying to push it out of my head. Before when I said it, I wasn't actually thinking it would be my future. I feared it would be, but I didn't honestly believe it. But now it feels real. It will be me and Charlie, together forever... Or Charlie II, Charlie III, and so on. Who knows, I might have to get a couple more cats just to keep us company. Anyway, I think I am in the acceptance phase now. Before was the denial phase, now I am embracing it, no longer fighting it.

I've been going to bed early these last few weeks since I started at the bakery. It solves many problems. Most importantly, going to bed early makes it so I'm not a complete zombie when I get up in the morning to go to work. Second on the list of importance, if I go to bed early, then I don't have to remember Spectraltech and Jared. The nighttime, when I am totally alone, is when it comes creeping back into my head like dark slow-moving clouds. Sleep helps me not to go there. I can keep pushing those memories back, and soon they'll fade and won't haunt me like they still do.

I'm excited for tomorrow at the bakery; I am going to make Pithiviers. Beth has actually tasted them in Paris and so I'm feeling a little intimidated that mine won't be as good, but I am willing to risk it. I know I've said it before, but it feels fantastic to love what I do. It really, really does. I'm glad to have one positive thing in my life.

I guess the ladies I work with are also a pretty positive thing. Beth has become like a pseudo parent type, taking me under her wing. She's very mothering by nature, which is why she makes a perfect bakery owner. She puts a lot of love into her work. Patti and Debbie are hilarious and make me laugh with their crazy notions of things. Patti especially, with her southern background and thick accent, she keeps me laughing all day. She has these ridiculous southern sayings that she's always using, and I rarely understand them. Stuff like: "Why are you smilin' like a goat in a briar patch?" or "Don't stand there like you're bein' milked," and my favorite one so far, "Excuses are like backsides. Everybody's got one, and they all stink."

My accounting background has come in handy at the bakery, actually. I've been helping Beth with her books, and I'm surprised I enjoy it. I guess even doing accounting at the bakery is fun. Maybe it was just Spectraltech all along sucking the life out of me, not my actual job. No, it was both. Well, whatever, it's gratifying to be able to be multifaceted at the bakery and I know Beth appreciates it.

It feels good to be needed and appreciated.

The bread baking in the ovens blasts me as I walk into the bakery the next morning. I will never tire of that smell, ever. It's on my top ten list of the best smells in the world. I actually don't have a top ten list of smells I love, but if I did, it would be on it.

"Well, look what the cat dragged in," Patti says in her thick southern drawl, looking up at me as she's rolling out the dough for the scones.

"Sorry ladies, hit the snooze too many times,"

I say and blush a little. I have yet to be late to the bakery, and I am feeling a little self-conscious about it.

I probably do look like something the cat dragged in. I didn't have much time to get myself ready. I just saw the time and jumped out of bed, threw on my tee-shirt and jeans (which seriously needed to be cleaned) and ran here as fast as I could. It's a good thing I mainly stay in the back, so no one sees me anyway.

"No worries, darlin'." She winks at me. "Happens to us all. Besides, Beth ain't even here yet."

"You better get working on those Pithi-whatevers," Debbie throws out from behind the giant KitchenAid. "I'm excited to try them."

I put on my apron and get to work. Somehow I have become the person in charge of creating the daily special. It's fantastic because I get to do whatever I want and try out new recipes. So far, everything has been a hit and has totally sold out. I am always amazed when Beth makes the announcement that the "Jules' Special" is sold out. That's what she calls it — the "Jules' Special." She even made a little sign and displays it by my daily creations. Every day I like to sneak out of the kitchen before the lunch rush comes and look at my baked goodies in the display case, with my name attached to it. Makes me feel, I don't know, proud? I haven't had too much to feel proud about in my life. It's a good feeling. Strike that. It's a great feeling.

The morning goes as fast as it usually does. Beth shows up around six thirty, which is odd for her. She is usually here from open to close. Patti and Debbie are always here early in the morning, but leave just after the lunch rush. I'm supposed to go at that time as well, but I always end up staying and helping Beth with the preparations for the next day. She doesn't give us a reason for why she is late; she just jumps right in and starts helping us get everything done.

We get the front of the bakery set up for the morning customers, and then, as usual, Patti and I head to the back to get ready for lunch. In the state I'm in, I'm glad I will be in the back of the kitchen today where I belong. I saw myself in the bathroom mirror earlier, and it was a frightful sight. Hair pulled back in a ratty bun on top of my head, no makeup at all. I've actually been trying to make myself look somewhat presentable since I've been working here. I'm not sure why, I guess I've become accustomed to how I look with makeup on now, so I'm just sticking with it. Not today, though. Today I definitely look like something the cat dragged in.

I can hear chatter coming from the front, which means the doors are open and the regulars are filtering in, getting their daily coffee and pastry fix. I stay in the back, working on my

Pithiviers and getting the bread loaves sliced and ready for the lunch rush. I just adore how even the mundane things, like slicing bread, are actually things I enjoy doing. There isn't one single part of working in a bakery I don't love. Even the clean-up. I love to see the kitchen clean, the days' work wiped away, ready for the next day. Each day is different, no continuing project to take with me from day to day.

Patti and I are baking away, and she's in the midst of telling me some story about her crazy dog that had chased a squirrel into the house, when Debbie comes in the kitchen. "You're wanted up front, Julia," she says, pointing toward the swinging door leading to the front of the bakery.

"Me? Why?" I ask, wiping my flour-covered hands on a towel.

"Somebody asked for ya." She raises her eyebrows in my direction.

I scowl. Who the heck is here? Who would come see me at the bakery? Then it dawns on me, it has to be my dad. He's been threatening to visit me. I sigh to myself, but then get a little tingle of excitement. Perhaps seeing with his eyes how happy this all makes me, he might get off my back about finding a job. Even if just for a little while.

I walk out of the kitchen and look around a bit, but I don't see him. "Someone's here to see me?" I ask Beth as she gives a customer change.

She doesn't say anything, she just points over to the corner of the bakery.

Sitting in a leather chair in the corner in perfectly pressed pants and a blue shirt is... Jared. My heart drops into my stomach.

He's looking away, out the window, so he doesn't see me. I start to back up, trying to escape back into the kitchen. I'll just send Patti out to make up an excuse. I don't want to see him, ever. And especially now, in the slept-in state I'm in.

"Julia," he says my name as he sees me trying to escape. He stands up and comes toward me, the counter being the only thing between us as he closes in.

I look around the room, nervous. I'm suddenly extra cold and my hands clammy. I don't have a speech ready. Normally, I would have a speech ready because I would have replayed this moment a million times in my head: Seeing Jared again. But I didn't think I would ever see him again, and I've worked so desperately hard not to think about him, and now I'm speech-less. No freaking speech. Why *am* I seeing him again? How did he find me?

"What are you doing here?" I ask as he comes up to the counter.

"I wanted to talk to you," he says, a serious look on his face.

"We don't have anything to talk about," I say, and then bite on my lower lip nervously.

"Jules, come on. Just let me explain." He holds his hands out in a pleading way.

"What? Oh no, you're not allowed to call me Jules. Only my friends can call me that. And you0... well, I don't even know what you are or who are you for that matter." I pause, sucking in a deep breath. I'm confronting Jared. I'm actually doing it with a bit of a backbone and no prepared speech. This is new for me. "Anyway, what is there to explain? You used me and then helped me lose my job."

I fold my arms and stand there. Jared takes a moment, maybe trying to gather his thoughts or something. I'm not sure what he was expecting to find when he saw me, probably the co-dependent, subservient person I used to be. Well, things have change, all thanks to him really. I'm now cold-hearted and hate-filled.

"How did you even find me, anyway?" I say, breaking the silence.

"Brown told me."

Brown told him? Why would Brown tell him where I am? I'm so gonna punch her in the face.

"Julia, look, can't you just hear me out? Just go to dinner with me tonight. Let me explain everything, and then you can go back to hating me." He looks me in the eyes with his piercing blue ones and I feel my resistance waning ever-so-slightly.

I shake my head, bringing myself back. "No. There's nothing you can say to make any of it better," I say defiantly.

"How do you know that? How can you make that call when you haven't even heard my side?" He scrunches his eyes at me, frustrated.

I don't respond. I just stand there, arms folded, boldly holding my position.

"Are you serious? You really won't talk to me?"

"Well, we're talking now," I say flatly.

"Not here. We need to go somewhere quiet, not so crowded…" he trails off, looking around the customer-filled room. I glance over at Beth who is staring, open-mouthed in our direction. She quickly goes back to work when she catches my glance.

"You really won't have dinner with me?" He looks at me like I'm being ridiculous. Maybe I am, but I actually don't care.

"No." I shake my head. "It's a waste of your time and mine. There's no point. It won't change how I feel."

"You don't know that."

"I do."

"You…" He trails off, running his fingers through his hair, frustrated.

We stand there in an awkward silence. I consider walking away, leaving him there.

"Okay, fine," he finally says, giving me a smirk. "I have some time off right now, I'll just come back here every day until you agree to have dinner with me."

Oh, please. I am calling his bluff on this one. "Well, you can come back here every day if you like, but I'm still not going to dinner with you."

"Maybe. But I will see you tomorrow, anyway," he says, giving me another smirk. The feeling of wanting to slap it off his face is back in full force.

"Yah, okay. See you tomorrow," I say, rolling my eyes. Like he's actually going to come back here.

I don't even stay to see if he leaves, I just turn and go back into the kitchen, passing Debbie at the door as she comes back out to the front of the bakery. Once I'm in the kitchen, I walk over to where I was making the Pithiviers and lean with both hands on the table, looking down at my shoes, breathing deeply.

"What was all that?" Patti asks. She and Debbie must have been listening by the door. I would call them nosy little snoops, but that would be the pot calling the kettle black.

I exhale deeply. "Just some jerk I used to work with."

"So, why was he here then? I didn't get to see him, but Debbie said he was a good-lookin' fella," she says, as she walks over to the ovens to pull out the cookies she's making.

"It's... it's a long story," I say, still not believing he was here, my heart still pounding in my chest.

"Well, we got a while," she says, nodding her

head over to the clock hanging above the door. The lunch rush usually doesn't start for three more hours.

Just then, the door swings open as Debbie comes back into the kitchen. "Who was that?" she says, eyes bugging out at me.

"She's just about to tell us, ain't ya Julia." Patti gives me a look.

"Oh, okay fine. I'll tell you." It will actually be good to talk about it, tell them the whole sordid story. Maybe finally saying everything out loud, rather than keeping it bottled up inside like I've had to, will actually help me to get some closure.

So, I tell them the story while we bake. I tell them about how I first met Jared Moody. Okay, I don't actually tell them that it was under a conference table, I leave that part out. I tell them about the gossip, the flirting, the lunches, the kissing, and then the layoffs, and finally, the total deceit. They sigh and gasp at all the right parts as they both listen intently.

"Who does he think he is, coming here to talk to you like that?" Debbie says, exasperated after hearing the whole story.

"And why did that gal — Brown is it? Why did she tell him where you were?" Patti adds.

"I have no idea. But he says he's going to come here every day until I agree to go out with him," I say, rolling my eyes.

"Oh!" Debbie says, smiling slightly. "That's kind of romantic." She looks over at Patti who nods her head, agreeing.

"Ladies, did you not just hear the whole 'he betrayed me and took my job' part of the story?" I say, incensed. How did they change their minds so fast?

"Yes, but maybe you should just hear him out?" Debbie shrugs her shoulders at me. "You never know?"

"No, thank you," I say, shaking my head at the two of them. Honestly, I feel like repeating the story to them so they can get it into their thick heads. Saying it out loud, finally telling the story from beginning to end, did not give me the closure I was hoping for. Instead, it made me even madder and even more confident in my decision not to give him a chance to explain. There really is nothing to explain. Jared is a jerk. Plain and simple. I wish Anna were around, and we were talking, she would understand everything and would be on my side.

Anna, like me, would see there is nothing romantic about this. Anyway, it doesn't matter. Jared's not really going to come back here every day. He was just saying that to try to get a reaction out of me. He won't even be back tomorrow. Debbie and Patti will see and then maybe they'll understand.

# CHAPTER 16

It's been a week since Jared showed up at the bakery. And true to his word, that a-hole has shown up every single stupid day. My only reprieve was over the weekend when the bakery was closed. I figured then, with a break, he would come to his senses and leave me alone, but no such luck. He was there bright and early Monday morning, getting what has become his regular order—coffee and a scone.

Every time he comes in, either Debbie or Beth come back and announce his presence and smile slightly at me. Beth has now been brought up to speed, and the traitor joined sides with Patti and Debbie, telling me I should talk to him. I thought at least Beth would have some sense.

I just roll my eyes at them. They're all crazy, hopeless romantic types. They don't understand that this isn't romance. It's someone feeling sorry for his many grievances and trying desperately to find forgiveness. That's all it is.

I called Brown that afternoon after he came to the bakery for the first time, and demanded an explanation.

"I don't know why I told him, Jules. He wore me down. I caved," she said, guilt oozing through her tone.

She told me he called her like five times (I found out later it was only twice—clearly she is not the pillar of strength and determination she makes herself out to be). She said he kept asking her to give him my phone number so he could at least call me. She finally told him where I worked, thinking it was a good compromise and not expecting him to actually show up.

But show up, he did. I'm not really sure what I'm feeling about it. It's a bag of mixed emotions with annoyance being the main feeling. Every once in a while, my mind runs away with itself and I start to feel a little flattered by it all. Then, I have to find my center and bring myself back to reality. The one where Jared used and hurt me. As much as my mind would like to conjure up notions of grandeur and other stupid girly things that it does, I have to remember the truth. His actions are all out of guilt, nothing more.

The ladies at the bakery are all Team Jared. Every day he shows up, they get more and more pushy with me to talk to him. Beth has even made me come out and work in the front when he's there, saying she needs my "keen young eye" for the display case. Such a lie. She never needed me before. I just roll my eyes and go along with it.

Jared never tries to talk to me, though. He just

comes in and orders and then sits at the same exact table reading the newspaper and sometimes working on his computer. He obviously has no idea how to stalk someone. If he really wanted to bother me, and get under my skin, then he should be trying to get me to talk to him. But he doesn't. He smiles at me, will nod his head in my direction. I'll even catch him laughing quietly to himself when he overhears conversations that I have with other customers. I usually just scowl at him and try to mosey my way back into the kitchen, until Beth, Patti, or Debbie drag me back out to the front.

Speaking of Beth, she has been coming in later and later to the bakery. It's fine, we always seem to get everything ready on time without her. And isn't that the goal of a bakery owner? To have a team of people you trust to be able to run everything even if you aren't there? It's mostly disconcerting to Patti and Debbie who find her actions to be totally out of character. I haven't known her long enough, so I've been told (at least I think that was what Patti was trying to tell me, I didn't actually get the metaphor). To top it off, she never offers a reason why she's late, she just comes in and joins us in whatever we are doing, without a word. I asked Patti and Debbie why we don't just ask her what's going on. Patti made a disapproving clicking sound with her tongue and said something like "Ya'll get your straw out of her Kool-Aid." I found this to be funny since Patti seems to always have her "straw" in everyone else's "Kool-Aid" (ahem, the Jared situation). I'm not sure why Beth is the exception.

This morning, the bakery is especially bustling with regulars and a slew of new customers. The new business is great but also stressful. Beth was late again but got here in time for the morning rush, thank goodness.

I'm in the midst of putting fresh blueberry scones in the display case when I see Jared walk in the door. He walks right up to the counter, not seeing me because I am still kneeling down loading the scones. I could see him, though, perfectly pressed pants and all. I debate crawling back into the kitchen, but knowing that's a little over the top, I stand up instead.

"Can I help you?" I ask in my very distant I've-never-met-you voice.

He smiles when he sees me. A genuine smile, the kind that used to make my heart flutter and butterflies multiply in my stomach. I'm not going to lie; my betraying heart still flutters a little at his smile. But I suppress it and remind myself that his smile, amazing as it is, belongs to a liar and a user.

"Morning, Julia," he says, ignoring my fake distant tone.

"Do you want the regular?" I say, still playing it cool.

"You know what my regular order is?" he asks with a smirk on his face.

"Um, no. Sorry, I thought you were someone else," I say quickly, wishing I wouldn't have admitted I actually do. I don't want him thinking I care that much because I don't. I'm just good at remembering orders. One of my many useless talents.

"What can I get for you today?"

"The regular," he says flatly.

"And that is?"

"Coffee and a scone—I'll do blueberry today," he says, pointing at the fresh scones I'd just placed in the case.

I get his coffee and scone, and then point him in the direction of Beth so she can ring him up at the register.

"Thank you," he says simply.

I don't respond. I go back to the display case, arranging the remaining pastries and muffins, trying to figure out if we need to make more muffins. I decide we do, and then head back to the kitchen to start up a quick batch of almond poppy seed muffins (my favorite). I love that I can make executive decisions about what's needed, without getting the approval of Beth.

At first, I was always asking permission, not wanted to step on any toes. Beth finally told me whatever I thought we needed, I should just do it. She told me she trusted me and would let me know if I ever stepped over the line. I've worked for Beth for nearly a month now, and I've yet to find that line. It's so refreshing to work for someone like Beth. I actually feel like I'm working more for myself.

It turns out that my "young keen eye" Beth used to get me out in the front when Jared was there, is actually quite useful after all. I'm actually not too bad at counter design and display. Something I didn't know about myself. Beth is always impressed with my ideas and I've even rearranged the tables a bit in the front to make the bakery a little more Zen. Okay, I don't really know what being Zen entails, but it feels super Zen-like to me.

While I wait for the muffins to bake, I go back to the front and take an inventory of what else we might need.

I squat down so I can get a good eye of the inside of the case. I can hazily see, through the case window, Jared coming back up to the counter. I don't move. I just stay there, arranging and rearranging. I know it's ridiculous, I'm being childish. I just don't feel like talking to him again, it's tiring. With my brain reminding me to hate him, and my heart fluttering shamefully at his smile, it's an internal struggle best left avoided.

I can only see his legs as he closes in on the counter. He doesn't say my name or try to get my attention. He just puts something on the counter, then I see him turn and walk away, out the door. I wait until I hear the door shut completely before I stand up.

On the counter in front of me, condensation twinkling under the overhanging lights, is a can of Dr. Pepper. A fresh, cold Dr. Pepper.

I stare at it.

Beth comes over from the register and stares at it, too. "What's the deal with the Dr. Pepper?" she asks, pointing at the can.

"It's my favorite drink." The gesture takes me by surprise. He remembered my love of Dr. Pepper. A small, unimportant detail about me.

My heart flutters and then my brain reminds me to ignore the fluttering. I turn and head back toward the kitchen, leaving the Dr. Pepper sitting there. But then, on second thought, I turn around and grab it. No use in wasting it.

The following day, Jared comes in as usual and requests his standard order from Beth. They're on a first name basis now, the best of buddies (oh, brother). He's his annoying, charming self. Debbie gets all dreamy-eyed when she sees him, and he's always complimentary with her and she giggles like a little teenage girl. Gag. Patti, who rarely comes out to the front, has even started to be seen more when Jared is there.

I was wrong, Jared is better at stalking than I

gave him credit for. He has wormed his way into my new life pretty seamlessly. He has shown up every day like he said he would, charmed my new coworkers and boss. He's even made friends with some of the other regulars.

The morning rush has calmed a bit, and after fiddling around with the display case, Beth comes over and tells me she wants some creampuffs for the lunch rush and that I should go get started. Excited to get away from the front and back to the kitchen, I don't argue. Not that I ever would, really. The kitchen is where I belong and where I want to be.

Debbie is in the back working with Patti as I enter the kitchen which has a strong lemon smell wafting toward me. I send Debbie back to the front to help Beth, as she had asked me to do so when she ordered the creampuffs. As Debbie leaves the kitchen, I swear I catch her giving Patti a little look.

I ignore it because it's not that unusual for those two. They are always giving each other little looks.

I get to work on the creampuffs. Patti and I work in silence as I separate yolks from whites for the choux dough.

"Jared still here?" she asks, breaking the silence. She's measuring out flour for some lemon bars (hence the lemon smell in the kitchen). I made them one day for a special, and they were such a hit that we've added them to our daily desserts.

"I guess," I say and shrug, pulling down a large metal pan from the shelf above the stove.

She slams down her measuring cup on the metal table making a loud bang. "You know you're throwin' the baby out with the bathwater, don't ya?"

I scrunch my face at her. "What are you talking about?" What does she even mean? Who throws a baby out with the bathwater? That saying ranks up there with "She wants to have her cake and eat it too." Who doesn't want to eat cake if they have it? It doesn't make any sense.

"I'm sayin' you can't see the forest through the trees," she says, now pointing her measuring cup at me.

"Okay, Patti—I'm sorry. I think you're going to have to explain what you're saying in Midwestern language."

"I'm just sayin' that I think you're makin' a mistake not lettin' Jared explain himself. 'Specially after he's been comin' in here like he said he would. You might be throwing somethin' away that could be good because you can't see past the bad."

"You don't understand," I say, shaking my head. I don't know how many times I will have to repeat myself to these hopeless romantics before they actually get it. None of this is about romance.

"Oh, I understand all right," she says,

dipping the measuring cup back into the flour. "You wanna know what I think?" I don't bother answering because no matter what I say, she will still tell me anyway. "I think you don't want him to go away. I think you like seeing him every day."

"What? That's ridiculous." I scrunch my face at her. She couldn't be more wrong.

"If ya didn't want him here, then by now ya woulda let him have his say so he would leave you alone," she says, raising her eyebrows at me.

"Oh, please. That's totally not true!" I roll my eyes at her.

"Ya oughtta think about it. I mean really think about it." She shakes the measuring cup at me again.

Defiance boils inside me. "You're wrong."

"Am I?" She cocks her head to the side and purses her lips in a know-it-all way.

"Yes, you are. I'll prove it. I'll go talk to him right now," I say, standing up straight with resolve. This is actually good. I can talk to him, agree to let him explain. Even though I didn't want to give him the pleasure, at least that will get him to stop coming here, and I can finally close the door on that chapter of my life.

"You do that." She gives me a smart-aleck look.

"Fine, I will," I say, having to have the last word.

I walk out the kitchen door, still carrying the whisk I was going to use on the eggs. I spot Jared in his normal seat, working on his laptop.

"You want to talk?" I say boldly as I walk up to him, pointing my whisk at him.

He looks up from his laptop, his eyes surprised to see me and possibly alarmed at my whisk-pointing. I look down at my whisk and quickly put it behind my back.

"Fine. I'll go to dinner with you," I say flatly.

He smiles slightly. He's won. He wore me down. But not really because I'm just letting him explain so he can get this off his chest and we can all move on. And then I can prove to Patti and the others that I don't need Jared to come in here every day. I need him to go away. I need to be done with all of this and move on. So really, I will be the winner here.

"Okay, how about tonight?" he asks, slightly ruffled. He was not expecting me to come up to him like I did. I've unnerved him a little. It feels kind of good to have an upper-hand.

"Fine. Pick me up at six-thirty," I say, keeping up with my upper-hand. "Actually, no, I'll meet you at the Paramount Café on Sixteenth at six-thirty," I add quickly, not wanting this to sound anything like a date because it is certainly not.

"I'll be there," he says, picking up his coffee and sipping it. I stand there looking at him. I'm not sure what I expected. I guess I thought now that he'd gotten what he wanted he would pick up his stuff and leave. But he looks like he has no intention of leaving. So, I about-face, and my whisk and I head back to the kitchen.

Just before I turn to go through the door that leads to the kitchen, I see Debbie give Beth a little high-five in my peripheral vision.

Realization dawns on me rapidly: Beth wanting me to leave the front to make creampuffs... the out of the blue, jump-down-my-throat conversation I had with Patti... the conspiratorial look Debbie gave Patti as she left the kitchen. Those three nosy little witches! They bamboozled me. I can't believe it. Actually, I can. But how did I fall for it so easily? I should've seen the signs.

Whatever. It needed to happen, regardless of how it did. I'm just glad tonight Jared can free himself of his guilt, and I can go on with my life and not have his face show up every day to remind me of my old existence. Jared Moody will finally be out of my life.

Surprisingly, a little spark of sadness touches me as I come to the realization. I quickly push it out. This is what I want. Closure is what I need.

Beth and I work mostly in silence as we clean up and get the kitchen ready for tomorrow. I know I've said it before, but I love making the kitchen sparkle. The smell of bleach washing away everything we made today, giving a clean slate for everything we will make tomorrow.

Beth stops and looks around the kitchen, leaning on the mop she's using to clean the floors. A sudden look of sadness crosses her face.

"Everything okay?" I ask, looking at her, concerned.

"Yah, just a little melancholy, I guess." She smiles slightly at me.

"Why are you melancholy?" I ask, curious.

She sighs heavily. "Can I tell you something that you have to promise you won't repeat to Debbie and Patti? At least, not until I've had a chance to tell them myself."

"Sure, of course," I say, feeling a slight twinge of nervousness. It often seems to go wrong for me when someone asks me to keep a secret.

"I'm selling the bakery." She smiles sadly at me.

"What? No!" I say, louder than I expected. Sickness instantly balling in my stomach.

"It's time," she says sadly. "Time for me to spend more time with my husband, my grandbabies. I love this place, but I think it's time for me to move on. That's why I've been coming in late. I've been discussing things with my husband, trying to figure out what to do."

"What does that mean for Debbie, Patti, and I?" I ask. I want to be more supportive of her, but I can't help my selfishness. I just found a workplace I love, and now it might go away.

"I don't know. I guess it depends on who buys the place," she says and sniffs slightly. She starts mopping the floor again.

I look around the kitchen. Is this all suddenly going to go away? Now that I've found a place to work where I feel like I belong — where I actually feel useful? "When are you going to sell it?" I ask, hoping she will take her time and then maybe during the process she might end up changing her mind.

"I promised my husband I would put it on the market next week," she says, concentrating on the mopping, not making eye contact with me.

"Next week? So soon?" My heart sinks into my stomach. "Who do you think will buy it?" Maybe it will be someone who just wants to keep things the way they are instead of turning it into something else. It's not like the formula we are using now isn't working. In fact, the bakery is doing better than ever.

"Not sure. Could be anyone, really." My heart sinks even further when she says this. I was hoping she would say that she wouldn't settle for less than anyone who would keep things the way they are. This bakery is her baby, after all. Why would she want to sell it to just anyone?

We continue cleaning-up, with me quietly contemplating. What would I do if someone comes in and changes this place to something completely different like a full service restaurant or something? I could hope maybe I would stay on making desserts. But I'm not even a real certified chef. Beth accepted that about me, would the next owner be willing to as well? And if not, then I don't know if another opportunity like this is out there, and I would be forced to get another desk job doing what I hate. I shudder at the thought. How can I go back to that life when I've had a taste of this one?

I knew this would have to end at some point though. I only have two more weeks of stretching out my severance to compensate for what I'm not making here. But I had other ideas in the works—like selling my car and possibly doing something on the weekends. Who knows if it would've worked? Maybe this will just get me back to where I should be, working for some corporate dumb-stupid-idiot-crap job. I feel ill.

"Here's a thought," Beth says, pulling me back from what could possibly start turning into a panic attack. That's where I'm pretty sure I was heading. "Why don't *you* buy it?" She looks me in the eyes, eyebrows raised.

"Me? Buy the bakery?" I look at her dubiously, like that could ever happen. How could I own a bakery?

"Well, why not?" She gives me a look like this is the best idea in the world.

"Because I don't know the first thing about running a bakery, that's why," I say, shaking my head. This is the most ridiculous idea. Me? Own a bakery?

"Oh, you could do it, Julia. Look how much you've learned in just the month you've been here." She gives me a look of confidence. I wish I had that much confidence in myself.

I shake my head. "I don't think I have what it takes, or the money for that matter."

"I think you've got what it takes, and what you don't have I could teach you. As far as the money goes, we could figure something out. Some sort of payment structure. You wouldn't have to come up with everything at once." She smiles at me, clearly excited at the thought. Maybe she *was* actually struggling with the thought of just selling it to anyone.

"I just don't think I could do it, practically or financially. I'm not a very good risk-taker, and it would be quite the risk." I look at the floor. I hate how I have never taken any risks in my life. It seems like all changes I've ever made are ones forced on me, not by choice.

"Well, you should sleep on it," she says, not giving up. "I think you would make a great owner of my bakery, probably even better than I have." She smiles brightly at me.

We finish cleaning up the rest of the kitchen. As we leave, and she is locking up the doors, Beth turns to me. "I'm really serious, Julia. Consider it. Consider buying my bakery. I think you would be great."

I don't say anything back, I just smile at her. I can't own a bakery. It's too much to wrap my spinster brain around. I'm not that kind of person. The thought of it though, even if I just recently had it, makes my heart practically jump out of my chest. It's an exhilarating thought. A dream I've never had before, but yet, it feels like it has always been a dream of mine locked up somewhere.

My phone rings and makes me jump a little, pulling me out of my trance as I walk down the street away from the bakery and toward my condo.

I look at my caller ID, and it's Anna. Anna is calling me?

"Hello?" I say, questioning if she will actually be there. It could be a miss-dial or something.

"Hey," She says plainly.

"Anna, how are you?" I say cautiously. I need to tread lightly, not sound too desperate to talk to her, even though I truly am.

"Fine." She sighs heavily.

It's quiet on the other line, and, for a second, I think we've been disconnected.

"Are you there?"

"Yah, I'm here. Look, Julia, I'm calling to tell you that I guess I'm sorry. I mean, I was pretty pissed at you for a while for your big mouth. But it's not your fault I was an idiot and messed things up. It would've come out eventually. I don't know what I was thinking. I guess I just hoped it wouldn't."

"Anna, I'm so sorry. I've wanted to talk to you so badly. I miss you." The words slip out of my mouth before I can stop myself. That ranks under the dreaded cheesy-after-school-special moments with Anna. Telling her I miss her is just a little too gag-inducing. But it's out there, and it's true.

"Yah, I've actually sort of missed you, too," she says, clearly having the same issues as me.

"So, tell me what happened," I say, wanting to know all the details about her conversation with my parents and how much information she told them.

"It's a long story. What are you doing now? Wanna go get dinner or something?"

"Yes, let's do that. Oh wait, no, I can't. I'm going out with Jared tonight. Crap," I say Jared's name with disdain.

"What? Really? So, are you two together now?" she asks, sounding excited, clearly not hearing the annoyance in my voice when I said his name.

"Oh, no. No way. There is so much I need to tell you, too. Hey, I'm not going out for a few hours, wanna come over to my place?"

"I could do that," she says, clearly intrigued by the Jared story.

"Okay, good. See you soon," I say and end the call.

I pick up speed to get back to my place. I'm

trying not to get ahead of myself, but hopefully being able to hang out with Anna and talk to her about everything will be the tiny silver lining to this pretty crappy day.

"You are kidding me, right?" Anna says exasperated after I fill her in on what happened with Jared. "He used you for gossip and then got you fired?"

"Yup," I say, nodding my head. It's so great to tell her all the details, especially right before I meet up with him because it will get me all pumped up and mad again. I really need to stick up for myself, and telling Anna the whole story is giving me the gumption to do just that. Bring on the confrontation, I'm ready.

"So, what happened after that?" she asks as she goes to my refrigerator and grabs a soda.

"So after that, I got a job at a bakery on Sixteenth Street."

"Yah, dad told me about that. How do you like it?" She takes a hefty swig of her soda and hiccups from the bubbles.

"I love it. Seriously, love it. But I found out today the owner is going to sell it," I say, remembering my conversation with Beth, and my stomach immediately starts to ball up again. I go to the fridge and grab a soda, hoping the bubbles might soothe it.

"That sucks." She frowns slightly. "So, why are you seeing Jared tonight then?" She asks, confused.

"Oh yah, forgot to tell you that part of the story. So, Brown told him where I was working after the layoffs."

"Brown told him? Why would she do that?" Her eyes widen with disbelief.

"I still don't really know. I guess he was pestering her for my number, and she thought telling him where I worked was a better idea. She was wrong. At least I could've ignored his calls. Instead, he showed up at the bakery one morning."

"And?" Anna leans toward me in her seat, needing all the details. I can't even say out loud how much I am enjoying this right now because it will put us in that cheesy category again. But I am so happy to have her back in my life.

"So, he showed up and told me he wanted to go to dinner so he could explain. And I told him no way, that there was nothing to explain. Then he said he would come back to the bakery every day to get me to agree to go out with him. I didn't believe him at first, but then he did. He's showed up every day for practically two weeks," I say and exhale deeply, letting my shoulders sag. So. Much. Drama.

"Wow. So, I take it you caved, then?" She gives me a little smirk.

"No! Well, yes, I guess I did. But I was sort of

forced into it by my coworkers at the bakery. They seem to have this crazy romantic notion of Jared, and so they did some psychological reversal Jedi-mind trick thingy. Whatever, it's fine. It needed to happen. I just need to let him explain himself, and then he can get it all off his chest and feel better about himself or whatever else he needs to do so I can be rid of him for good."

"Hmmm," Anna says contemplating. "That's interesting."

"I know, isn't it?" I agree.

"No, I mean it's interesting because guys don't really care about getting things off their chest or having some sort of closure. That's a girl thing."

"What are you saying?" I ask, confused.

"I'm saying it's not closure for him, Julia. He wouldn't go through all that trouble just to make sure you didn't hate him so he could feel better about himself." She shrugs her shoulders, displaying confidence in her knowledge of men and what they do and don't do.

"Then, why would he go through the trouble?" I scowl slightly.

"The only reason he would do that is because he cares about you. Maybe he even *looooves* you." She raises her eyebrows slightly as she looks at me.

"Oh, geez. No way," I say, shaking my head. "He doesn't care about me, not like you are

315

insinuating. And he certainly doesn't *love* me. He just cares that he hurt me and wants me to forgive him. That's all."

"Um, yah, guys don't do that," she says and raises her eyebrows at me.

I shake my head. She's wrong. Whatever guys *do*, Jared must be the exception to the rule. He's just having some guilty thing going on that he really needs to repent for, and that's it.

"Well, I guess we'll find out tonight won't we," I say, and then take a drink of my soda. "Anyway, it really doesn't matter if he cares for me. Nothing he can say will make up for what he did."

"We shall see..." she says in a little sing-song voice, clearly not believing me.

"I'm serious. There's nothing he can say. Nothing." Why is no one on my side? It's getting super annoying. "Anyway, so tell me what happened with you after I let my big mouth run off."

"Yah, thanks again for that." She smiles slightly and sarcastically. "It's not surprising what happened there. Mom and Dad confronted me, and I admitted to them it was true."

"So, you told them about using mom's info to get the credit cards, then?"

"Yep. I told them." She nods her head.

"What happened? Did they flip?" I ask, eyes bugging out of my head. I thought she would pull an Anna and conveniently leave that part out when she told them.

"Oh yah, totally. They flipped out big time."

"So, what did they do?"

"Well, it's not like they could ground me or anything. I'm sure they wanted to kick me out, but that would've been no use because what I really needed was to have a place to live cheap enough so I could earn money and pay everything off quickly. So, I'm working at Dad's firm." She takes a drink of soda.

"Dad told me you were working for him. How do you like it?"

"It's okay, not the highlight of my day." She shrugs. "But the pay is good, and, of course, Dad put me on a super crazy budget schedule to get the debt all paid off quickly. It sucks, really. I can't shop at all." She frowns.

"So, aren't you supposed to be at work right now?" I nod my head toward the clock which says four-thirty.

"I took a half day today, I had things to do like open up my very own bank account."

"Well look at you, all grown up," I say and smile slightly.

"I know, it's kind of annoying." She turns her head to stare out the window. We sit in silence for a moment and then she turns to me and smiles. "You know what we need to do?" She nods her head conspiratorially. "We need to get you all dolled up for your date tonight!"

"It's not a date," I say emphatically.

She rolls her eyes. "Well, whatever it is, you need to look hot. Nothing says revenge like totally looking like a hottie," she says and gets up from her chair.

"This is not about revenge, it's about *closure*." I point my finger at her, correcting her.

"Fine. You still need to look hot, let him see what he's really losing." She grabs my hand, pulls me to standing, and heads toward the bathroom. "Come on, let's find you something to wear."

I don't argue because when Anna gets that look in her eyes, there's no reason to try. Plus, she sort of has a point. I should look good. It will give me an edge of confidence I really need to have.

Anna goes to work, back in her element like she was when she would take me shopping for clothes. I take a shower while she goes through my closet finding me something to wear. After my shower, she plucks my eyebrows and does my makeup. I insist that I not look like a hussy, and she pouts a little at that. Her definition of made-up is a little on the hussy side to me, so she has to tame it down. Plus, I don't want Jared to think I tried too hard, like meeting him tonight all dolled up means something more to me than it does.

Once she's satisfied with the makeup, I get dressed in the outfit she picked out—a basic black skirt with a short sleeve soft pink cashmere sweater. She quickly does my hair—blowing it out with a round brush, so it falls simply and softly on my shoulders. She then takes me to the full length mirror in my room and puts me in front of it.

"Now, see how pretty you can be when you just make a little effort," she says in a smart-aleck way.

"Gee, thanks," I say as flatly as I can. I turn from side to side to get different angles. Okay, I do look good. She might be right, but I won't be telling her that.

I let out a big exhale.

"Nervous?" she asks as she flattens down my sweater in the back and does a little tweaking on my hair.

"A little, I guess." I look at myself in the mirror. "I'm just nervous about what I'll say. My mouth gets all tongue-tied at stuff like this, and I would just really like to say what I want to say."

"You'll be fine." She smiles slightly at me.

"Thanks," I say, then turn and give her a hug. It's a little awkward. Anna and I aren't really huggers. But I don't care. I'm just so glad to have her here, and it's the best way to say it without actually saying it.

"Okay, it's just past six," she says, pulling away and pointing at the clock by my bed. "You better go."

"You'll wait here until I get back so I can tell you what happened?" I ask, a slight unintended begging tone to my voice.

"Um yah, duh. I've been cut off from shopping, remember? What else is there to do?" She half-smiles.

"I won't be too long, promise." I walk toward the door and grab my purse.

"Good luck!" She opens the door and ushers me out.

I walk out the door and down the hall to the elevators. As I walk through the lobby and open the door to the street, the light breeze hits me just so, and I get a little chill. I'm a big ball of nerves right now. But at least when I get home tonight, it will be finally done.

When I arrive at the Paramount Café, it's just past six thirty. I look around the room a little to see if Jared is there yet. The hostess sees me looking and asks me if I'm Julia. I confirm, and she takes me to the back of the restaurant, to a more secluded area I've never seen before. She guides me to a half-circle corner booth where Jared is sitting, waiting for me.

I see him smile slightly at me as she ushers me toward the booth. He stands up as I take a seat on the opposite side, as far away as possible. I'm quite sure he smells good, and I do not want that to detour my thoughts.

"Hi," he says simply as I take a seat. He looks

me over, not even trying to conceal it. "You look really pretty." His smile brightens more. "Thanks for finally agreeing to dinner."

"Yah, well, I was sort of forced into it, now wasn't I." I give him a sarcastic look, the best I can muster. How times have changed. Just a few months ago, I would have been oozing lust and hanging on his every word, thrilled for the chance to spend time with him. Now, I just want to get this night over with.

The waiter approaches our table, tells us about the specials, and takes our drink orders. He leaves to get our drinks and give us time to look over our menus. Honestly, I have no intention of eating dinner. First of all, I want this night to be short. And secondly, I don't really think with all the emotions and nerves I'm feeling right now that there is any room in my stomach for food.

I pretend to look at the menu for a moment, and then I put it down on the table. "Okay, I came tonight to hear you out, so let's hear it," I say coarsely, ready to get started.

He shuts his menu and sets it down on the table, running his finger along the crease of it, deepening the fold. "Okay, yes... good." He looks up at me, eyes meeting mine. "First of all, I want to tell you I'm really sorry. I didn't expect things to turn out the way they did."

I scoff at that. "You mean, you didn't expect me to find out who you really were." I roll my eyes.

"No, I didn't want you to find out the way you did." He moves his head trying to get my eyes back on his, but I look away. "I was going to tell you."

"And how do you think I would've taken it, even if it came from you? 'Gee, Julia, remember how I pretended to gossip with you and that you were my friend. That was all a lie!'" I say, doing a pretty bad impression of a man.

He shakes his head. "It's not like that."

"Oh really, what's it like then? Because that's the way it sure seemed to me." I meet his eyes this time so he can see the disdain in mine. I'm feeling pretty good about myself right now, at least at how I've handled things so far. No tongue-tying whatsoever.

We sit in silence as the waiter drops off our drinks, and taking a cue from the obvious tension, he walks away without taking our order.

Jared runs his hands through his hair, frustrated. "Just let me explain, okay?"

I give him a slight nod with my head, "Let's hear it then."

"Yes, I was consulting for Spectraltech. The board hired me to clean house because they needed to find ways to cut spending." I flinch a little at the "clean house" comment. It's such a harsh way to talk about employees that give the better part of their life to an establishment. Like we're crumbs on a counter, wiped away with a blue envelope. "The consulting firm is my design." He continues, "As far as I know, I am the only one who does things this way."

"Go on," I say, not impressed.

"Anyway, I come into a company under the guise of a new hire. There are many statistics showing that productivity goes down greatly when employees know consultants are there. This way, the way I do things, people aren't nervous, aren't so scared that anything they say and do will get them fired. Then, I can see them actually at work, not putting on some show like they would if they knew who I really was."

"So, then you find people who know what's going on within the company and use them for info. Got it." I fold my arms.

He shakes his head at me. "It's true, I do need to know what's going on in the company I'm consulting for, and it's also true that there are certain people who tend to know these things — gossips. There are some in every company."

"So, then people like Brown and I basically do your job for you." I frown, annoyed that there are people like us in every company. How unoriginal of us.

"Not really. I can't take what I hear as gospel. I have to check it out myself — but it helps me get on the right path," he says, leaning back against the booth.

Suddenly, a flash of relief washes over me. I'd

been beating myself up for so long now, thinking Jared had taken everything Brown and I said literally, instead of as speculation, which is a lot of what gossip is. I had so much guilt that I might have inadvertently gotten someone laid off who shouldn't have been. All of the sudden, I feel lighter, my shoulders a little less tense. It doesn't change the fact that he lied to me and used me for information, though. That part is still the same.

"So," Jared says bringing my attention back to him, "then once I have a list of people I think are redundant, I present the list to the board. They go over it as well and once they all come to an agreement, they do the layoffs, including me in the mix. Then, no one is the wiser." He looks down at his hands.

"Okay, got it. Thanks for the explanation," I say, starting to edge out from my seat.

"Julia, wait. We aren't done," he says, frustrated.

"I don't really know what else you can tell me," I say, scowling at him.

"Don't you want to know why you were on the list?" he asks.

"What's the point?" I shrug my shoulders.

"Just… just hear me out, okay?" He puts his hand through his hair again. "My gosh, you are so frustrating." He shakes his head, closing his eyes briefly.

"Fine. Go ahead," I say, and exhale deeply.

What could he possibly say that will make me change my mind about him? There's really nothing.

"So, after a while, after spending time with you, I started to feel bad about everything, about not being totally honest with you. I guess... I don't know—it's never happened before. I didn't feel bad about Brown, I couldn't care less what she thinks about me. But you, for some reason I cared what you thought." He pauses letting the words seep in. And they do. I try to shake them off, but I'm finding it difficult.

"So then, if you cared what I thought, then why did you put me on the list of layoffs?" I ask, bringing myself back to where I need to be — mad.

Jared looks down at his hands. "When I made the list, I was up all night going over everything." He looks up, making contact with my eyes. "You kept going through my head. Calhoun had told me that due to everything going on with Nguyen, they were going to revamp that department. He wanted to keep you on, though—but put you in another department. I assume it had to do something with your baked goods." He flashes me a small smile, and then quickly a serious look comes back to his face. "But I talked him out of it."

"Why? Why did you talk him out of it?" I say, anger rising in my face.

"Because you're better than that place, Julia.

You are. You deserve better," he says, looking me in the eyes.

"Who are you to decide what I deserve?" I ask, incensed.

"Well, I guess I don't have any right to decide what you deserve." He shrugs his shoulders slightly. "But let me ask you, are you happier now? Are you happier away from Spectraltech? Do you miss it?" He looks me in the eyes, searching.

I look away from him, down at my hands sitting in my lap. I don't even have to contemplate his questions. I *am* happier. I've never been happier with a job than I am now. I do not miss Spectraltech, not even remotely. In fact, if they asked me to go back right now I would give them a big resounding no.

"You are happier now. I know you are. I've seen you at the bakery. You're in your element there." I look up at him and meet his eyes.

I sigh. "Okay, fine. I am happier at the bakery." His eyes brighten, hearing me admit it. "But that still doesn't mean you had any right to make those kinds of decisions for me."

"You're right. I didn't have any right. I took a chance, went with my gut. I'm sorry, it wasn't my place." He shakes his head. "But if I hadn't then you would still be back at Spectraltech. Taking smoke breaks with Brown, trying to find excuses to do anything but work." He gives me a small smile.

I look down at my hands again, now twiddling nervously in my lap. He's right, he didn't have any right to do what he did. But if he hadn't gone with his gut, I would still be back at Spectraltech, miserable.

I sigh heavily. "It doesn't matter much at this point, though. Beth is putting the bakery up for sale next week," I say and slouch in the seat, sadness balling in my stomach as I contemplate life without the bakery.

"Why would she do that? With business picking up like it is?" He furrows his brow.

"She said she needed to spend more time with family… And how did you know business has been picking up?" I look at him confused. He hasn't been coming to the bakery long enough to see how much business has grown. Actually, if I think about it, business started to really pick up only after Jared started coming in every day.

"Well," he looks down at his hands resting in his lap, "I did a little social media marketing for you guys."

"How's that?" I say scrunching my face. I have no idea what he means.

"I tweeted about the bakery." He looks up and gives me little smile.

"You what-ed?" I ask, still confused.

"You know, tweeted… on Twitter?"

"Oh, yah. Okay… Twitter. Got it. I didn't know tweeting was part of Twitter." I look down at the table, feeling silly for my lack of social media knowledge.

"Anyway, I have a pretty large following of people in the downtown area that I post information to. Business stats, growing trends, things like that. Anonymously, of course. So I thought I would see if I might help you guys out by posting about the bakery. It appears to have worked," he says, looking a little proud of himself.

I probably should feel happy for his help, but instead I feel like he is being overly smug about his masterful twittering skills, or whatever you call it.

"Gee, and all this time I thought it was my daily special bringing in the business," I say and give him a thin, bratty smile. "Looks like you saved the day at the bakery too, just like you thought you did at Spectraltech."

"Wait... what? Are you mad that I posted about the bakery? Geez, Julia. I was only trying to help." He furrows his eyebrows at me, the frustration creeping back.

My shoulders slouch, down-trodden. I am being so petty. I'm not a petty person, at least I never thought of myself as one. It doesn't feel right on me. "No... sorry. You're right. You were just trying to help," I say but don't look at him. "Thanks for doing that. Anyway, I guess it was all for naught since the bakery probably won't be around much longer."

"I still don't understand why Beth wants to sell. Doesn't she like it?" Jared looks at me, disappointment on his face.

"No, she *loves* it. I don't think she truly wants to sell the bakery. I get the idea that her husband wants her around more and wants her to sell. I think she'll be devastated to sell it to someone who wants to make it into something else. She had this crazy notion I should buy it." I shake my head, rolling my eyes.

"Julia... That is a great idea. You should do it." He leans in toward me, a serious look on his face.

"Me? Oh, please, that's not going to happen." I fold my arms and lean back in my seat.

"Why not?"

"Because I wouldn't know how to run a bakery. I'm just not the kind of person who owns a business."

"Do you even hear yourself? You never give yourself any credit." He looks at me, aggravation on his face and in his tone.

"Why would I? Anything I've ever done in my life has practically been forced on me. I don't do big changes on my own." I look away from him. How is it that everyone cannot see this about me?

"So, then do something on your own. Make a change."

"Yes, well, that's something probably easy for you to do. Not me."

We sit in silence for a minute, maybe he's finally conceding to the truth. I am just not the type of person to own a business. It's not in me.

"You should do it, Julia. Take a chance," he says, ending the silence, his eyes searching for mine. I look away. I don't know how other people have so much more faith in me than I do. True, owning the bakery would probably be the most amazing thing in the world, but I know myself. I know my limits.

"Anyway, that's not the reason we are here tonight," I say, changing the subject back to our original topic.

"Right, right..." he drifts off, clearly having a hard time transitioning back.

He sits up straight in his seat and clears his throat. "So, knowing what you know about me and the whole Spectraltech thing now... do you think you can look past it all and maybe forgive me?" He swallows hard. It's probably hard for someone like Jared Moody to ask someone for forgiveness.

"I don't know..." I say quietly, looking away from him. "It's just that, I feel like I don't even know you, you know?"

"Julia." He leans his body into the table, toward me. "You know me. You do. Everything I told you about me, it was all true."

"But there was a big part—a huge part—that wasn't true. I don't know if I can get past that. Maybe I can..." I look down at my hands, indecisive.

"Well, maybe is good enough for now." I hear him reply and look up to see him smiling slightly.

"Okay, then." I put my hands together and place them in my lap, looking up at him with resolve. "I guess now you can sleep better at night, having gotten that all off your chest."

He gives me a confused look. "You think I went through all of this so I could sleep better at night?"

"Well, didn't you?" I raise my eyebrows at him.

"No," he shakes his head, frustration emulating from his face. "I mean, yes, I want you to forgive me, but not so I can rid myself of some guilt."

"Then, what was it all for? Why go to all the trouble?" Was Anna right? Was there more to this than I allowed myself to believe?

"Julia, you are so thick-headed sometimes," he says, running his hand through his hair once again. "You don't get it." He looks at me, "I care about you. In all the years I've been consulting, not once have I ever met anyone like you. I couldn't get you out of my head from the first moment I saw you and that stupid red stapler."

My eyes dart around the booth, unnerved. "Oh," is all I can say.

"I... I want you in my life," he says softly, uneasily.

My heart starts to speed up. This is not what I was expecting to happen. I'm not really sure what I was expecting, but it wasn't this. Confusion sets in quickly. I've spent so much time hating him for what happened. Feeling used and lonely and hurt. I had made up my mind that he was a jerk. But now, I see he wasn't, at least not intentionally. And he cares about me. In my whole life, no one has ever said that to me to my face. Of course, I have had people care, but it's always been implied, never said. It's all a little too much, though. I didn't come here expecting this, and so now I feel so torn and lost even more.

"Jared, I'm sorry..." I hear myself say, trailing off. I shake my head and look down at my hands, and I feel like I want to cry. My thoughts are a jumbled mess. It's like that angel and devil on the shoulder thing they do in cartoons. Only it's not an angel and a devil. It's my mind and my heart. On one shoulder is my brain telling me he used me, lied to me. On the other shoulder is my heart, telling me he cares for me and I must care for him and to forget all the other crap.

In my state of fighting with myself, Jared has slid around the booth, closer to me. Then, right next to me. He takes my hand in his, weaving his fingers through mine. I want to let go of his hand and run away, but I want to stay there, too. It's not fair that he is doing this to me. Tears well in my eyes, emotions I did not want him to see.

"Julia…" He places his free hand under my chin and lifts my face to his. He's barely inches away from me, his face is so close. The way he smells, the heat from his body so close to mine. It's breaking down my walls, even though I still struggle to keep them up.

My eyes refuse to find his until I can't fight it anymore and I look. A tear escapes down my cheek. He wipes it away with his thumb, gently. He puts his hand on my cheek, cradling my face. And then he moves his head slowly toward me, and softly his lips touch mine. He lets go of my hand and his other hand comes up to my face, cradling it. His lips are soft and sweet and tender. They speak volumes to what he's feeling. I give into the kiss and stop fighting with myself.

My heart flutters and skips feeling victorious in the kissing. But my mind — my mind keeps bringing me back to the feelings which are still there: the feeling of being lied to, used. I ignore my brain and give into my heart, and I kiss him back, slowly at first, then I move my hands up to his back and pull him into me, tight. He responds by letting go of my face and putting his arms around me, pulling me into him.

I can't breathe, and I don't want to think. This feels good, right even. But then so wrong at the same time. I can't lie to myself. I want him, but I want who he was before. Not this Jared. Not the

Jared I don't trust.

That's the problem here, isn't it? What's been underlining my confusion is that I don't really trust him. Isn't trust the basis of a relationship? Isn't that what should be the foundation? If we don't have that, then what do we have?

Suddenly my mind is clearing, the fog lifting a little and I can see what I am really struggling with here: Trust. I force myself to pull away from him, and I let out a small whimper as tears explode from my eyes. "Jared, I can't... I'm sorry." I grab my purse and I walk as fast as I can to the door.

Outside of the restaurant, my first impulse is to stop and breathe for a second because I am practically hysterical, but I don't know whether he will follow me or not. So I just start to run. I run and cry all the way back to my place, and I probably look like a complete idiot. I don't care, though.

"Hey!" I hear Anna say from the couch as I walk in the door to my condo. Then she sees my face. "Oh no! Julia, what happened?" She gets up from the couch and comes over to me.

"I... I... I..." I can't talk. I'm practically hyperventilating from crying and running back from the restaurant. I catch a glimpse of myself in the mirror I had hung by the front door, and I am a disaster. Makeup is running down my face, and my hair is a mess. I go over to the couch and fall into it face first, and sob.

Anna is at a loss. She keeps asking me what happened, keeps asking if there is anything she can do. I can't even answer her. I just keep my head face down in the couch, crying my eyes out. She gives up trying to get me to talk, sits down on the floor next to me, and rubs my back intermittently while I try to gather myself.

After a while, I finally calm myself enough, and I move slowly to a sitting position on the couch. Anna grabs a box of tissues and hands them to me. I blow my nose and try to wipe my eyes. Tears keep reappearing, not as quickly as before, but they're still there, streaming down my face. I try to think back to when I cried like this last, and I don't even know. Even when I lost my job and then found out about Jared I didn't cry this hard. I was angrier then, so the crying was colder and harsher. This time it's different, and I can't pinpoint it.

"Are you okay?" Anna asks me as I attempt to gather myself back together.

"Yes... No... I don't know," I say through the hiccups and tears and snot.

"What happened?" She furrows her brow, concerned.

"He... he kissed me," I force out, and the crying starting up again immediately. I breathe deeply, not wanting to go back to the hysterics I just came from.

"Um... okay?" She gives me a strange look. Like why would anyone cry that hard over a kiss?

"No, it's just that..." I breathe deeply, once again, trying to gather myself. "He said he cares about me." The tears once again explode from my eyes.

"Julia," Anna says, frustration looming in her voice. "He cares about you and he kissed you. I'm confused. Why are you crying then? You need to start from the beginning." She sits down next to me on the couch.

I sit for a minute, breathing deeply trying to bring myself out of the tears. Finally, I am able to gather myself enough to tell her everything. And so I do—I tell her every detail.

"Okay, wait. I'm still confused," Anna says when I finish telling her what happened. "Why were you crying so hard?"

"Because! Did you not hear anything I said?" Does anyone ever listen to me?

"Julia, you're confused, I get that. But he wants you to forgive him, he cares about you, he cares enough to try that hard. Most men wouldn't do that. What are you so sad about?" She squints her eyes at me.

"Because I don't trust him!" I say loudly, slapping my hands on my legs for emphasis. "That's the big problem here. I don't trust him, and I don't know if I ever can. It's like my mind and my heart are fighting and I can't get them to just agree. I want him, but I don't trust him. I'm a mess. A complete disaster."

"Wow. Okay, you're being super dramatic." She leans back on the couch.

"Yah, I know," I say sniffling. "I can't help myself."

"Look, Julia," she says as she sits up and grabs my shoulders, turning me toward her so I can see her face. "I understand you don't trust him, I understand you're confused. What you need to do is figure out if life is better with or without him. That's all there is to it. If you decide life will be better with him, all of the other stuff will resolve itself. He already told you he wants you in his life. So, that's what you need to decide." She lets go of my shoulders and looks me seriously in the eyes, almost as if she's talking to a child. Which, let's face it, when it comes to relationships with the opposite sex, I am a little behind. Childish, even.

"Okay, okay," I nod my head, "that does help break it down." I exhale deeply, my breathing becoming steadier. Just like that, she broke it down into one simple question. Do I want Jared in my life, or not? That's it. How is it my little sister, who is ten years younger than me, has so much more life experience than I do? It's a little embarrassing really.

"I think you should sleep on it," Anna declares, patting me on the shoulder.

"Yes, that's probably a good idea." I slouch back on the couch exhausted from the day's events. It really has been a long day. "Will you stay over? We could have a slumber party?" I smile sheepishly at her. The thought of being alone sounds horrible, plus I just got Anna back in my life. I need to take full advantage of it.

"Okay, but only if you bake brownies." She smiles brightly. "I've really missed them."

"Wouldn't be a slumber party without them." I smile back.

We spend the night eating brownies and watching sappy chick flicks which do nothing to help my situation. I keep tearing up at dumb parts where no one should be tearing up. But my emotions are raw and at the surface, so I can't help myself.

I make Anna sleep in my bed, using my sad puppy dog face to guilt her into it. She agrees, but stipulates that if I try to snuggle even slightly with her she will push me off the bed.

It's late when we finally go to bed, and I know I'll regret it in the morning since I still have to get up so ridiculously early for the bakery. My stomach sinks a little as I think about the bakery and I remember the conversation with Beth, which was only earlier today. It seems like so long ago.

"I forgot to tell you something about the bakery," I say to Anna as we settle in.

"What is it?" She fluffs her pillow and nuzzles her head into it.

"When Beth told me about selling the bakery today, she told me that she thinks I should buy it. Don't you think that's crazy? Me? Running a bakery?" I say, still slightly stuffed up from all the crying I did earlier.

"Doesn't sound that crazy," she says, her voice muffled in the pillow.

"Doesn't it? Jared said the same thing."

"Might be just what you need," her voice slurs slightly at the end as she starts to drift off.

We lie there in silence. Anna's breathing becomes heavier, patterned. I stare at the ceiling, sleep not hitting me so quickly. Could I actually own a bakery? That doesn't seem very spinsterly of me. Of course, not much about my life right now seems very spinster-like. But to actually do something huge like that? It's way out of my comfort zone. I'm not good at stepping out of my comfort zone as I have established so many times before. It took forcing me out of it to make the changes I have made recently. I was forced out of the basement, forced out of my job. No one is going to force me to buy a bakery though. That will have to be up to me. Could I actually take the plunge, though? Maybe Jared's right, maybe I could take a chance. Maybe Anna's right, even if she did say it while half-asleep.

Maybe buying the bakery would be just what I need.

# CHAPTER 17

I think I've already established what spinsters do. They get stuck in their life, and then slowly they deteriorate until they are left with only some cats as companions and a braless muumuu to wear. That is my definition, at least. Webster has other ideas, but I won't go into that again.

I have learned that to move away from the dreaded life as a spinster means you have to get yourself un-stuck. I wasn't in any place in my life to un-stick myself until Jared came into it and really mucked things up. But in good way, I suppose.

It took me some time to see, but it wasn't until he came into my life and turned it upside down that I finally was able to make changes, and to find... well, me. I got out of my parents' basement, got a job I love, and now I'm taking an enormous plunge (the biggest of my life thus far)—I'm buying the bakery. Yep, you heard right, I, Julia Warner Dorning, am going to do something completely unspinsterly and buy Beth's Bakery.

It took me a week to fully decide to do it. I did

a bunch of research. Okay, not so much. All I did was ask everyone's opinion, and they all gave me a resounding yes. Then, I asked my dad to invest (which he agreed to whole-heartedly — thank you, Daddy!), and now I am currently working on getting a small business loan. It will take a couple of months before it's all done and the keys are mine, but I'm doing it. I am going to own a bakery.

The thought makes me feel many things. Happy, excited, sickly. The sickly part only creeps in sometimes when I freak out and think I should just drop everything. Luckily for me, I've had Anna, or Brown, or my parents around to help talk me down. Thank goodness for all of them or I wouldn't be where I am.

It's been just under two months since I was let go from the shackles of Spectraltech. Probably the hardest two months of my life, thus far. Everyone has a turning point in their life — one that makes them do an about-face and go down the path they were meant to. These past two months have been my about-face, my life changer.

Who knows where this path will end up taking me, but I'm excited to find out. I also know I can't go down this path without the person who basically started it all in my life. It didn't take me long to realize that.

So, here I sit on the patio of the Paramount Café, waiting for Jared to meet me. I have so much to say to him. I've actually rehearsed the speech in my head a million times (or so). I need to tell him so many things. I want to tell him how much my life has changed because of him. Although he doesn't deserve all of the credit, it wasn't until he showed up in my life that everything started happening. And I want him to know I thought losing my job was the worst thing that happened to me, but it turns out it was probably one of the best. It's changed me in ways I never thought possible. Instead of being ashamed of the direction my life was going, I am now... sort of... proud.

Most importantly, I want him to know that I trust him. I trust his judgment, I trust his expertise, and I trust that I will trust him even more as I spend more time with him. A lot more time. Like, hopefully the rest of my life... I am not actually going to tell him that part, though.

I hope he hasn't given up on me in the time it has taken me to get this all figured out. I needed to do all of this on my own. I needed to be ready for a future when I saw him again and asked him for one.

"Hi," Jared says and smiles when I look up at him. He sits down next to me.

"Hi," I say back simply.

My heart flutters and my stomach does flips just at the sight of him. We sit in silence for a moment as I try to muster up the confidence to tell him everything. But suddenly my speech has disappeared when I see his smile. Speeches are overrated anyway.

I reach over and grab his hand, intertwining my fingers with his. I don't really need to say anything, the gesture speaks volumes. He looks at me and smiles brightly, making my pulse speed up. I don't know if I will ever get used to the effect that he has on me. I hope I never do.

# THREE MONTHS LATER

The grand opening of the bakery—my bakery—goes off without a hitch. After I bought it, I made a few minor changes, making it my own. I changed some of the colors of the interior and hired an artist to paint cutesy things on the wall. I also had her write "You are what you eat, so eat something sweet" in curly letters above the wall behind the cash register because I loved the saying too much. It was also a shout-out to Beth, and she loved it. I also changed the name since it was really no longer Beth's Bakery. It took me a long time to decide what to call it, but in the end Julia's Bakery just had a good ring to it.

I decided to kick things off with a grand opening. I invited my friends, family, and even some of the nerds from Spectraltech to celebrate. Mr. Calhoun even showed up (of course he did). Patti and Debbie were there, keeping the desserts coming. It was amazing and exciting and everything I ever dreamed it could be.

Jared was by my side the entire time, being his usual charming self, smirking slightly at me as he toasted the red stapler that "brought us together" in front of everyone (I need to remember to slap him for that later). I think, hands-down, it was one of my best days yet.

At the end of the evening as we were cleaning things up, Jared comes up from behind me and wraps his arms around me, nuzzling his face in my neck. "I'm proud of you," he says softly in my ear, sending chills down my spine. I turn my head just slightly so his lips meet mine and he kisses me tenderly, lovingly.

So, here's what we now know about Jared. He's all mine. My boyfriend. I actually have a really hard time calling him that, because it just sounds so cheesy coming out of my mouth. It's hard to get used to. Maybe I would do better calling him fiancé. Yes, I think that rolls off the tongue much better. A girl can dream...


The End

# ACKNOWLEDGMENTS

I must give shout-outs to Lori Schleiffarth, my sister and greatest friend, for helping me edit along the way and telling me when I was being a complete idiot (in a loving way).

Robin Huling for being the best cheerleader and BFF a girl could ask for. I would not have finished this if she hadn't pushed me (gently, of course).

Nikki Sanders, my BCF (Best Cousin Friend) for editing and giving great advice and making me laugh all the time.

Julie Dirks, for her hilarious stories which inspired me to bring Julia to life. And no, it's not a coincidence that their names are similar. We didn't become spinsters like we thought we would! Yippee!

Prascilla Park, Sarah Sutliff, Kelly Glave, and Molly Rosenlund for reading the less edited versions, and still cheering me on.

Brad Condie, for my amazing cover art. You are one talented guy.

My mom, also a writer (much better than I am), and my dad, a comedian. I hope to be like them when I grow up.

My other siblings (Dan, Jenny, Carol) who inspire me and support me. My extended family who are some of my most favorite people in the world.

My immediate family. My babies: Audrey, Max, and Violet. And Rob, who saved me from my future life as a spinster. I love you tons and tons.

Made in the USA
Lexington, KY
04 June 2014